D0931406

17

FIC   Major, Clarence.

My amputations

$15.95

DATE			

Clarence Major

My
Amputations

a novel by

Clarence Major

fiction collective
new york
boulder

Library of Congress Cataloging-in-Publication Data

Major, Clarence.
  My Amputations.

  I. Title.
PS3563.A39M9   1986   813'.54   86-6408
ISBN 0-914-59096-0

Published by the Fiction Collective with assistance from the Publications Center, University of Colorado, Boulder, and the National Endowment for the Arts.

Grateful acknowledgement is also made for the support of the College of Arts and Sciences and the President's Fund for the Humanities at the University of Colorado, Boulder; Brooklyn College; Teachers & Writers Collaborative; and Illinois State University.

Text and jacket design by McPherson & Company. Manufactured in the United States of America.

The Western States book Awards are a project of the Western States Arts Foundation. Corporate founders of the awards are The Xerox Foundation and B. Dalton Bookseller. Additional support is provided by the National Endowment for the Arts Literature Program.

Author's Note: The characters in this novel are products of my own imagination and are not in any way based on actual persons or actual experiences. Any resemblance to actual persons anywhere is coincidental.

To the people who must find themselves

*"You are you because your little
dog knows you."*   *—Gertrude Stein*

My Amputations

Again, as in a recurring dream, Mason opened the closet door and stepped hesitantly into its huge darkness, its nonlineal shape: he pulled the door shut then crouched there on the floor—which seemed to be moving—with the breathing of The Impostor. This dimness was not illuminated by the glowing Mason felt. He could smell the man: his sweat, his urine, his oil. The skin of Mason's eyes was alive with floaters. Faintly in the background—perhaps coming through the wall from the next apartment—Sleepy John Estes was singing "Married Woman Blues." Mason pushed hard for *the* beginning, some echo or view. Anglosaxon monosyllables clustered there. He couldn't remember how it all started nor even his muse's birth. He called her Celt CuRoi. Yet memory was expanding... Low clouds crawled against a terrible sky. Lots of rainstorm-damaged trees, houses, fences. His birth—?—came like that. He swore to the date, the year, the damage, the blood. *And* afterbirth... and his broken-grasping for sea, land, form. Why'd he remember overturned cars, the Great Flood, a woman up in a tree, words: nigger, jig, darky, convicts at gunpoint working to rebuild a broken dam, a six-hundred-or-more death toll...? and, and from eighteen Woodrow Place? river moving out to lake, to sea, to ocean. Sea?... already searching for it: to float upside down in its membranous-liquid grasp. Giant sharks might be deep in it but Celt would guard... yet she, too, was only a beginning—not a sailorette, joe, just ah... bug-examiner like Lil Massy: transparent wings, pink underbelly bright and silky as panties—mating dogs smelled like a rain forest full of moss and rotten logs. First letter of alphabet fascinated them: a house: Egyptian pyramid, farmer's joke; picture on box of crayons; then D: door to darkness, closed-off mystery. Together they went down the earth-passage—at underworld's first level Celt and Mason dimly expected to encounter themselves waiting—locked in a dark, secret, everlasting closet. Instead, they stood uneasily on the bones of a dog-like animal dead a million years. On level two they plowed through the remains of a dinosaur already taped and labelled MRF. They uncovered the majority—but were too innocent to connect...*to force*. Strutters, diwalkers. V was clearly an upside-down hat: it protected them the way back up where—just before the exit—they stumbled into the clutches of cruel aunts with syphilitic-eyes, long-eared witches, drunk crab-shaped uncles, the broken—yet joyous, powerful, love-bound—spirit of a people: his—and by spirit, hers, too. They tasted salt, sugar and felt the frozen ground in winter; watched bird feet, were stung by fish fins. Turkey rot! Mason and Celt discovered it was possible to fly—even with broken wings: flying was not *why* you are but *how:* and *then* why: it was also not rushing downstream on a raft or being engulfed by a storm or swept away in a flood. It was how he got to know Celt. Before Celt he'd been a blind bat struggling to embrace the sky: his spirit existed before he was born: he simply stepped into it—as though it were a Union Suit. At sixteen he was unfinished; eyes: large, blank brown things. Did his mother Melba love him? She was certainly not his muse. Look at her apron: too clean: something is wrong. Is it that she doesn't like him much but loves...? Her eyes: unfriendly—yet she's a person of responsibility as big as the Atlantic. Small, tight mouth—Anglosaxon. Her skin was lighter than his. He was—in color—between her and his father Chiro: nutmeg. Her Irish-African eyes? His were more in the tradition of Chiro's. As Mason grew: there was laughter in his thunder while he beat his wings against the page—attempting to become a good writer. He jus' grew: Chicago, 1955: there's Mason along the lakeshore: gulls cry. In the stockyards: pools of blood from the slit throats of hogs. He heard Wind Voice here howling in from lake Michigan. He claims he swallowed the lake. Art Institute's lions roared at traffic. Ashtrays and pink salmon. Calendars without dates. A private collage: he was reborn constantly in it: to the gills he settled in this stuff. Distractions, *spectacles*—where'd he find the force for his connections, a vent for the smoke clouding the thrust of *his* crisis? And how to fit in simple things, moments, only he knew the shape of—or so he claimed. Hold his hand, reader. Example: a particular line in the sky, skywriting—a particular rose on a particular bush—bushwriting. No echo; no snow in the hills—which hills? Wyoming, of course. He tried too hard to be, uh, profound. But he was young: eighteen. Take him by the throat, dear—. He thought himself, he says, Rimbaud or somebody. The sky, roses, appletrees, you name it. He says William Carlos Williams wrote him, encouraged him. He came to realize he wanted it all flat or upright and permanent like cubism—like things: surfaces. Now, here in the closet there was a feeling not of claustrophobia but one of plague, glut, glue; a sense of pestilence—and redemption—worse than East Africa—1368, a glut worse than Henry the Eighth, a glue thicker than Egyptian cement. Mason: holyshit: heard the pained-breathing louder than ever, smelled The Other with pity and contempt. He was no longer squarely sure these sounds, these smells, were not his own.

Mason, early in life, got slapped in the face by the unmistakable separation of Church and State. Hard-headedness made the hit come easily and irreversibly: his "innocence" became irrecoverable: he'd traded it in for an existential shot in the dark: A bidet was not a toilet without a seat; whores didn't necessarily kiss better than housewives; but . . . yeah, you're getting warm (take your time—as Mississippi Fred McDowell used to say: time, time . . .), even hot: keep the Clean (Church) separate from the Dirty (State). Point: early Mason lost faith in *both*. Remember, he was a rat from the get-go. The *separation* itself: his stepfather, for example, never taught him anything except the separation part: his sensibility was a peephole through which you could see frost gathering on military sternness. He polished his old army boots every Saturday morning although he'd been discharged twenty years before: spit-shined, spotless dude, he was, who chopped beef, not pork, not lamb, for Swift's at the stockyards. Could barely write his name: connected crudely printed letters with cross-bars: was not visibly intelligent either: just noble—full of nobility. Mason's mother caught her bottom lip between her teeth and chewed on it thoughtfully: held it that way, puzzled by the demands of the Church on one side (forced connections?) and the State on the other: that lasted for two, no, two and a half years. Mason's youngest sister, Maureen (never thought of her as *half*), was the offspring of that civil wedding made holy between Wilbur Young, The Man of Rules, and Melba, Woman of Blues. In six months he'd be fourteen: after school Mason walked to the cleaners—Rapid Magic Delux—his mother and stepfather owned on Forty-Fourth and Langley, South Side. It was December—it had snowed heavily three days before: snow now muddy, slush. He had the sniffles, a runny nose, chills. His pea jacket, though warm, had no buttons. When he entered Rapid Magic he saw Melba—thin, chilled, with folded arms, walking toward the pressing-machine, barefoot. At first glance nothing seemed unusual. As Mason went behind the counter, Melba turned and came toward him. He *knew instantly: something was wrong:* her eyes: it showed in her eyes: they'd never been *that way* before: they were, how d'ya say, blank crazy . . . ! He spoke: "Are you all right?" She gave him a glazed look—unfocused . . . His mother didn't *know* him. He felt shot-through-the-grease. Mason watched his mother count the money in the cash register; then she wrote down the total on a scrap of paper alongside the machine. He stood at her side: she'd already totalled the same amount eight times on the same sheet. Had she forgotten? Obsessive fear of—? Mason's fear raced out of him, flapping, bloody, like a rooster with its head just chopped off. He felt desperation: a mindless mother meant being at the mercy of The Man of Rules. As usual, Mr. Young left his gig at Swift's at five, got to Rapid Magic at quarter-to-six. He normally ran the deliveries in his old car. Today when he came in, he casually spoke to his wife—who didn't return the greeting, didn't seem to recognize him—then turned to the boy who was pretending to read *Catcher in the Rye.* Mason quickly put his book aside, seeing that his stepfather hadn't even noticed the change in Melba: Mister Rules was busy gathering garments for delivery. Mason went to him. "Mister Young" (they were *that* formal) "uh, mother is . . . there's something *wrong* with her . . ." Young continued to sort through dresses, suits, jackets, slacks on the rack, separating them by address, street, city section. Young said nothing. (Melba, though able to hear this conversation—she was perched on the high stool by the cash register—was clearly *not* hearing it.) Then without looking at the boy, Young spoke: "Get the bucket and mop. The floor is dirty." Mason, tenderfoot, foolish, didn't get the connection, he stood there with his mouth agape. "But—" "*I said get*—" Young turned his violent deadfish-eyes on Mason—the skin of his thick, bulldog face, which was the color of potato skin, sunk to a splurgy purple-brown. Mason wiped a tear—which tasted like salt-pork—out of the corner of his mouth. "But *look* at her!" Young raised his hand, as though ready to strike. Mason turned and ran to the toilet at the back of the shop where the mop and bucket were stored. Trapped, framed, he filled the bucket at the sink, dumped Liquid Magic from its plastic bottle into the water. He was sobbing. Taking his equipment out by the pressing machine, he dropped the mop, then lifted the bucket with both hands and threw its contents across the shop, on Young and the garments he was fussing with. Before Young could respond, Mason ran out the back door, dashing through the smelly gangway, he reached South Parkway (later called Martin Luther King Drive); and it was while running, as though carrying the pigskin of his future tightly gripped under his arm, that he had a vision: Celt CuRoi would guide him firmly from the middle ground of *separation* sprawled there between Church and State. He would not fumble—would kickoff with skill unbound: would not need the *protection* of anybody else—ever. It was midnight before he climbed the steep stairway of the apartment building at Church Avenue and State Street where the family lived in Apartment C.

But it was *only* a vision. Before long, in Cheyenne, on an Air Force base, he sat at a typewriter. Knocked up girls floated through the balloon of his thinkbox. In high he'd already impregnated three or four fast members of The Jailbait Society. Each night now, while asleep, Pony Express gallopers brought him summons to appear in civil court to answer contributing-to-juvenile-delinquency and bastardy charges. It was hard to get up early enough to be there on time. He couldn't get permission to leave the base. Meanwhile, he was trying for a kind of literary apprenticeship. Mason's apprenticeship started like this: after reading and imitating Dumas, Dickens, Conrad, Baudelaire, Rimbaud, Verlaine, Zola, there were Richard Wright, Gertrude Stein, Ellison, Baldwin, Himes, Toomer, Hemingway, Faulkner. Yes, *yes*—Faulkner! Well, you know old Joe Bullock, Jr., the guy who cut his girl's throat and threw her body out back behind the shed? (The yella girl story was the one Mason could hear—not just in Faulkner, in Stein, in Toomer! his mother was one too.) Yella was a waitress in a greasy-spoon in 1921. They made her wear a hairnet. Joe thought she was stepping out with John the white boss. *Scribner's* turned down their attempt to make their story known to the public. That was in 1930. *American Mercury* published it in 1931 under a title the town leaders later changed—by forcing previously unknown connections. It all went back before the fury and in some of the early versions you could hear at the redneck barbershop or general store (where old white men spat tobacco juice into the flame in the stove) in the winter: Yella was a decent young woman, not just a part-time colored (Faulkner would've said "nigger") prostitute: More to her life than contrast of southern grotesque and racial irony: more than fear and hopelessness. A boy, Bobby Joe, went about telling the story from his own point-of-view. People liked his version. Mason learned about first-person-plural from it. H.L. Mencken, however, cut the "white" baby out of Yella's womb before revealing her story to the public. While here nearly freezing in the snow and filing military documents at Stock Records, Mason made an earnest attempt to write. Results? I clear my throat.

What—fifty-five, fifty-six? One instructor was screwing one of the enlisted women—a blonde, sort of fat and dumb. They'd do it each morning before class: they'd arrive an hour and a half early—screw in the dark classroom on the floor and by the time the rest of them got there blondie'd have her hair combed, clothes back on but she'd always smell of sweat and sperm and her cheeks and earlobes would be sending out crimson signals. All the other guys, Mason too, felt it in the groin. Imagination was a bitch. They were all just a bunch of lonely Cheyenne cowboys. Mason was a devil of a guy in an early morning outfit, a dreamer of sex frames, a drinker in base beerhalls. Rumor was they were all being fed saltpeter anyway: desire was supposed to be undercover, like winter roots under a blanket of Wyoming snow. Mason sent his little sister, Maureen, a leather cowgirl dress, with frills, bells. Melba wrote: "Gwen gone wild. Lord, save us. Glad you're in the service. The checks I get help a lot. Any chance of re-enlisting?" Church and State matters: exchange and conflict: still strong back yonder in Chi-town. Mason was not homesick though. At the same time he was becoming aware of something else: he was going to die: sometime. This was a pain in the ass; got his quills up: he'd surely miss out on some important moment up there in the cooking-with-gas future. Attaboy!—but rotten luck, eh? He was nearly twenty-one and as Gide said after that it's all downhill. Clara Downhill—wasn't that her name? South Side. Big sister Gwen . . . into drugs and booze, who knows whatall, living life in the fast lane: turning out like Clara Downhill, all the rest. This was Mason's reprieve? Had he bought the ghetto system, could he change . . . ? Well, he *thought* he wasn't going to have his balls hung from the church bell and his brains splattered all over the courthouse lawn. He *thought* he'd write his way out. After Cheyenne, he'd be carted off to Valdosta, Georgia: Monkeyshit! On the way he visited Chiro whose eyes were bloodshot, yellow, red, gray. Mason's father's fingers and feet were swollen with disease. Mason cried up to night stars—a bull's bellow—in sadness and rage . . . In three days he was just north of Florida— where runaway slaves once established a human community ("state"? "nation"?)—stepping down from the hot, grimy train, at Valdosta. (Why were so many black guys from the North assigned to these southern backwoods...? where they were afraid to go into the towns filled with rednecks.) Yet in all fairness to poor Mason, we must observe the contents of his sadness: it was a team of butterflies galloping and snorting like sweating, wild horses. One Saturday night, he and a couple of other brave dudes caught the bus to town—*anyway*. First person met was an old black man weeping on street corner. Reason? Daughter'd just been thrown from a police car—she lay at his feet, bleeding— after being gang-raped by a squad of fat, red-faced cops assigned to the "nigger section." Mason, Churchy and Dossy O got a colored lady—driving by—to take the girl to a midwife (—no hospital for black people). It was dusk, Jean Toomer dusk. Red dirt. Half moon. The whole bit. Fishfry in back of an old house that resembled a burnt elephant, a cat house. Mason's fear: skulls with black skin stretched across them were drying in moonlight. But the fishfry was for fun—wasn't it? *Huh*? Yellow electric lights—night bugs—strung above blue-silver smoke and the hot steam from black cooking kettles, grills with years of red Bar-B-Q sauce blackened to their racks... Smells mingled: tangy innards, catfish, sizzling ribs of pork. You could hear the chicken backs and wings, gizzards, thighs, legs, popping their grease. Everybody was happy. Dancing. Louis Jordan rippling through "Saturday Night Fish Fry": from the record player on the back porch plugged-in in the kitchen. Mason, too, felt good—at the edge of anger, though, and Richard Wright-fear. Agony, really. The flesh of a mature sheep? He could eat *more* than mutton. His hunger was gigantic! Was that a sheep or a pig on the spit? He felt the presence of Celt here, just above him—like a winged siren. He, a griffin. And Chiro, too—at least in spirit: because of Jordan and Mason's memory of his father's, "*Hot dog*! Listen to them keys—" Sweet, sad legacy— "Ain't nobody here but us chickens!" And here one could be one's *self*: even if population was being checked by murder just beyond. People glazed in warm sweat were doing the bebop-touched Boogie-Woogie, crying, "*Hi de hi de hooo-hoo!"* and dudes sporting the hip Billy Eckstine rolled-collar—in powder blue or butterfly yellow. Cab? He was always there as background. You bet. Mason held the legacy like an instrument, a relic passed down so the warriors of the enemies could not see it: part of his survival equipment, his force. Yet he defied the cliché: he couldn't strut his stuff, point a toe, tap: not then: too self-conscious, stiff. He watched the others with Bar-B-Q sauce on their chins—licking the last drops from their fingers—; watched from warm shadows, warm and wet; drank white lightnin' as they stepped to the rhythms, inside them, defying *and* obeying them. The shy young women and men, wallflowers like himself, smelled of lye soap in their cheap cotton summer clothes newly bought that morning at the dime store. Unlike the black women in southern literature these real women didn't "laugh easily, with deep-throated pleasure," rather, they smiled gently like Jean Toomer's mysterious, dark and light, sad, women. Everybody had a country hip-walk. Mezz. But the food ran low, got cold, the sauce achieved its crusty lardlike surface, the hips—real ones—felt tired, eyelids ached, night lights filled with bugs, even the music got sluggish. It was after midnight and everybody was either ready for love action or sleep. The last bus to the base—a dragon designed to fly one above danger—would leave in five minutes. Hubba hubba! The three comrades checked their Timexes and got the "Last Bus Blues." As they ran their heritage music chased through cobwebs of their headflesh: Burgundy Street, Canal Street, Clark and Randolph, Decatur Street, Beal: "You Got The Right Key But The Wrong Key Hole," "It's Tight Like That," "Barb Wire Blues,"—ol' Georgia Tom, them Mound City Blues Blowers, ah, and . . . They leaped into a trot, self-consciously keeping a city cool in the sticks: a new form of manhood. At a lighted corner a cop car stopped, dark like a hearse without lights. Two gray faces, swollen from beer, glared at them. Lights flashed. Sirens went up like a flock of gannets—only harder. Cops looked very moral—and fictitious (many years later Mason would swear the Moral Majority and Moral Fiction deserved each other). The car jerked forward and shot fast toward them—flying onto the sidewalk. Realism? Not really: spaceships were more impressive. It stopped before the guys. The car radio—just a touch of profound irony, huh—was playing "Ah Leu Cha," by Bird straight from Radio Free Europe. But there was *some*thing *else* coming from that car radio: the car hemmed our guys against a greasy showcase glass behind which monkeys on sticks and paper whistles were suspended on strings. Mason feared death. Like Bob Crosby's Bob Cats, Mason wanted to do a "Big Foot Jump." Now folks, you know brown or black folk running *had* to be guilty. They'd forgotten—in their haste: with only five minutes. ("I know I am guilty but what is my crime?") The cops, with their huge pistols already drawn, got out. "Against the wall, niggers." The heroes obeyed. Were these the rapists? With hands against cold glass, legs spread, Mason felt his balls swing inside his Jockey shorts. Mason got a closer look at the showcase: Tom Mix smiled from a Bubble Gum showcard, a model airplane—on a piece of thread—was about to enter a thunderstorm filled with lightning, taking off from, *ah shit, who knows where* . . . Mason—and the others—felt the thick rough insensitive hands, searching for . . . *knives?* They *never* had knives. What a cliché. "You niggers from the base? What's the hurry?" The bus was coming now—filled with ugly light. It went by.

Back to the South Side—a mistake. Mason was lonely and listening to music. Discharged, he heard the whine of: "Biscuit Roller Blues," by Kokomo Arnold, Bessie Smith's "Black Mountain Blues," and the lament of Marcus Garvey's dream: Hazel Meyers' "Black Star Line." Then he met—in a moment when faith in his muse was a stuck slush pump—the cheerful, eighteen year old Judith Williams: in a living room? on a street corner? in a five and dime . . . ? They hustled each other down to City Hall. She was warm: a catalyzing refinery. This civil attachment was to last: an assembly of flowing connections, wobbly Christmas tree lights, the wedding of sucker rod and clamp grip, spit, glue wrench and oil fever. Judith wanted to be a movie star: to shine, be bright: she was beautiful, *beautiful:* plum-cocoa colored—Indian, Central West Africa, shades of islands long beneath the ocean. She didn't know "Aunt Jemima Stomp," from a foot-warmer. But had a wonderful, fluttering voice full of bird cries, torches, Dixie, Soul, branches in the breeze, trombone, sax, and it was easygoing, husky, sweet, any way she wanted it to be: a passionate canary without the screech, churp, tonsil exercise, ear-splitting C's, crooner's frogs, sentiment. Yet, y'yet: where could she go with it—except to the shower, the kitchen? That eat-dog world out there contained only a few successful satchelmouths, catchers of the wire, canners of music, side-makers. Mason loved to listen to her day and night. Listening often took his depression away. You know Judy's story: it's the same ... She'd grown up with two younger sisters, an illiterate, cheerful mother who worked hard as nails housecleaning for wealthy folk in Evanston, Trumbell Park, Oak Park, Elk Grove; from turnip greens-South, she knew no other way. Boop-poop-a-dop. I won't tell you the whole jaded story: but, this: there was a stepfather, not the father of any of the three. Never mind that Judy *seduced* him: at twelve. At seventeen she started dating and this shook him. He drank heavily, spied on her in theatres, drive-in snack bars. Tra-la-la. She came to her marriage curvéd with guilt ("*Now,* Mason, *you know* my ma *must've* known ... How *could* she've *not—*?") and hatred for her mother, herself. Judy and Mason got their first furniture from Sears and the Salvation Army: a let-out couch in a studio apartment with a kitchenette in a basement where they could hear rats in the walls playing chase scenes for screen tests. Mason wanted to be a writer, yes, still; and the Salvation Army typewriter worked and that mattered. As he worked at the kitchen table Judy sometimes sat beneath it playing "Doctor Feel Good." Kids together, unschooled; fumblers with their Salvation

Army spoons, broken cups, Sears blankets, forks, dusty books, knives, sheets, they had a sort of life, a hey-nonny-nonny chance, hope. Before Judy and Mason came to their whipped senses they were up to their hairline in oozy babyshit, soggy diapers; their ears clogged with choking screams from Salvation Army cribs. The tone of her songs changed: her pair of pipes stumbled and fell down from G above high C to a gutty, inky-dinky low E-flat. With half their Heart in the Church, half in the State, the couple felt trapped between the Devil and Next Month's Rent. C above high C was a thing of bygone giggle-time. Yet Judy held off on the Blues—for, uh, two months. Okay? Then wham: into them lip-quivering mammies she dug: choking up "If I'd Listened To My Mama I Wouldn't Be In This Mess Today," with the "Bearcat Shuffle" body-shakes. Stingy welfare checks were stolen from their broken mailbox, and (white folks on TV talk-shows Sunday mornings kept saying "If *they'd* only try to do something for themselves and get off welfare, they'd . . .") the babies, three, no, four, no, five, were all crying at once, midnight, sun-up, three in the afternoon tea-time, anytime. Their Salvation Army washing machine broke down like their yellow-back radio with the 1948 dials: every month. Repair bills came wearing ski masks. The Platters didn't help with their high harmonizing. Mason didn't feel so smart anymore, was less of a smartass, a pisser-in-pockets, a sitter-on-the-dunce-stool, a spitball-thrower. He *did* consider robbing a bank. But the nerve was on a long vacation, down in some swampy terrain where the blood was thin, cool. He was waiting for a telegraph message: about what? The future? He tried playing the ponies but gave up the sport of kings when, first time out at Arlington, he went to the dogs in a photo-finish. The South Side was a madhouse of stumbling losers two-timing playgirls doublecrossing husbands failures and sneaky wives in search of a break in the flux; Muslims, junkies, devout simple-minded fire-and-brimstone-church-going handclapping holy folk. Judgment Day was only theatre: this was another cantaloupe, a wopper, kicked dust. Who needed it? Judy and Mason had six children in the wink of a birthcontrolless eye. Even his mother, a tough, hard woman, felt sorry for him. Twins, then twins again, two boys, two girls then a boy and a girl: Linton, Arthur, Patricia, Tina, Keith and Irene. They had big hands and narrow hips like the Williams lineage. They had Chiro's eyes. Mason's mother's mouth; curly hair, full-moon faces, roller-skate-fast minds. Mason lost his interest in fucking. He considered jumping off the Wrigley Building, driving a Suzuki a hundred miles per hour into a stack of old bathtubs, hanging himself with the umbilical cord of a satyr-raped she-goat. Yet there was a small comfort obtained from the government's poverty report: at least they weren't alone. A caseworker pulled his coat, showed him why he felt a draft: "Listen, if you leave, she'll get *twice* as much..." After many weeks of sizzling in the blues, juggling guilt, Mason took the step. Go go go. They had a strict tearful parting: strained: kissed all the brats, gave Judy one last sideways look of heartbroken disapproval. She looked him back: with strait-jacket-fury. They promised to keep in touch. But it was time. (He sent money—thousands—to buy his way emotionally *and* because he cared. Eventually, Judy was afraid he wanted to *take* them from her, so she started moving a lot, concealing her address, maintaining an unlisted number...) It was a private matter: the world had no business looking in on it. He was still lonely, had a firm weakness for Touch: warmth, friendliness, comfort, companionship: was still prisoner of his wing-tipped erections. Not a cold fish, he met Mary Lou the day he left Judy. Six months later she gave birth to triplets. Mason wanted to do King Oliver's "Alligator Hop." *Six*...? What happened to eight and one? big universal everlasting nine? That was not the worst of it. He couldn't grab a handful of rods: he was hooked into her, flapping but caught firmly through the gums. Mary Lou, magical Mary Lou: mysterious, secretive, sucked him in slowly, grinding-ly, leaving him light-headed, restful, unable to move. She was tall, slender, strong, brownstone-brown. I could tell you endless stories about her, her shady past. But—another time. She was so clever the cute girl triplets were dead ringers for Mason. Yet he had no faith in the quality of his spit. Figuring he could get out later, in fair weather, he decided to spend the winter between Mary Lou's spread thighs. (Mary Lou's mother was a raggedy half-crazy baglady who secretly owned dozens of apartment buildings all over the South Side, a slumlord who ate out of garbage cans; her father, thirty years older than her mother, raised turkeys in El Reno, Oklahoma. Mary Lou had a crazy sister who played piano for a storefront church, was wedded to Jesus; and a younger brother: shot through the head in the Army while crossing in the wrong direction on a firing range in Weatherbeatened, Mississippi.) Mason was hopelessly stuck? Jude the Obscure—worse? *he fucked and fucked till his house fell in!* Mary Lou was a Queen Bee, all right: they fucked up a storm; steam rose from their rooms; lightning struck in the night. Trips to Cook County Hospital became so frequent they lost track of the brats they brought back. Like Frank Buck: they brought 'em back alive! Mary Lou and Mason couldn't get near each other without going apeshit, ripping each other's clothes off: his tongue in her ear or her mouth full of his cock or . . . you name it. They'd lost any hope of extracting themselves from the abyss, the vortex. Every time he turned around she was unzipping his fly. (Celt watched from a distance but kept out of it. Mason's dream of becoming a famous writer took a walk.) Something had to be wrong in nature, ya know. All these babies and money problems gave Mason the "Coffee Grindin' Blues," the "Dipper Mouth Blues." He had a lot of names to memorize: plus he was still in *touch* with Judy and the kids . . . just down the street around the block up the avenue. This was a high price to pay just to have somebody be there. Although Mary Lou was an artist and sensitive and all, she was not talkative. He wasn't either but her silence seemed to compel him to flutter and stammer out an unending stream of obscure sentences adding up to intellectual void-filling nonsense. So love-making was their only natural, *un*affected event. Also Catholic, she was Mother Earth: fuck and be merry was her motto: populate the land, carry on the race. Plus she *loved* children, especially infants. Jude-Mason lay beside Mary Lou through the cold nights listening to her whimper: "Nobody can do me like Papa Cow Cow can do," and clawing at him. She often imitated Sara Martin singing, "Eagle Rock Me, Papa." But Mason was crying the "Bullheaded Woman Blues." He lost his slave and it took three months to discover he wasn't qualified for unemployment compensation: hadn't been standing tall on the job long enough. He sneezed at snazzy dudes in the street: suspected Mary Lou was stepping out on him. (She *was*—and he was cheating, too. Ugly scene.) The welfare cycle hit: Mary Lou could become a prostitute and he could join a gang of thieves. Consider this: Mary Lou could confess to the priest and kill herself. The children might be adopted by happy, well-adjusted middle-class Negro families making it on the outskirts of town. (Liberal whites hadn't started adopting black kids yet.) Mason, in all fairness, could also kill himself. Everything after that... Smooth sailing? He split for New York.

The background of such a madman is at least of clinical interest. I strain to find something good to say. Does such a personality evolve from insecurity, a feeling of worthlessness churning beneath the facade? Mason's father didn't find his handsome mother tied to tracks. He was not deceptive—and that's not a family secret. You be the judge. Mason, here speaking: My father comes back to me often. He came back last night; with a flat wide nose, a plate in his lip, a sculptured skull, looking through a mask. From the inside of his head I now look out at you: you are wearing my face, yet you are not me. I lost a forefather in the bush—on the q.t.—one in the gas station while the Cadillac was being filled, the oil changed. My father has grown fat. He's a model of virtue yet he has cloven hooves. He smokes and rubs his red eyes. He has forgotten the taste of innocence: he has nothing to declare. His head and especially his sad eyes are not truly his own. He is up against obstructionists. He is a fat, fat man sunning himself in the sunchair. There's wet, cut grass before him: something he has accomplished: the beer he holds is his reward. My father liked seeing my mother, when they were still together, in summer prints. Now he is discussing symbolism, the conflict and exchange between Church and State, the value of a muse, with his smart girlfriend, a college dropout. His African nose flares, just slightly: this happens when he's tense, excited. He now looks less like a prince of rogues. His complexity is authentic. Skin? The inside tissue of darkness turned the blowup-blue of the Black Hole. Every night I dream of my father—now that he's, how'd ya say in Anglais? *dead. Is* he dead-*dead?* I ask 'cause he comes cloaked in his own flesh, even now. See him coming across the night sky which is like a sheet of fifty-by-fifty black metal—used in bridge construction. He's dangerous yet undefined: he has nothing to confess. He's wet from the rain falling from the white moon. He's reachieved innocence through having emerged from that romantic ooze of damnation known otherwise as Getting-Along. The setting is not bleak not a trap and there is no charm in the spell he conjures. My father is still sad. And still. Sadness swallows him. He is also a stranger to me, as I am to my sons, my daughters. He's slightly on the lunatic fringe, yet somehow free of dereliction. At least *he* believes in me. He's a stranger coming in lightning, crossing the construction site. My father gives in to a dream of the werewolf. His howl sticks in his throat as he pulls himself to the edge where he falls peacefully into a muddy swimming pool in a backyard in Atlanta. I am in Chicago. A foghorn is the last sound he hears. The light from my welding rod, his last light: this is lineage. Then he recovers *for* me: old Clootie. Infernal Angle. There's no bilking in his action. My father's face multiplies in the night. Is there such a thing as interchangeability with one's father? I could not imagine my father a hero—Salt of the Earth. To his generation he is a constant threat because that whole generation was *caught in the act*—and he wasn't. He is the Marquis de Sade, the eternal infidel, Lucifer, victim of meddlers and muddled affairs. I sleep dreamless in self-defense, taking transmigration with Kafka seriously. Outside the dream, in a barbershop, he looks out the window: through it, the Deer woman walking up a path. She could be Painted Turtle's mother. All flat surfaces. My father's metabolism is slow. He worries about his feet and his heart and his ribcage and his fingers—he has arthritis. He worries about the chemical balance of his body—yet he isn't health conscious exactly, sees no trapdoors, steps on no thin ice, does not have the "Bullfrog Blues." The moon outside above the road lights the way for my father, like D.H. Lawrence's, when he is stumbling home drunk. Except my father does not drink—is not a drunk. A lame duck, yeah, but not a scoundrel. My father has a gun in a gun-holster strapped to his chest. He is unbelievably like a Hollywood gangster in the way he carries himself. Yet he has no hideout, no illusions, no contact man, fix, hype, buster-and-screw man, no biter, no acetylene torch. He says don't be like me, be an artist. In the sand my father finds a skull-bone. He places it on his dresser. He watches it for a week then decides to paint it yellow. Why yellow, which yellow? What kind of paint? My father often feels unloved—and loved, by the wrong women, too passionately. His secret life is inflamed with the quality of hurt. His facial muscles won't relax. The nurse takes his blood count at the free clinic, his girlfriend counts his socks. Holes. A peewee soft-song man sings outside his window. He waits for the train. It arrives late. Although it is late it's still the seven-forty-seven. As though walking into a hornet's nest, he steps up onto it. Through the window he sees the rotten roof of the station. It's raining. The roof leaks. On the platform eight virgins are collecting for the March of Dimes. At his foot is a shopping bag. In it: the infamous skull-bone. He's a bagman. Smell the cool wet morning? Where's he going? He gets off in the city. We watch him walk with his bag. Slightly stooped. He enters the Magnan-Rockford building. With one of the keys on his key-ring he unlocks the basement door marked *Janitor*.

Mason's father, I'll have you know, wasn't a janitor for *anybody*—ever. Something too inconsistent in Mason's collage, back there: those shifting contradictory images. They disturb me. Chiro may have had his fingers in many pies, a thumb or two dripped (dipped in) blood, perhaps. Surely he was a peccadillo, maybe a chiseler but he was not inconsistent. It's Mason who's...Ellis Sir met the world bravely, without tosh. No rift in his life: nothing was rubber-stamped; everything done in the original. Why do I defend his father and damn him? (Well, you heard the phoney voice in the previous chapter!) Mason's father, for example, often walked—he did not use his, uh, wings or Cadillac to show off. I can see him now: he's walking along Peach Street in Atlanta. It's early morning. He looks distastefully at his surroundings. Yet he is unable to leave. He projects himself into another time, another place: the cobblestones beneath his uneasy feet are slick from too many years of slime, blood of bull-runs, urine. Here he's not full of the "B.V.D. Blues," but a respected Model of Virtue, perhaps a doctor, a man of trust. All his life Mason's father has thought the word father and now it breaks down into two parts: "fat" and "her." Is a father hiding the female *her* in himself? Another view: he's riding a bicycle high on a tightrope...Mason's father willed his wings to Mason. Remember the escape? They were made of mutation itself, of conviction, and of impeccable iron feathers. And here is Mason's fat-her as Red Charleston with a history of backdooring, listening to Duke Ellington in Kansas City directing his band through "Chocolate Shake." Cats outside in the alley gambling, [a passage between buildings—not a path through a lovely garden, this alley]. Many of the lames in the turnout are talking trash; trotters angling for attention. Duke keeps on keeping on. Up there—big smile. It's Saturday night: somebody feels mellow, somebody else feels deadly. Frankie and Johnnie meet C.C. Rider. Coppers are pulling coats, police swinging billysticks. Some up on china white, others down on sneaky pete. Mason's father was a music lover who danced a trickbag step to Louis Jordan, to Benny Carter and his Chocolate Dandies ripping through "Cadillac Slim": splib-oh-do-be-ooop, bob-bop-ah-do-ooop . . . Chiro understood the Body by Fisher. Saturday night: the lights are still greasy from the baptized bird. All around Mason's father a hawk flapped and stabbed. He did the Cootie Crawl, too. He moved through honkytonk changes, buying drinks for unemployed dudes, hot mamas, Kants. Completely qualified, folks. Another shot of Mason's father: in buckskin. "Got my gun, got my hoss." He takes off with Cab Calloway toward the sunrise in one of those twenty-five minute colored shorts. He told stories of genocide and mass murder around the campfire. He worked the chain-gang, helped to build Atlanta. Chiro poured the cement like sperm. The wheels of automobiles stuck to the shadows of churches. Chiro's mother was a preacher in one of those churches, his father—a jailbird, a heel grifter, a lady-killer. He was not exactly a dangerous nightwalker but he knew them all—knew which pockets concealed their knives, their smokers; knew the crooked cops, the ladies on the lookout, the secrets of them all. Chiro hung out at card parties and Saturday night fish fries. Did the Lindy. Chased chippies. Was a cherry picker. Did the Chitterlin' Strut. Could even sing Indian rain songs. (Indians were part of his heritage, too. So were the people shipped here from the prisons of England.) Cab taught him to sing "Chop Chop Charlie Chan." Chiro strutted around in a zoot suit and quoted the scriptures better than a country preacher. Was perfectly at home in any schizophrenic city—especially Atlanta. Even his pain was sort of sweet: "Sickness and Benny Goodman's Sextet." "Buttermilk and Fats Waller." "Neckbones and riverbeds of garbage." Mason's father didn't come from the Broken Hill in Australia, never walked in the tides of the Coral Sea: he was of the place where streetfights and cockfights reigned. Here is an easy early snapshot of Mason's father: fingernails neatly cut and polished; felt hat at rakish angle; no scar, no conk, no smell of Okefenokee, red dirt, not even Cadillac grease, perfume, Royal Crown. A cat rejected by the World War Two draft board, he was a sharpshooter. Some swore he had one eye, nine fingers. At least one lady called him Mack the Knife, one other Fisheye. But they were both confused. At the point of orgasm, one lady grabbed his Saturday Night Special from its place tucked in his pants at the base of his spine and pulled the trigger—she was that excited. The bullet went through the mattress and lodged in the rattan carpet beneath the bed. He bit her neck till he got blood. Yet this witches' brew was not his thing. He could do the Twist. Had no real use for the Frenzy—untying the knot. Mason's mother wrote this historic letter to his father in March, 1941: "You are a beast. You had your son by the hand, remember, and his steps equalled one-fourth of each of yours on that hot dirt road in an uncertain place where the Cadillac broke down. You always walked too fast. And your daughter: what of her? Haven't you betrayed her, too? I'm not surprised that the woman in the passing car gave you a ride into town and *her* car broke down, too: You're just bad luck, Mister. You got the 'Dipper Mouth Blues,' and you look like a forkbeard two days out of water. I remember many nights when I didn't want it and you forced me: I hate you for raping me. Good-bye, Melba." Although Chiro was a conscious dresser, he never wore gold suspenders and tap-dancing shoes (although, in *The Memoirs of Madame Rose Marie Butler Williams, Grande Queen of The Best Time in Town Bar and Hotel on Butler Street*, Chiro *did* wear shoelaces made of gold thread.) Near the end of his life, Mason's father ate regularly in the restraurant he once owned. The lady next door always tried to get him to go to church with her. He never did. So she gave him church flowers she brought from the altar. He was by now an old man bent low in his dim room. No other person ever entered it. It was crammed with the bad odor of an old man who smoked too much, whose wings were damaged and musty...

Mason and The Turtle (an Indian he picked up along the way) arrived: Times Square: glitterbugs, honks, dash, punk, chump sex, jackleg-caviar mobs, teenieboppers galore. Then downtown, The Other Side Hotel was steamy. He and Painted Turtle leaned against the piss-stained wall, outside, on Third just off Fourteenth. They checked in. She was on her period, felt sick, dizzy. Mason peeked inside at the tiny lobby. The Lower East Side hadn't changed. But being back churned up mixed feelings: filth and freedom. His aim in Amesville while on release time had been to restore himself, get the bats out of his attic, the burlesque-kickers outta his midnight show, Lady Macbeths off his trail, to redeem himself, purge himself, get the cuticle cuties out of his system, to *forgive* himself for the mess he'd made... On the wall of the booth was a drawing of an octopus: on its belly, this: MRF. What polpo-bullshit was...? Not Mister Roy Fart—not Mad Rat Fink. Mason Ran Fast? Never mind. With a shaky finger, he dialed Ferrand. The Private Eye spoke: "I got your man: I'll have the full report typed by my gal by the time you get here with the balance." As he walked back to The Other Side he smelled a rat. A couple of cheap fannyshakers winked at him from a cabbage-green doorway. Duchesses, dicty chicks, dukes and pantie-peelers, breezed by. This was a grimy area. Streakers and stripteasers went arm in arm. Mason had the bread in the suitcase with the books. The Turtle was writing a letter to her folks in Zuni. She seemed only mildly interested in Mason's Ferrand message. And finally: "You giving him *five hundred dollars?*" Her sigh was resignation: she groaned; her neck cracked. He felt tangled—apologetic. "I thought you *understood?*" She did, she did: *said* she did. He smelled a skunk. Maybe he'd write a novel about—this. He could just see the reviews: "This is a novel about a man who... the author of... Although The Narrator of... denies... seems sympathetic... his quest... who pretends..." Giving Ferrand the loot would leave them with eight bucks. The Turtle did not say: The Lord will make a way. She went to Eighth Street and window-shopped while Mason, as light-stepping as a snipe, returned to fetch the "infamous" report. Ferrand's office was above a Boop's Super-Duper Fast (Four-Hour) Service Cleaners. Talk about being taken to the cleaners! Ferrand looked up when our antihero walked in. Girl Friday, apparently, was out to lunch. To Mason he looked like an efficient man, with Henry Fonda-integrity, honesty, the whole bit. Even the slow speech. The droop, too. It could be raining cats and dogs and he'd get from point *a* to *b* without getting wet—and without an umbrella. Mason's confidence was informed by his, uh, savvy. "Seat." "Thanks." Cut the formality: long story short: the report: "After receiving a large grant from the Magnan-Rockford Foundation, the man who claims to be the author hired a bodyguard. Unsatisfied with living in fear, a month later, he dismissed the guard in favor of changing his name and thus living a clandestine existence. It was less expensive. He assumed the name of Clarence McKay. (My secretary, Mrs. Scalamaltzy, did a little research at the main branch. The author's choice may have stemmed from a quaint respect for a forgotten Jamaican writer, Claude McKay, who thought of himself as *international*.) McKay's address: Eight-sixty-four East Eleventh Street, third floor, Apartment Ten. At this address he pretends to be poor: wears sandals and jeans around the neighborhood, has a white girlfriend, etc. In actuality he is relatively wealthy: he just purchased a country estate in South Hadley Falls, Mass., near Mount Holyoke. I spoke on the phone yesterday with a Mister Shabbi in Zurich—where the author has an account at Swiss Bank Corporation International, Limited. Shabbi told me he'd just been contacted by real estate brokers in the South of France who were about to sell the author a piece of old French property with a view of the sea. The brokers were checking credit. The author also has accounts with Chemical Bank New York, Saudi International Bank, Banque Nationale de Paris. His other investments are managed through banks in Hong Kong, Luxembourg, Dusseldorf—exact nature: unclear. His broker in New York is Mister Stephen Gracio, Morgan Grenfell and Company, Limited. He has "friends" at Baker International Corporation, and, according to unconfirmed reports, is seeking information about ways to exploit the rubber business in Liberia, the gold in Ghana. His telephone number: Five-five-eight, eight-seven-three-four." Mason scratched his bloody mudfrog till the itch turned to pain. He found Painted Turtle in McDonald's on Sixth and Eighth eating a Big Mac and absent-mindedly dragging the crisp tails of one frenchfry after another through a bloodbath of ketchup. He gave her the scoop, while checking out the screwballs and seedy, the schlemiels and sheiks, "gracing" the counter in disdainful sluggishness. He ordered the Filet-O-Fish, and bit into the trust-company of its crust. The Turtle was reading the report. When she finished she handed it back without a word.

Mason shot through The Impostor's apartment: desperately, hastily overturning chairs, books, pillows, lamps; dumping the pathetic contents of dresser drawers; raking out the tacky, broken, random things in the dark, turn-of-the-century closet. With Jesus' help he overturned the ratty mattress in the tiny bedroom. One smudgy small window imprisoned in its dirty, battleship gray wall. They moved like charged sentences—with that old infamous thrust: wrenching, tearing, kicking, stabbing, bursting through things with the spikes of their fists. Secrets were sought? What else? Hide and seek? Whose hide—? What could McKay (*they* called him this) have . . . ? Would they find Truth skewered into The Impostor's messy belongings—his dirty jeans, pots, plants on the window-ledge? This guy: McKay—a social climber? Ha! a member of the international jet set, with chic Parisian girlfriends, ah—No. No way. Barking up the wrong double entendres. No place could be farther from the charmed beau monde glitter than this dump in the Lower East. It stank of rotten chicken heads, rabbit guts, piss, dog shit, eighty years of grime, not of satin linings, pink mink, sugared café au lait. No Flauntleroy here, yall. But I will restrain myself: no point in talking about absurdity. Mason and company had the stylistic verve of a polar bear. Brad was guarding McKay—tied to a white wooden kitchen chair, by the bathtub. At the same time he was going through the wallet again, checking the checkbook: everything, yup, said *Clarence McKay*. No question. McKay, handsome devil, was babbling like crazy—clearly not sure of their intentions. He kept saying he had no money, nothing valuable. Mason went over and slapped him. "You stole my manuscript, while I was in the joint—" "What?" "From Zimmerman—Don't try to deny it!" *Whack! "Think hard, motherfucker!"* McKay's wrists worked hard against the expertly knotted rope. (Big blond Brad had been a piss-poor bluejacket in Hawaii with flatfoot blues, a blue-eyed rover boy with gambling problems who fistfought other belly mates, but he had a talent for dogging a rope; and this old hot-headed Joe Gish threw a pretty good hook, too—could answer, marry, and take in the washing.) McKay's naked crusty feet strained against the old flowered linoleum. The popping muscles in his neck gave reality to the vertical thrust of his anger—humiliation, fear. *Whock!* "I don't know *nobody* named Zinnerman." Whimpering now. Say the secret word and ... Mason grabbed the guy's shirt front, shook him vigorously, shouting, *"Think!"* in his face, spittle flying onto McKay's eyelids. (The loudness of Mason's voice brought to his memory a time in prison when a loud shout like that saved his ass from being raped by a gorilla with a scar down the center of his left cheek, his hair in pin-curlers, pumps on his thick feet, who ate rusty razor-blades, tin cans, ship screws, mine cables, Boy Scouts and mousetraps for breakfast—and never got a tummy ache.) A button came off in his grip. "... thief, rotten sonofabitch, lowdown pig ... snake-in-the-grass, yellowbelly, bullshitting mother—" McKay was now crying, sobbing. This fella *did* look enough like the picture on the book jackets ... but, then, the earlier books had carried pictures so different from each other. It was hard to tell, for sure. And then, who could trust those damn bookjacket shots? The phone rang six times.

Edith Levine had dyed-blond hair and yellow blue (green) eyes. She'd gained weight. Was nervous as she held the closet door opened. The crafty dudes pushed the captive in and Mason locked it. "...some mistake..." McKay was still whining in a voice with the plaintive yelp of a kicked pup. "*Now* what?" Edith wanted to know. "He can't stay *here* long. You gotta do something—" "Don't worry. We'll—" Mason squeezed her thin shoulder. Brad: "We got techniques. He'll come around in no time." Pretty nice pad ya got here, Edith. Seventy-second and Riverside Drive ain't bad. Mason'd already been told Edith was hanging out (drinking with) a different crowd: Joe Valenti, Gianni D'Amico, others down in Little Italy and some heavies up in the Bronx. Rumor also had it she was doing a sideline Call Girl-act for Guy Flotilla, Porn Boss of Times Square. *Edith?* a college graduate—smart, expert on... What'd happened to those mushy marriage plans—the bacon and eggs popping in the skillet at sunrise with the tangy smells floating up to the ranch-house kiddie bedrooms...? Had they gone down the drain in the same splash with the dream of a brilliant career in sociological research on one of the big teams? Edith'd already heard through the gossip-vine about Painted Turtle and was curious. But Mason wasn't talking. His mind was a battleship full of stampeding torpedo experts crazy with war lust. Brad lit a stick, passed the joint to Edith, she hit and passed to Mason. They sat around like Farrell nitwits except in a classier setting. Mason knew Brad and Edith now had a thing going, sort of. Well, nobody had serious relationships: right—but they had serious mutual you-scratch-my-back-I-scratch-your-back interests.

Days later the man in the closet still insisted he had no idea what the hell was coming off. The idea was to brainwash—? beat him into submission—? agreement? You tell me. Was it possible anybody could be *that* good an actor and not be paid for such performance? Still here at Seventy-second. Mason sipped a 7-Up. It was Jesus' move. Checkers were a bore. Brad was watching TV. Edith was downtown making a porno flick with Mighty Mo, a new star. They planned to call it "Happy Valley." Painted Turtle, here for the first time, was restless. She'd already gone for one walk—was thinking of going for another. Definitely she was against the *idea* of that human being in the closet. All this shit made her nervous and Mason knew it and worried. And that dud McKay was a bomber and tomorrow he was going to Chemical. He had to. No point in waiting. Just walk right up to the window—with a powerful scenario; like, hey, I lost my checkbook, or, uh, I gotta big oil deal going in Saudi Arabia—need a quick loan, know my credit is shipshape here. Tell the prez I'm here. *He* knows my name. One of your biggest stockholders. But Sir, do you have an appointment? No, but got a point. Not funny. Give the clown a pentothal injection. He has no ace in the hole—just playing against—. He was cold footed, all right. His gold colic was out to lunch. He'd reach the bank's entrance at United Nations' Plaza, flannelmouthed with no hold on the jerk line. He needed a hymn, a chance to put the saddle on the right horse. No private apocalypse to foretell him of an end to his checkbook blues. Mason was a quivering nerd. Mister Bogus'd step into the revolving door. It'd stick.

When Mason came out of the bank his color had changed: he saw himself in a showcase window: dark gray-purple— not his usual earth with tree bark and leaf and sky in the pigmentation. He could still hear the clerk's laughter echoing in his unclogged ear. Had she seen him as the wretched of the planet? Surely she instantly took him to be an archfiend, a liar, a nut. He felt lucky to have gotten out without a police escort. It would take time to establish his "rightful" identity. He walked back to The Other Side. Painted Turtle wasn't in the room. Probably up at Edith's. That damned cretin in the closet: he'll *crack*—imagine coming up with a name like Clarence McKay! What could be phonier? Until the masquerader cooperates the MRF bread won't rise. Hadn't the other winners been announced in the news on TV in the rec room at Attica? Robert Penn Warren, Donald Barthelme, novelist Charles Wright, and another name Mason couldn't remember. Sorta like that old TV show called *The Millionaire*. They seem to give money to people at random for no clear reason. Imagine! Fifty thousand smacka-roos a year for life! Mason, feeling the depth of his human impediment, remembered an inmate who'd swindled a bank out of a hundred and fifty thousand by simply calling the president, telling him he was some Arab oil magnate with a son in Attica. The bank sent the inmate the money the next day. Most of it went to an account number the inmate had given the president and about twenty grand came to Attica. Even after the dude got ten years added to his sentence he was still a hero to the guys. So what was Mason's excuse? Not a *real* crook? Oh, I forgot: he was a novelist. *Is* a novelist? A poet, a sensitive man, a man of convictions; a person of "true credibility"? And although, like his father, he'd been framed and lost part of his life rotting away in a prison cell, he was not bitter enough to further destroy himself. He had to now go slowly, reestablish himself with skill, smoothly. The Wolf in Sheep's Skin was the immediate hindrance. Just ahead waited riches and respect: yachts, bank accounts around the world, the good life—where the chance of social pain, sudden death by stupid accident, insults, violence were reduced. And Painted Turtle would *be there* to enjoy it all with him. His stupid mudfrog itched but he refused it the comfort of a scratch. Oh, well. He subwayed to Edith's. Brad was in the closet with The Impostor. Mason looked in. Brad was stuffing Wonder Bread into McKay's mouth. Where was Edith? And Jesus? Search me. Brad giggled as the captive gagged. Don't feed him too much—the brains will never clear: empty stomach opens way to vision.

Water twice a day. Bread every other. Enough. Mason'd lost track of the schedule they'd laid out for reprogramming this guy they held in darkness. What's wrong with his nose—? it's all purple. He fell. Mason felt like an hombre with athlete's feet between his fingers: watching Brad struggle with McKay gave him illicit shivers. Was life itself some kind of virus? Never mind. He and The Turtle had made the best of it. The others weren't going anywhere though they claimed they were. Edith knew what she'd do with her cut. Jesus, too. And Brad. And Rob. The immediate problem was this impersonator: Mason had to deal with this shammer in the only way one deals with a conspirator: to out-do him he had to become a supreme impostor himself. He scratched his mudfrog with gentle schizophrenic devotion, as he watched Brad's savage action... What lessons had Mason learned in prison? Public Enemy and Grits had taught him— perhaps—too much. What would Public Enemy advise? He'd say, Listen to me, jack, you gotta give up this bullshit about gettin- yo rep back. What difference do it make, huh? The important thang is: *you,* barnstormer, baby-lifter, bootlegger, boozehound, cake-cutter, garbage-kisser, *is* you! You gotta outsmart that sucker. He outsmarted you, so you got to throw a double-whammy on him and hang him by his balls. Be a quick-change artist! Listen to Public. I know what I'm talkin' 'bout. And he'd throw his chin out. Smirk. You say the *name* is part of the deal? I hear ya. You can't get the dough without the name being restored. Well, if that rotten egg-sucker ain't around then where's your competition? See my point? Drop the joker in quicksand, send him skating across thin ice, stand him on his head in the bottom of the East River. That's what a snake-in-the-grass deserves. Don't dangle and fart around. You got to *create* yo identity! So you once owned it, so what. Who cares. You don't anymore. You're just a greenhorn, a sucker, a laughing-stock. What you want now is to get a passport, bank account, driver's permit, whatever you need, in the name of... you know who. You'll have to *buy* them. Go to my old friends Valenti and D'Amico. They can help. Once you're legal and clean as a chitlin' nobody'll be able to touch you. Sitting pretty and ready to fly, you won't even need them dingy wings I seen ya with... Yup. That's the advice Public'd shoot. And he'd be right. Jesus came in out of breath—shot into the bathroom and started washing under his arms. What happened to you? Nothing. Mason moped in the doorway.

In the porno films—for money—he didn't have to be Hambone nor Cotton Mouth Joe but he had to shine. Damn Edith! Jack Pradel, Director Supreme, told Mason his instrument was impressive. After the checkup Mason handed Jack the doctor's report. Green light. He'd get three hundred a flick. They'd shoot for a week. Each morning from ten till noon. Okay? The cameraman was Joe Wembly. Nice guy. Edith herself was stuck in another series. Just as well. Mason didn't want to screw her on screen. Sordid? Too moral?... He showed up early—nine-fifteen—for the first. Faye (Undressed-to-Kill) Daltrey was to be his co-star. Brunette. Big hips. After the shower and make-up Mason stepped out under the lights. Faye had an instant eye for the camera. He approached her as she watched the lens. She winked at it as he slid her panties down. Title: Diamond Legs. She had long ones. Shapely. Kept stepping and moving. Twitching. This was a reflexive one: no story-line. She slid back on a leather couch and he went at her till body and spirit closed. Then she made her mouth into the C-shape of a clay pot as she pulled at him with great linear strokes. Next scene: he entered her from the rear. She was energetic. Her wide hips were gyrating, rocking: it was like disco dancing. Faye winked at the camera. Blew a kiss at it. When he came she winked again at the Eye... Next morning he got it on with Little Sally Walker—a grown woman dressed to look like a twelve-year-old. Sally wore bobby socks and had a mouth full of bubble gum which she kept smacking. Her blonde hair was in pigtails. She had a jump-rope with blue handles. Story: Mason was supposed to be a farmhand and she was the daughter of the farmer. First shot: Mason quickly, expertly driving the tip of a blade into the neck of a calf just behind the jaw. Little Sally Walker wanders into the shot. Hello. Good morning Miss Sally. And there you have it. Within minutes she's playing Pony Express with his Messenger. Next he's tonguing her lava in search of a formula for clarity. Then Coca-Cola Max Sanderson, a white guy from down-the-road-a-piece, arrives. Together he and Mason romp with Little Sally Walker making use of all her orifices... Then Lilia Pant on the third morning. Mason liked her best. She was a real actress. Dreamy. Dreamy, dreamy. Lilia's hair was some sort of iron ore color: thick fluffy. She too kept up a permanent relationship with the camera. She was supposed to be a call girl working in the back room of a bar called Pink Pussycat Lounge. The bartender sends Mason back to her. As he goes back he thinks: "You are not yet the casting director: save your energy, man. You're one with a future. Don't blow it on fuck films." Joe Wembly follows Mason's erection to Lilia's face. Her crunch was crowded with charm and dance music and air-conditioned erotic finger-licking-good messages... Then Eve Hott, in Chatterley's Lady. Mason's Chatterley: a Black mafia Boss in Harlem. Dressed in tux. The first four scenes show him unfulfilled by his harem of hot mommas. Then Galaxy Creole, a thug from downtown, sends Louisiana Eve Hott up to see him. And, wouldn't you know, the show...

Mason *was* a motion picture: you could run him forward then backwards. He split, resisting the temptation to squat in the Mickey Mouse closet with his "enemy." He was in reverse at the moment—anxious about Painted Turtle, he went to Forty-second Street and sat in a dark theatre, watching celluloid clambake, cluck, all the screensation of a quickie: couldn't keep his mind on the bark, the gelatin: something about a prison break. They have no *idea*, baby: one day he was bopping along First toward A when two plainclothesmen jumped out of a squad car before it even stopped. Sluff action. Gave him a one-eyed-fadeaway. Grabbed him. Twisted his arms behind him, banged his head against the building. Roughly rammed hands into all his pockets. He was clean. Slapped handcuffs on his wrists. Threw him in the back seat: barred in. The trial was quick. He couldn't afford a lawyer: at the mercy of city service, he lost and the next morning was driven out early in a huge Black Maria—a battleship floating on quicksand—with fifteen other black dudes smelling of sweat, grass, and rotgut... Up there Mason had lots of time to review himself: he'd grown up watching the chitlin' circuit, waiting to see the half moons in Freddie Washington's pretty eyes. When he daydreamed teachers shouted at him. Everybody was a potential enemy. If one wasn't playing with loaded dice one was about to bilk you in another way. He was just a run-by—out of focus. Every day was April Fool's: don't give a sucker an even break. One had to be a magician in such a world. He got a custard pie in the face at every curtain call. But at Attica, Mason was a model prisoner: with a head full of canned music, funnies, giddyappers, still he read books, books, books. Few others did: they were mostly into hick pics, horse stuff or close-up shots of Dirty Rats. (The young ones got raped: fucked in the ass by studs and jocks and heavy queens. The boys surrendered their assholes in exchange [so they were told] for protection from the bellybutton sweat of mass murderers, hit-men, and crazed maniacs. Public Enemy, Mason's old pal, was too old to get it up, although he, too, had, in his day, been one of these protection-granters.) In the joint Mason woke every morning with a bullfrog-headache and smelling like a shrike and unwilling and not ready to face the daily hullabaloo. His mind was a camera mount imitating the motion of a boat: seasick, ugh, vomit: his mother's words echoing just inside his eardrums: you, like your father, ain't never been no good . . . his side of the family . . . rotten. Before Mason realized it he was grown, his father dead, his mother old: not even a dummyhead focused on the action! Growing up he executed cats, frogs, grasshoppers, snakes: had a definite criminal streak—struck out with redhandedness at the "degenerate" world around: nothing was "innocent"—not even insects. With pals Mason discovered the mysteries of Halloween, New Year's Eve: a feeling of craziness and anarchy were everywhere on such nights. One could do almost anything—*anything!* He was restless, when he wasn't interested in lessons, a future, but maybe in girls, his own "importance." Interest in girls [as *sex* objects] came the year after sitting on the dunce stool in the fifth grade: stuck his tongue out at teacher when her back was turned: made the other kids laugh: Mason liked the attention: wanted to grow up to be a comedian. He threw chalky erasers at girls, jerked their pigtails to hear them squeak, shriek; tripped fat boys in halls and in the cloakroom, peed in pockets and ate other students' lunches. He stole money, too: it was fun: everybody *noticed* him: he was at the center of the camera-eye: All he needed was a cast of thousands: Cecil. He screwed his first girl in an alley—Chicago type: felt like His Satanic Majesty. Other boys still virgins looked up to him ("How'd it *feel?*") and followed him around on the playground. Then high school: here a thousand-watt spotlight was not focused on his curls, no sky panning behind him with overhead reflector. He couldn't stand it: he spat at the truant officer and quit before he could be formally suspended. He wanted to knock up a nun like that French boy in that French novel; wanted to run off to Malta or Delfi or . . . do *interesting* things. But that was sort of out of character for a ghetto kid. Damn character. Yet he managed to run no farther than the Air Force draft board. The sergeant promised him Europe and he got Texas—San Antonio. Hot dry dusty. Basic training was a blip: falling in mud holes, dodging blanks, hiding in bushes, jumping in and out of shacks freshly sprayed with deadly gas, drills, bland food, more drills, itchy wool blankets, swimming for non-swimmers once a week.

Phew! Then the boys got their first town pass and went into San Anton'—being boys they got hungry as hogs on the way and the first thing they did was find a lunch counter called Blinkies Hamburgers and Hotdogs. Mason, two other Afro-Americans and three Polish kids from Chicago's West Side. Mason noticed right away the walls contained blowups of electric stars, heavenly bodies and cinema lasses: Shirley Temple, Tex Ritter, Lana Turner, Roy and Trigger. They sat at the counter. The napkin holder had an embossed head of a roaring lion. The toast-thin waitress—blonde, wearing pink rimmed cateyed specs—came. She asked the white boys what they wanted, then said to Mason and the other two, "We don't serve Negroes here." Mason noticed the salt and pepper shakers were not C-shaped. The fat sloppy owner came over scratching his red neck. "All right, I want you niggers to get. Y'all must be from up North some whah. Well, dis is Texas, byGod. You white boys can stay." No hostility in his voice: only annoyance. "Niggers from 'round heah'd know better'n t' come in a rest'rant and sit down wid white folks." Celt CuRoi whispered in his ear: "You are not yet the casting director: save your energy, honey. You got a future. Don't blow it on this fly-speck in the shitpile." Yet Mason could not resist: "You got catsup on your chin. Mustard on your T-shirt." The Fat man swung at Mason but missed. They all jumped up and ran out. A couple of blocks left of shooting they stopped. The pink boys sheepishly went off in one direction—toward white-town and the brown boys pointed their noses toward black-town. Mason wondered if the rest of them felt the sour something coming up the throat. Now, he and the other two found Mama Minnie's Chili and Tripe Parlor in the black section next door to The Camelback Shoeshine and Barbershop (that day he started smoking Camels). It was midmorning and sunny. While they ate, three fat prostitutes came in from their gigantic Buick parked out front. And so it went: there was Mason soon in motion again. Texas was no picnic: a couple of days later he had guard duty from late afternoon till midnight. Here his motion was slow. Not even Celt came to keep him company. A kid named Rubinstein from Chicago relieved Mason at twelve. The full moon was Hollywood Boulevard on opening night for *Gone with the Wind.* Mason was upstairs undressing when he heard the voices. Careful not to wake the bigot who slept above him, Mason looked out the window. The moonlight showed Rubinstein down there on guard duty between the two barracks—but who were these three other guys? Drunken voices. *Ah!* One was, you bet, their Tactical Instructor, Airman Gimbal—a warlock with tangled hair and insanity in his eyes. He was holding Rubinstein by the front of his shirt and repeatedly slamming his back against that barracks over there. Saying, *"You sonofabitching Jew! You kike, you money-hoarder...we should stomp your ass into the ground! Hitler was right—"* He went on, as the other two drunk TI's watched and giggled and swayed at the end of their high-hat-shadows while holding beer cans in yellow-lighted paws. Rubinstein was crying. Mason felt helpless—rage—as Airman Gimbal punched Rubinstein in the stomach again and again the way you'd sock a punching bag. The other two drunks now held Rubinstein's arms. The plump kid took one finisher, corker, sleeping potion, slogdollager after another. He *had* to be biffy-batty by now but he hadn't yet reached out for hearts and flowers. Though he whimpered and puffed in a wham-whoozy voice, that victim of the washboard blues, the hammer, refused to be creamed. Losing control of himself, Mason dashed downstairs— a cyclone in the stairway—and ran outside, skipping the steps, hitting the grass, feeling the sting in his spine and knees, his teeth banging together. He saw them over there. The blow-by-blow report kept up a bonebending racket in his ear. Grunt-and-groan response: Rubinstein. The TI's were growling and...Celt suddenly tapped Mason on the shoulder. He ignored her. Then it happened: he started gagging, vomiting up his guts, stewed potatoes, boiled chicken, spam, Wheaties, milk, potato chips, ice cream, cobwebbed fears. And now *they* saw him, on his knees, in the moonlight. *Holyshit!* So guilt and shame were following Mason like mad hound dogs tracking an escapee from rock-splitting "justice." Ah, yes: he was riding the delivery bike back to the Edward Hopper drugstore. Headlights, like swacks in the dark that made the floaters fly, came at him. A wind machine on stage behind him? *Stage?* Hush yo mouth! Motion on Mason! The dirty slush of a recent snowstorm was good for deep, thin tracks—you could even *write* words with the tires. But now rain. The car came *at* him. Fast. Getting out of the way of this left-hander, he fell between two cars, losing the bicycle—as it flopped, hit by the swooping fender. Mason looked up from the wet, oily gutter. It was night. The car's side window was lined with gray menacing faces; griffins, buzzards, sharptoothed rats. What North Side gang was this? Maybe it wasn't wise working up here near Loyola University. He thought Jewish boys were more human than this. He ate his humiliation and rage, as he lifted himself and his bike, up: they did not taste like strawberries, cornflakes and milk. It was enough to make one realistic. And that time in Cheyenne after basic with the Spanish exchangees. Christ, those guys! sitting around the barracks flipping through their Merriam-Websters pathetically in search of "fuck" and "cunt" and "cock"—how could they have so misread Henry Bosley Woolf's intentions? These hombres, from Madrid, from Barcelona, old enough to remember their fathers' talk about the Spanish Civil War, and still feeling South/North antagonism, knew those words existed in the wallop, smell and cheesecake of America, so why weren't they in your everyday, honest-to-goodness dictionary. Mason nor the others could answer. And why was it so important to find *those* words? Still Life with Dirty Words. Did they really *scratch* the itch? They called the real one Miss Cunt. She was brought in a truck every Friday night. The driver of the pickup said he was her husband. Guy obviously had a deal with the guard at the gate? Miss Cunt was not handsome, nothing to write home about: over forty, bleached hair, lots of veined fat. She and her husband were a couple of rednecks from around Laramie where, they said, they had a few chickens, a hog, and got by. Well, the Spanish guys couldn't find *cunt* in the book but they got her in the cab. Mister Cunt just sat there in the driver's seat, on guard. Only two or three of the American guys—

boys really—had her. The Spanish airmen'd get up there and sit her on their laps. One at a time, with their cocks up in her fat, she'd wiggle around till they found the speed of light through the sounds she made. Sometimes Mason lying way away in his bunk could hear her grunts. She had one kind for grinding and another for derby. As I said, hubby counted the wet loot and kept top eye opened, and this service was provided the Spanish men in search of "fuck" and "cunt" and "cock" for as long as they were in military records training. There was no way to avoid their bragging. Mason was still in motion but the camera wasn't on him. Then he got shipped *(shipped?)* to Valdosta where commanders laughed at him when he requested transfer; said he'd been promised Europe. It wasn't till a doctor treating him for an ulcerated stomach said racism was killing him that the commanders unpacked their sense of humor and gave him a screen test for another location: he won a deeper degree of South: was given a ticket to a base in northern Florida. Here he discovered rocks had souls: discovered ancient Greece. Books were not shot from guns. He lived in himself since there was not space worthy outside. Finally, honorably discharged, Mason made the mistake of returning to Chicago.

The plan was simple: Jesus, Brad, Edith, Painted Turtle and Mason would knock off the Chemical Bank at United Nations' Plaza. They'd be successful and Gianni D'Amico and Joe Valenti would in exchange for heavy bread get Mason his booklet and plastic. Plus: everybody would get a lot of loot—split equally. They'd go separate ways: for safety. But first: in order to get the Hotchkiss—maybe two of 'em—they needed quick, easy money: they'd hit a bodega—a thing Jesus knew how to do—to get cornmeal for the Japanese ninety-twos and, if lucky, even a W two-sixty-three machine pistol. Brad had a misfiring Smith and Wesson twenty-two, Jesus owned an old forty-five with a worn pin. They sat in Edith's place planning the downtown hit. Mason, who owned no gun, pranced back and forth in the room like a torero escaping a bull. Now that Mason had improved the quality of his imagination he enlisted Jesus, impulsively, to test him: good bank robbers had to have incontestable imaginations. Image? So assume a secret plan concealed a design: he had to know the wire-works of it. Jesus said: "Okay. Ready?" "Yeah. City with yellow light on scrapers. Black water beneath iron bridge?" Jesus shook his head. "No." "Church windows glowing from inside?" "No." "Hillside with frame houses facing sunset?" "No." Mason began to feel tense and angry. Jesus, casually sacked out in a beanbag, looked up. "Well?" "A nervous horse being operated on in a veterinary center?" "Wrong again." "Going downstream on a quiet river surrounded by plush exotic Conrad-trees at dusk under a blue African sky with red clouds?" "Naw—give it one more shot. One more for the imagination!" "Okay. Ah—" but the doorbell rang and they all jumped like wall-wire short-circuiting. They didn't buzz and nobody came up. Mason opened a beer. He figures better with a drink? He puzzles me. If I tie a string to his nervous little finger and connect it to a large C hanging, say, in the sky, then connect the C to Celt and from her stretch it from myself to Mason, then jerk the end of the damn thing—what would happen? Would I get any added up, totalized meaning, plot? Here they go: they, say, strut into the bank: "Motherfucker, open the cash drawer. Give me all the hundreds you have." No. They gotta be smarter than *that*. What if they take along a duffel bag? While Mason and Jesus hold the clerks and guard at gunpoint, Brad could fill the bag going along the counter. Or Jesus could fill. That'd give 'em a hell of a lot of carrots and potatoes. Of course they'd be putting all their rotten eggs into one basket but what the—. No matter what, they couldn't go in with a stupid sticking hammer nor a rusty cartridge-chamber. Painted Turtle was in the dark bedroom, alone, brooding. Mason went into the kitchen where Edith was boiling gun metal-colored water for her three-minute egg. Still on a diet. They won't let you fuck in films if you get too fat. Jesus started talking excitedly about the old PR who ran the bodega on the corner of Sixth and C. Edith brought out tea and even PT came out for some. Public Enemy used to get high on tea: just drank it hot and got smashed. Only person on earth who got drunk as a skunk on Lipton's. Like Public, he was still doing time, wasn't he. At one point Mason had so little time to do it seemed to him crazy to join Public and the others in a break. But wasn't this yet another kind...? Anyway, Mason threw a Milton Bradley softball against the wall: surrounded by gentle murderers, cute armed robbers, depressed rapists, big, dark drag-queens, punks, jocks, hit-men, wire-tappers, mass murderers, and generic types who ate razor blades for breakfast and cut vein-lined throats at the frenzied high point of prison sodomy-rape. Mason—who was nervous—had a problem catching the ball on its return. Public was waiting there for an answer. You with us or not? Man or mouse? Bull Moose, who'd casually cut off his woman's head and carried it in a plastic shopping bag over to the East River five years ago, was laughing at Mason's hesitation. Squirrel, a pretty boy, who got gang raped every day, was biting his nails. Grits'd whispered to Mason that morning: "Shotgun's gonna waste you just before the break if you don't." Just like in the movies: taut social cables between them. These men, dear reader, were not polite beachgoers saying *Ouch!* to the rocks along the shore near Eze. Mason felt his life about to hit the fan. All because of silly tea. But the break was called off at the last minute because the Governor had gotten wind of it and sent a secret message by way of the warden: "I will shoot to kill." He might have been drinking tea, too. Who knows. Oh, the woes of a life of crime. Although Mason thought of himself as innocent, a victim, he had not managed to completely erase his memory of his days of catgut-slick petty theft. Listen to this: the fifth floor was dark except for hard light from the street. Swiftly Mason quietly checked all the cash registers: locked locked locked—*ah!* *un*locked. He stood there, tense as a long-legged cowboy badly breaking a broomie. Then: with his upturned index, holding the drawer from its bottom, so as not to leave prints, he gently pulled, hearing the sweet turn of the smooth rollers in their grooves: he lifted the paper money out from under the bars—feeling a kind of bronco-buster's victory over a gut twister. His bad actor was Life-Up-Till-Now. He felt no sympathy for society, folks; didn't feel he was doing anything wrong. Cheated from birth, he reasoned, he was simply a rat stealing a crumb. That sluttish rush of excitement he felt, as he stuffed the loot into his jeans, was hoedown-swoon he could live with. Then Mason went on through the dark before him. Surely there had to be another—greater mistake. That was the thing about it: it got good to you. He woke up often in confinement: drenched in his own bile, sweat, urine. His own hopeless face, mirrored, shared nothing with him. It belonged to another guy he'd never met. Miss Hand and Her Five Daughters were his female companions. The queens and jocks didn't want him—luckily—because he was too *old.* As I told you, Mason was a reader: he read Verlaine, Oscar Wilde, Chester Himes and Iceberg Slim and Genet and Cassanova and Villon and Cervantes and, draw iron, that victim author of modest rep.

When Mason and Jesus stepped into Sanchez's Bodega at Sixth and C a gray stickup artist was already holding a nervous W two-sixty-three on the leather-skinned old man and his single customer, a gaudy Puerto Rican woman in a Sears & Roebuck blue flower print who was whimpering in terror. The gunman, with matted long light hair, looked like a burned-out flower child. His trigger-talk was unconvincing. Yet, uh, y-yet . . . it took Mason and his sidekick a full minute to comprehend what was happening. A sluggishness held Mason right up to the moment of Judge Colt-perception. The gunman, a boy excitable, impulsive, grouchy, hog-wild, nuts, was a true danger—

and Mason and Jesus knew it. And moved *like* they knew it. He waved his impressive machine pistol at them. "All right, get over there with her—" California accent? And as Jesus and Mason obeyed, Mason's plan was to stick up the boy after he stuck up Sanchez. Why not? He had to get *there* by hook or crook. No moron could be tolerated in *his* path. The old man handed over the stack of dirty bills to the kid. As the flower child stuffed them into his jeans he relaxed the gun slightly. When he looked down at his own hand, Mason rushed him—pushing Jesus' old, worn, rusty forty-five into the boy's right ear. "Make one move an you're a goner. Hand it over." Mason meant the W two-sixty-three. The kid obeyed. Mason stuck the weapon down in his belt under his jacket. "All right, the money, kid!" He handed it over and the hippie shot. Mason's mudfrog itched but this was no time to scratch. While the old man was profusely thankful, and reaching for the money, Mason was opening the machine pistol—no magazine. "It's empty!" Sanchez took the dough out of Mason's hand. Mason gave the old guy a startled look. "Gracia, gracia . . . !" And guess what? Mason nor Jesus had the twist of heart to tell him he was not truly in spirit vindicated. Meanwhile, Mason saw the kid hauling ass through traffic against red. Mason and Jesus, embarrassed, stepped out backwards, ruffled and guilty, as the grocer offered them ten bucks reward. Some Witches' brew this venture turned out to be. Well, at least they had an impressive weapon—exactly the one Mason dreamed of. In fact, perhaps there was more irony here than farce: the machine pistol cost more than they probably would have lifted from the cash register. Was this the same Mason who in the joint had read The Author's works over and over again till he convinced himself he was the writer and no longer the reader? Paradoxical or not, he was still the imposterous bilker! Quoting Conrad!—and I'm sure he could quote Melville's *The Confidence Man*—and might yet. I grant him agility in his mission but little else. Was he a single snow-rooted and arctic flower-weed in a storm? The Island, of course—as corny as it is—was himself, and he had, in a sense, not left it, not reached it. Although Joyce

Kilmer's so-called tree was only a symbol, it spoke out of a complex anxiety in this drinker of scamper juice: namely his need to maintain a sort of membranous contact with nature through the printed sheet held to light. "Naked he was forced to stand in the sunrise, his incisions bleeding..." That confidence now shaken by insistent irony, one so penetrating Mason now felt was lost as, say, Conrad's Marlow when he found himself plunging on deeper into the hoosegow he called darkness. Mason's icky self-deception was excruciating: a madman, surely: a mirthlessly deranged four-flusher who meant to dream his way through very serious, ugly business. His mission, you see, had him rushing downstream toward a great waterfall. Painted Turtle had the potential—though not the willingness—to turn him into a respectable citizen, a man of true integrity and credibility, but never mind: he hadn't been ready even if she'd been interested enough. Plus she was moody, depressed, at the end of much failure, a helpless singer without a song, unable to return to Zuni where others still managed to be whole, she too was lost. So Mason fumbled on, hearing the buzz of C's and the drip of Z's deep within. A chiseler well-oiled by guilt and grief, Mason carried the weight of symbols: fish and bird ones. Walking with his "friend" Jesus, he now found himself on the filthy, desperate streets of the Lower East Side again, carrying a gun, a victim of many trick mirrors. Here no shade as under that jazzed up tree. No sir. This was jalopy, jellybean poverty—as background, and in the foreground, in himself: sluttish rage and self-doubt. No mandrake here. Grim, grim, grim. And it was precisely this contrast he needed now and hated: it blazed in him with its discoloration of his so-called lyric nature. Lyric, uh, nature? So be it. No one escapes romanticism: not even tough guys. In fact, I swear, especially not tough guys. He surely needed a formula for clarity *of direction:* perhaps this: in a mixture of bay leaves, rosemary tops, two and a half pounds of pig fat, dump eight baby swallows (fresh out of nest with tails and longest feathers removed) then place in blender. Add salt and pepper to desire. Switch on. While at Attica, Mason read the *Book of Knowledge*

(1687) and now seriously tried to remember some of the ancient formulas for "clear sight." Who was to swear the 1654 Pharmacopoeia entirely out to lunch? Moral guy, this. Morality applied only to the content of one's attitude. Hem was right: it was what made you feel good. Don Quixote had good intentions but his attitude was without reliance. Clarity? Did Mason really want it, reach out decisively for it? I smelled a rat. Remember Nietzsche (not a friend of mine!) said, "Aren't books written precisely to hide what is in us?" And another dead man, also puzzling over the relation between "*clear* reality" and confessional writing, Jack Kerouac, in *Vanity of Dulouz*—go to it Jack: "I'll... get to believe... I'm not... Jack... at all and that my birth records... published books, are not real... that my own dreams... are not dreams... that I am not 'I am' but just a spy in somebody's body pretending... "

Being an electrician was not the world's truest vocation and although inkslinging was closer, you bet, it too was not. Old Jed Oxford out yonder in the sluggish Amesville air, standing ankle deep in the rich soil was in his work closer to the ultimate one. Mason'd learned Jed's deepest commitment was old as humanity itself: to nature. Jed'd believed human beings were bound to and shared nature like all living things. Yet Mason, crazed with his notion of being somebody he wasn't, hadn't found in himself any willingness to follow Jed's calling. Danny Kreutzer was the electrician and he was expensive. But this way was better: no direct confrontation with nobs. Just walk in and take the pretty jewels, crisp money, silent ready stuff. Pronto: find a fence. Next the big guns. Then the driver's license; the passport. Like clockwork. Kreutzer himself was a picaro, so said pal Rodriguez. Mason and Jesus went up in a taxi. Kreutzer's was in the Bronx. They rang the door in a massive ugly building at Waterloo Place near Crotona Park. A happy Mephistopheles, he agreed to go to work for them on a ten percent commission. Usually got twenty. On the subway back down they idly read the grafitti and the names of kids trying to make their presence felt in this barking dog show. This far uptown Mason missed the vegetable carts of First. God, did he need clarity now—and where the hell was that eater of Irish cherries and grapes, Celt? Painted Turtle was acting funny. Melville couldn't be quoted ("I hope I know myself...") out of context. Well, rats, nothing was easy. In a voice happy-as-ducks-in-Arizona! Kreutzer said on the phone to Mason: "Come on over. I got the roundup. Bring a hundred—fresh lettuce." An hour later, Mason and Jesus stepped into the apartment of one Danny K., for the second time in one week. Kreutzer's shit-eating grin was loaded with sandbags and heretic clouds, a mist hung close to the floor of his swampy mind—all this: in his face. Mason's circumspection meant nothing to Electric Danny. Mason handed over the money scraped together from Edith's purse, Painted Turtle's savings, Brad's shirt pocket, Jesus' jeans, Mason's wallet. This was in exchange the scoop: The Berdseids, a sure shot, lived in Apartment Eight-F in a high rise at Riverside Drive and West Seventy-Eight: lots of valuable jewels, expensive dinnerware, antiques, perhaps stored-away cash, silk bedsheets. Mason asked Kreutzer if he knew a fence. We don't use that word around here, he said. "Transaction-agent" was the expression (Z state sez one thing, Z church Cs another: like Z difference between wiping ya arse with one hundred percent cellulose and steel wool.) Mason and his thuggish sidekick left armed with Berdseids' information and the address of Ota and Company. In search of their scheme they went down and checked out the Riverside Drive apartment door. Careful not to be too obvious. They'd have to take the hinges off? Natural movable joints these days were easier to crack than a hundred and eight varieties of dead-bolts. The Birdseids were always away mornings after eight and never home before three. Never? Well, risk was always. An old door with wood panels. Maybe they'd have to remove one.

Could turn out easier. Jesus had equipment. When they got back Edith was upset, said McKay had been crying for over an hour. No response. How was that fink Kreutzer? Edith said she'd never put *her* confidence in him: something about the curve of his face. They could hear the whimpering. Mason felt bad. But maybe they were bogus tears? He thought: shit, this guy *might really be* The Author or even Pep West, who cheated his way into college, through college, who steamed open other people's mail. Mason wanted to kick himself in the butt for his boneheadedness. Now the problem: what to do with the remains of the unbreakable, uh, mistake. But his train was derailed when Painted Turtle came in wearing black lipstick, with punk paint on her cheeks. Imagine, a woman *forty* or more—! but there was a white feather stuck in her hair. Brad, in the kitchen doorway, cracked up. Jesus was telling Edith rumors about Danny being fluff. Mason was depressed suddenly: no one here was a breathing living character: he went over to the closet and looked in. "You'll get your justice so shut up!" Painted Turtle behind him, yanked his arm. "I need to talk with you. It's urgent. Let's go for a walk."

Breaking and entering had in them the seeds of cherries, the mustard of virginity. Nervous saboteurs, Mason and man-Friday gave up on the crowbar. (Jesus stood on the lower landing while Mason rang the Berdseids' bell and the one across from it: all was clear and now...) Still, it was important not to wake the dead. Jesus was good with the small drill. It made only a tiny hissing. A round splash of daylight from the living room window inside gave them pride and hope. Couldn't use the damn hammer: big as an Irish banjo: too much noise. But wasn't it true New Yorkers minded their own... *(say what?)* "No, try to get the tip of the saw in—" "Yessir, boss." Jesus' Puerto Rican accent fitted the southern Negro attempt like catcalls at an opera.

"Gimmie the damn thing!" Mason rammed the little saw in the freshly drilled hole. Jesus whispered. *"Ouch!* it hurts so good!" "Use the next size." Jesus easily enlarged the opening. Then the saw got in and slowly Mason worked it back and forth. Slowly, at first—then in one fit of impatience and fear he swung the saw viciously in and the old panel wood split halfway down. Amazing. A swift kick from palsy-walsy's western boot sent it in on the apartment's highly polished oak floor. Jesus, smaller than Mason, crawled through first. Then Mason stuck his tense head in, ooly-drooly, pulled his tight shoulders together, with his slim arms inside, he plunged for entrance. Tut-tut, brash my boy. "Wait—I'll open the door..." but Jesus was too late. Mason looked up from his hampered posture like a humpbacked midget with a painful face stuck into the ridge. His eyes were those of a confused puppy. He could see Jesus grinning. "Don't stand there with that stupid grin—*do* something! I'm *stuck!"* No person claiming eight letters in his given name has a right to pull a vaudeville act when he should feel active despair. But the more he struggled the tighter in he got himself. Jesus: "Maybe if I rock the door." "No, idiot! Take my arms—" Mason gripped the slender wrists—yanked. Nothing. Mason began to doubt his future: home runs, the whole bit. What about human dignity? After all, to hear him tell it, he was *a writer.* The pulling caused fish-headed pains in his ribcage. Birds beat their lice-bitten wings in his lungs. The air smelled like a fallout shelter of wet kittens. Jesus was licking his knife: about to cut or saw Mason out? They heard the elevator start downstairs.

Roy Seidel Ota had a clean skull that reflected the light above it. He was counting out on the desk edge in back a stack of dirty tens and fives. "No got twenties?" Jesus wanted to know. Mason kept a tight jaw. He was counting with

Ota. With the loot in a paper bag they left Ota and Company, a crowded jewelry shop on Canal at the edge of Chinatown near the bridge. They knew they'd been gypped—one always was in this kind of transaction. Valenti and his cousin D'Amico had said they could get a couple of Thompson machine guns. Things were tight: at the moment they couldn't promise anything else. But first Mason wanted to get rid of The Impostor and he decided not to kill. Unnecessary. But do something with him. And Ferrand, mistake or not, he had to get even with that crook. Lots to do quickly. Take The Impostor to the edge of the abyss—let him jump: fall or fly. Give him to the clang-a-lang moonless night ride into a fuddy duddy region? The Impostor might even find a new life, settle down, marry, have an infant to play tulips with and never again become the target of captors or larks. If Mason could maintain a kind of stillness at the center of this frenzy he too might get through: right or wrong. Edith, when they got back, was relieved and waiting with the rented car. (She'd sold a helluva lot of hash and grass that morning and had extra bread. Naturally she was looking forward to the bank take: so it was worth it.) Brad had The Impostor ready with the blindfold and tied hands. It was already dark, safe. Edith told them they were gypped: five hundred, she said, was only a third what that stuff was worth. Painted Turtle was at a movie in the neighborhood. Edith said she seemed depressed. Mason grunted. The four of them went down with The Impostor. Brad held the guy's arm, leading him. Edith drove, still bitching about the five hundred: it all had to go to Valenti. Okay, okay. The rush hour traffic had passed. Edith wheeled the new Ford expertly out of the city, heading for Jersey. She came to a complete stop in a dark parking lot just outside the Lackawanna Railroad Yard in Hoboken. The street lights from Barclay didn't help down here. Mason was pretty sure he remembered the line they wanted was five tracks over from this end. Even in the dark nothing seemed changed from this morning. Yes, there it was: the door still slightly ajar. The engine would spit and cough at five in the morning. The Impostor would be tucked away behind a stack of empty burlap sacks. In his long journey west he might thank his stars—crossed or not: the injured free of the injurer. No law of opposites could be applied. If The Impostor had in the outer gray matter of his brain something even remotely associating him with the real master of ceremonies, then that cortex had been preserved as the ultimate secret with its thick Peruvian bark closed hermetically around the unbroken linkage of the two. Could he have been the author of such a mysterious disruption in the relation between cause and effect: if The Impostor were yin, Mason was not necessarily yang. Forced connections were possible. But this was labyrinth: like the outcome of Mason's romantic philosophy of asserting himself: *taking* the identity he wanted. If The Impostor was on a blind trip, so was your boy. And the rigor mortis of truth was with them both. Harebrained? You bet.

Money. Mason packed his W two-sixty-three. Money: a jockeyship itself: owing its fiber to confidence. Bamboozle there (even in his memory of child support which he paid, "buying his way out of guilt," one judge said to his lawyer) in that sandcastle. Now the "stolen" money given to Ferrand: stolen because Ferrand had no right to it. He'd walk in: "Fucker, you doublecrossed—" then shoot the cigar outta the joker's mouth. For starters. No, he'd be more serious, factful. After all he only wanted the bread back. Mason arrived. Ferrand in his one-horse office sat with his kicks on his desk. Calmly, sweetly Mason told the detective *the* truth. It didn't impress. Then with ten-speed passion Mason shot: "I don't like being deceived. Once I climbed a pole for clarity: I was deceived. Then you pretended to give me the hoof marks of the man who snatched my —uh..." "...your wallet?" "Ferrand, I came here to get my money back." He took out the machine. Ferrand's pig-smile didn't take wings. Mason plunged on, hysterically: "I came to you sincerely. What a fool I was. I'm going to shoot you, and you know it. I came wearing the ugly mask of a dead mullet with glazed eyes. I coughed blood on the way. Ferrand, I—" He disliked his own pleading. It generated his anger; need for revenge. Mason saw that Ferrand was mindful of the pistol: as though it had a life. "I tell you: no cheap, two-bit private eye's gonna stand in—" but as Mason talked he angled the W two-sixty-three away from Ferrand, carelessly, and in that moment Ferrand whipped out his own weapon, a forty-five, and in no time had it against Mason's forehead where his worried eyebrows met. "Nigger, don't you know I'll kill you. You mean nothing to me or nobody else! What kinda *dumb* nigger are you, huh? You talk like you just came down from heaven, boy." Ferrand was turning red as he backed Mason—at gunpoint— toward the door. "Now get out of here before I have you strapped and sent to the nut ward at Bellevue!" As Mason turned to leave Ferrand shot at his left shoe. The bullet hit. Close range like that it had to take off the whole foot, right? Wrong. This explanation is called instant gratification. I don't believe in bait, foreshadow, the Judeo-Christian work ethic, the Theory Z Management philosophy, negative votes, October, gold diggers, Freud's reality principle, so: the bullet bounced off left—leaving a tiny hole in the window as it sped its way across the abyss created by this building and the one next door: it smashed through the window of another office—that of an importer of Hong Kong toys. Of course Mason was wearing his steel-toed boots from welding days.

Halfway through the "daring" stickup Mason felt less like a greenhorn than he'd the moment they stepped into the glassed, sterile and staid enclosure. You should've seen 'em: Mason with a Thompson, Jesus fanning the silver thirty-eight (that probably would've misfired), Brad bullyng customers and clerks with Mason's W two-sixty-three. Two guards they disarmed and herded over with the jittery, dapper customers by teller windows. Mason and Brad held them at attention while Jesus jumped about—behind counter—with his potato sack filling it from cash drawers opened on command. The three saw everything they did through the dimness of nutmeg nylon smelling of Edith's Evening in Paris. Contrary to the plan: Edith was at the wheel alone. The Turtle did not show when the time came. Edith kept the Buick from Hertz hot. She was already dreaming of a vacation in Saint Tropez. While Jesus was busy with his Idaho's Finest bag, Mason stood firmly—yet with a mind as dreamy as Edith's: he'd *show* the world . . . that Ferrand hadn't been worth going back to though Mason'd had a mind to return and shoot up the place. And though they'd settled for one Thompson—look how things were going! Jed'd yakked on about the seasonal rhythm, a certain wisdom, yet he'd made a kind of sense about how human-rhythms turn out . . . in line with other life-rhythms. Jed'd yakked a lot, mostly about his great old pa, and his wonderful grandpa, wise men, in touch with nature, and the great simple life of hillbillies. Mason and Jed sometimes shared a bottle of booze after the day's chores and that character, Jed, would get so caught in his love for his hill folks and their "wisdom" he'd forget he was talking to a traditional enemy of his people. One time ol' Jed whimpered, "My gosh, boy, I forget you colored when I'm talking to ya. You just like anybody else. How you get *like* that?" Jesus finished his sack job. They all backed toward the turnable doors. Everything was going just dandy till Mason stumbled over a two-and-a-half-foot silver-coated metal ashtray filled with cigarette butts and decorated sand.

Boy, was *he* hot to trot! Mason'd just left the Valenti-D'Amico place of operations in Little Italy and was walking north on McDougal. He held in his right hand, at stomach-level, a dark blue booklet, looked with dancing eyes at its cover; the thumb and index of his left hand poised, ready to lift the cover back. As he walked he read: United States Government Printing Office. He looked at the snapshot of himself on the fourth page: didn't like the expression puttering around the full mouth. The passport photographer's fault: no sensitivity to subject. Too much a mug shot. Number J111967. Cover again: in gold letters: Passport. Beneath those precious words, also in gold, was the United States' seal: an eagle facing left with a left-talon clutching thirteen arrows and a right one clamped around a branch of olives—strength and peace. That's *me,* jack, *strength and peace!* Not a native son for nothing! Above the eagle's head: a mandala with stars at center representing the original (again) thirteen colonies. Well, this was Mason's passport and he felt close to the lofty efforts those sparkling stars represented. He'd get on a soap box for them: you bet your boots: after all this was his country, too. Wasn't it? Opening the booklet again with proper reverence, he whispered aloud the language of the third page: "The Secretary of State of the United States of America hereby requests all whom it may concern to permit the citizen(s) / national(s) of the United States named herein to pass without delay or hindrance and in case of need to give all lawful aid and protection." God! Just think! the support of the entire government behind his identity! Money talks, yessirree boy. He turned to the fourth page again: "Warning: Alteration, Addition or mutilation of entries is prohibited. Any unofficial change will render this passport invalid." Then this vital data: name, place of birth, date of birth, date of issue—which was February 3, 1980—and date of expiration—February 2, 1985. The picture again: although the expression was not his it was the face of "a serious writer" like those on the jackets of novels: the tormented look, the scowl, a permanent expression of cynical disapproval. A man of profound thought? Spare me. The next page gave him only a fluttering pause: "Notice: This passport must not be used by any person other than the person to whom issued or in violation of the conditions or restrictions placed herein or in violation of the rules regulating the issuance of passports. Any willful violation of

these laws and regulations will subject the offender to prosecu-
tion under Title Eighteen, United States Code Section fifteen-
forty-four." This followed by blank pages for entries and
departures, for visas. At the end of its last two there was more—
the highlights: "This passport is the property of the United States
Government. It must be surrendered upon demand made by an
authorized representative of the Department of State. The
passport is not valid unless signed by the bearer on page two."
Mason stopped at the corner of Prince and placed his heavy left
boot on the top of a fire hydrant, balanced the booklet on his
knee, and with his trusty Bic signed the thing. Happy day:
signature du titulaire. The gods smiled. Znotchy was in high gear.
Mason stepped briskly: he was making it in America. Hotdog!
Yet he was no penance payer: any judgment would be secular
since he wasn't a 1940s James Cagney of the Lower East Side
caught excruciatingly between Church and State. If repentance
must be then make it a civic sacramental ordinance: his forgiving
priest was his own knowledge that he'd done his so-called best,
that the Forces had been so powerful, so overwhelming, and
poverty and misuse so pervasive, that he could not have done
better *otherwise.* Lie? The Department of Justice would not
agree. So: absolution wouldn't be forthcoming? How about
confession? Had the system nailed him so profoundly to the
cross? He insisted that the angels of The System had lice under
their wings. He too? You bet. Was there guaranteed another *sea*
up ahead? No, but he had no trouble at all getting a driver's
license in the desired name. He went downtown to the Municipal
Building and stood in line like everybody else. That was the
hardest part. The passport did the rest. Applying for a Visa
Credit Card wasn't quite so copesettic. The computer said The
Impostor already had one. "Uh, excuse me, I forgot." A day later,
elsewhere, Mason applied—with fingers crossed—for a Master
Charge card. Luck would be with him.

Mason Ellis sang "Diddie Wa Diddie" like Blind Blake, crossed the street at Fifth Avenue and Forty-Second like the Beatles on the cover of *Abbey Road* and reaching the curb leaped into the air and coming down did a couple of steps of the Flat Foot Floogie. (Earlier, in his room at the Gramercy Park Hotel—just north of the park, he'd kissed himself in the mirror! Yes, yes he'd moved: did ya think he wuz gonna stay in that fleabag...?) He climbed the grand stairway. Inside he found Reference. Selected the volumes to update "his" activities. A photocopy machine added technological sparkle to a dreary corner by a drinking fountain. He took the books there and xeroxed the pages he needed. It was like discovering a map of the unknown world: The Grand Lake the Shadow Mountain the Rainbow Curve. Then: feeling paralyzed as in a dream unable to move he stood trim, halfway between sturdy shelves where he'd returned heavy volumes and a reading table, holding the copies at chest level. His cards exposed—? the dealer dealing from the bottom...? was his opponent putting the squeeze on him? Was there some recent history of "himself" he had missed out on? What madness was responsible? Was he a man who'd missed a train because of a threat-of-loss...? What'd The Impostor done since seventy-nine? Spare us. He longed for wish-fulfillment, it *alone*—and none of the above. Mason took the stairway down. Dazed—he started walking rather than taking any of the buses headed for Washington Square, or Cooper Square. As he threw himself against the Hudson winds sweeping up Fifth, choked on the gas fumes of the taxis racing down, he closed his eyes against Reagan posters pushing for president in November, against Carter posters too, everywhere—on the backs of buses, on billboards. Too much. Then *bong:* he bumped into—*what?*—a person? a light pole? a bus? Mason opened to see the big man stepping around him, cussing. But, uh, wasn't he Reverend Jack Mackins, the preacher of those wonderful reformatory sermons at Attica? Looking over his shoulder Mason felt pretty sure the huge wobbling fella *was* Mackins. A typical Sunday morning Mackins sermon: "One day each of you will open the closet door and step inside. You'll crouch there in the dermal membrane of darkness with the Lord. The darkness will not be illuminated by your whipped trust. You will have to earn strong faith. You must hear God breathing. The skin of his eyes will glow in the dark and fill you with fear and the nightfall cry of the loneliest whippoorwill on earth because of a light pouring out. Then you'll find yourself pushing like a sonofagun for the beginning. Your own, that is: you won't find it: what you'll discover will vary." Reverend Mackins raised his fist "to the heavens." "No matter what your experience may be in *that* darkness, *endure*—do *not* perish!... Now, bow your heads, boys. Lord, save and forgive these poor boys sitting here on this holy day of rest, before me, in your care, without citizenship, locked up like cattle going to slaughter. Lord, they are not hopeless. I have walked among them and know the richness of their souls, the keenness of their minds. Lift them to your bosom. Nourish them in the wind of your voice, the fire of your breathing. Give them a chance for a life outside of crime, a sinless life: deliver them to a safe place beyond the excruciating controls of ethnic ghettos. Give them at least a little Civil Rights Movement or something to believe in. It's hell down here, Lord. (Give the women too an Equal Rights Bill: deliver them from bondage!) Dribble something down. I beseech you, One on High, perform frontal lobotomy on anybody who wants to fuck over somebody else without it being in dire self-defense..." Jeux d'esprit? Mason remembered this sort of outcry as being better than gold, sharper than a Saturday-night-switchblade entering a cliché. Mackins, dammit, had imagination! Mason'd gotten ideas for stories from those upstairs-thoughts... One term in one paragraph on one page of the sheets in his pocket worried him. It was: "post-modern." Mason didn't know what it meant. As he strolled southward still, he puzzled over it. Aside from its strictly utilitarian purpose— uprightness and stuckedness—it declared itself separate from modernism (so he'd read). Modernism depended heavily on the metaphoric: as a rejection of 19th Century Romanticism and its sentimentality it was made possible by many factors—among them (and this with a straight face): one) psychoanalysis; two) Einstein's theory of relativity; three) in Physics, the breaking of that hussy link between effect and sister cause; four) the downfall of Joyce Kilmer's tree; then five) that ... locomotive; six) the rejection of the assumption that language offered a logical means by which one might understand—. (What'd all this wooden horse-trading talk really mean? was it some sort of new-fangled way of giving a bad weather report?) Then, what was metaphor? Was Mason to believe what he'd read about himself and metaphor? Maybe Garbo's "I want to be alone," was metaphor? or "I am." Model for reality? Marcus Garvey's headgear was metaphor for Malcolm X's eyeglasses. Jelly Roll Morton was metaphor for Stevie Wonder. Huh? But this rejection of letting one thing stand for another ... ? Interesting, yet ... Maybe The Impostor *believed* the text represented nothing outside itself. I don't, thought Mason. Reverend Mackins knew God by his first name: was the name the same as the, uh, ah, spirit, I mean, body ... ? Miss Inbetween was metaphor and Miss Acheass was metonymy. So be it. Text as permanent property—free of outside clut. Okay. Like Cubism: a peeled conceptual orange oozing Cezanne's blood and sperm: synthetic, analytical, geometric. Mason glanced up at the overcast dome. There was a promised full moon behind that shit. Hay-bob-a-re-bop. He was on his way. Hi-de-hi-de-ho. Mason still had the will to endure: while ten thousand people choked to death on their grub each year here. Saaay whaaat? To say nothing of ... *Hay,* shouldn't he cut out this shit and call a speakers' bureau? After all, he was a well-known author in need of some immediate action.

Everything changed. Jesus was now in jail baptized in a network of epileptic violence awaiting trial for possession. (He'd moved uptown into a foxy apartment on West

Eighty-Second and had started dealing heavy shit. So the possession charge was good luck.) Mason thought about Jesus: fed up with the witty and giddy and pleas and fleas. Blessed are the poor, blessed are the pure; blessed are the persecuted. Lying on his big bed, Mason, Mason. Busted a week ago, Jesus wouldn't get more than, say, a year, maybe two, if he got a rotten judge. Maybe he'd be lucky enough to get a liberal. Edith, Edith: where could she've hidden herself—with all her loose ends still here in the city. She'd sold her lease and split. And Brad. Well, Mason knew his story: dude living it up big, high on the hog, in the fast lane, jamming, strutting, buying drinks for his dizzy bunch of new friends, trying to fingerbop-pop with the jaded and slick crowds at the Brass Rail, Eddie Condon's, Basin Street and Max's Kansas City, and all the padded bars from Waverly Place all the way up to East Fifty-Seventh. (The hit had yielded close to four hundred-thousand split four ways: and the last time Mason saw Edith she was driving a Mercedes...) Mason looked at his new typewriter, a Selectric, on the table over by the window. A sheet was on the spool: the beginning of the vita he was typing for Moreparke at Cowie Speakers' Bureau. Miss Mufinsnat'd thought his first effort needed editing down. He'd reduce it from twenty-five pages to six: something she could send around ... Moving on with the change. Would Painted Turtle return? You're full of catfish. You flap like a bee bee-shot bluejay. Click, click. A little hemp wouldn't be bad right now. Help? He got up, went to the typewriter, sat, but only gazed out the window: sky full of goldfish. No, look again: that's the building across the street. No, I tell you it's a red sunset.

He felt it too soon to crack the ice at the invisible empire, the Magnan-Rockford Foundation. Maybe just scared? What was this nonsense about needing a solid base first?

Which base? More confidence? Step first into "his" old shoes, autograph a few books, speak to audiences from behind podiums? He'd been at Fifty-Two Gramercy Park North ten days before he broke down and bought himself a drink at the bar downstairs. It was in celebration of Moreparke's apparent trust and belief. Cool, but stay on your toes: bob like a buoy: because there's always the chance The Impostor might turn up, a-and, and what if Brad fucks up, Jesus squeals... The word is deep cool: swing low, sweetly. You got shoes, I got shoes. The Impostor could try a hoax. Mason sipped the White Horse hearing the rich click of ice against glass. He smoked a Camel. Hadn't it happened to Barthelme? Somebody published stories under his name. The real Barthelme got wind of it; asked the guy to stop; wrote a letter to *The New York Times Book Review,* denying authorship. And what about that guy who claimed to have collaborated with Howard Hughes on that autobiography? April fool! Simple Simon! Watch out for the trap-door! Pay attention: in a day or two, John Moreparke'd said, he might have a tentative tour outlined. They could discuss it. Moreparke felt the MRF grant'd given the writer enough recent publicity to make a domestic tour possible: people were interested in winners, in money. ("Are *you* with us Mister Mason?") Two protein-fed guys who were participants at the annual convention of organic chemists working in the polymer field were talking shop two iron stools down. Mason'd seen the banner out in the lobby. A bespangled husband and wife with a purse the size of a canoe, farther along, were drinking gin in blue silence. All realistic. All over fifty. Mason finished his drink. Back upstairs in his large room, with sitting room and French shutters, he sat himself down again at the cold, infernal machine. This he called moving on. Time. From day one till this circlet of anxiety he'd felt the uncharitable end—which, though, he could now reason, was only a transition, was still *an* end. The jammed-up feeling of having to move on, to flail against the quickly located details...

Everything continued to change: Moreparke's itinerary for Mason: unpromising programs at: University of Maryland; Howard University; Brooklyn College; Sarah Lawrence; University of Washington at Seattle; University of Colorado at Boulder. Miss Mufinsnat, a scarecrow with bug eyes, had neatly typed out the schedule, complete with names and numbers of hosts on twenty-five percent rag. Mason in jeans and sports jacket picked it up from John (it was John now "please") who was, bless his gut, a water buffalo in a suit. In defiance of "man" Mason pushed his way through the crowd at Kennedy. He was doing the "Big Foot Jump." With his new leather carry-on, he found twenty-eight C, Smoking. The gray-haired man next to him was reading *In Defense of Man.* The taxi out was smooth. That picture of the horsefaced woman on John's desk? Cowie Junior's daughter. And Miss Mufinsnat a cousin of the Cowie's. One of the top three of its kind, old grandpa Cowie, who started the business in 1895 had died in 1931 when Junior was twenty-five. Mason stroked his lapel at his curious good luck. Yet there were worries: what was left of the hundred thousand—most of it—was not in a safe place: (locked in the trunk of the VW bug he'd bought after the hit) but taking the chance was part of his so-called defiance. The beetle was itself in a garage two blocks north of the Gramercy, parked in a dark corner three stories below the sidewalk. They were ascending now. Now they were up. All was well. Now they landed at National. February cold: damp, freezing. The taxi to flat, bleak College Park was being driven by a brown-skinned man with weepy eyes and freckles. He kept watching Mason in the rear-viewer. What puzzlement. Looking out, Mason imagined he was in Africa, in a big industrial city: the faces along the sidewalks and at intersections waiting to cross were saffron nutmeg black ivory with an occasionally pink or ivory white. And government buildings with massive columns, clusters of shopping areas. Traffic was sluggish. A membrane lampglow over everything. Early evening drizzle. Miserable shit weather. The last time he'd been here was during Martin Luther King's famous March on Washington. He'd gotten sick from the spoiled mayonnaise on his salami sandwich. Now Mason (free of his guns) felt as "clean" and "respectable" as he had in those days: as credible. He certainly *looked* like a person of respect and position. In a way, this pigtail-jerker *was* flying "home." Like Lionel Hampton, like Ellison's character in the short story. Home, surely was *that* profound *and* elusive. How could it be otherwise? It was not the heart of darkness: not completely: not color: not completely. Not place. He looked out again at his dark people along the sidewalk. *My* people? No confetti floated over the city as he arrived. As the cab inched its way, in bumper to bumper traffic, on the Belt, he looked over through the trees and saw what he imagined to be the lights of Georgetown. O spirit of Toomer, stay, give me comfort, direction, in this chaos! (That night Mason rigged up a branding "iron"—made of a metal *E* on a key-chain and an *M* on a tie-clasp. He branded himself with this emblem: *M/E.* Almost passed out. Later, in the mirror he thought the view of his chest impressive.)

The campus—he would later discover—was typical: young people with pink or white or gray or olive faces and soft hands, carrying strapped to their backs packs and wearing synthetic green or blue or brown jackets and blue jeans and black or brown scuffed boots. That's it. They walked carefully on dirty January icy and snow-packed sidewalks. Buildings: red, sturdy: cold brick, abstract: indifferent. One could imagine green in the Spring. A tree, perhaps a row of trees along certain campus roads. The deadness of winter now clamped the campus in its mouth like a man with a smokeless pipe clamped between his calm teeth. (Men with pipes in their mouths remind me of dogs fetching things.) His host met him where the taxi stopped—all prearranged. She was all smiles. She led him now to her office. They sat for a half hour. They kept attempting to break the silence at the same time. Embarrassed, Mason looked over his lecture notes. Then to the lecture hall. Students coming in. After the host introduced him, Mason stood in *front* of the podium. I'll spare you the whole bit but you've got to get the drift: "Thank you," he said, "I come here with my life before you: I am a writer whose muse ran off. I'm just beginning to find myself on my own. I want to speak to you about my new effort to recreate myself..." the most interesting reference he made was to something he described as "self betrayal." Anyway, the "body" of his talk would make you hit the ceiling. And I like you too much for that. The questions were a curious set: "Did you write a book called *Native Son?*" "No? How about *Invisible Man?*" "Are you the author of *Miss Jane Pittman?*" "If you're so terrific how come I never heard of you?" "Do you know Toni Morrison? How about James Baldwin? What're they like?" "Do you make a lot of money?" "Why not?" Clear he wasn't getting the red carpet here: nobody's said the chairman was throwing a big reception. (Oh, even Mason—who'd never been inside a university building before—knew the routine.) After dinner with Edna Coddington, his host, at a two-star Italian restaurant, he and she were pretty smashed: ready to hang out the laundry. By the end of dinner it was clear she'd been the only one interested in having him there. She liked his work. In the little sputtering car, they tried to warm each other by kissing, rubbing each other's hands—giggling together. Cold but not a dry run. Then she got the engine going. She was driving him to Howard Johnson's Motel down the main drag when she told him her life story: she was living with another young professor—a dope addict who was trying to screw all his female students and who was also busy trying to screw and claw his way to the top and into tenure. They had an uneasy, off and on relationship. Shared a big house in Chevy Chase. She had a daughter in high school who lived with them. The girl was really smart and would grow up to be a writer of genius. Roger? Roger. This was *contact,* thought Mason. Edna was up: she wanted out but Roger was violent. She was afraid. He might try to harm her. Women in her women's group told her constantly she should leave him. He was a loser. Yet her best friend told her to hang in there 'cause he helped with the house payments plus she could see other men when she wanted to anyway. And that's the way she felt now. Her analyst hadn't given any sign of disapproval. Then she had a bright idea. If he weren't anxious to turn in, they could drop by her "best friend's" place. When he said sure she reached over and squeezed his cock and balls together in one big grip of her slender hand with its long white fingers. She turned at the next light. She'd gotten her doctorate from Harvard which gave her a certain status but she felt she wasn't getting anywhere. She'd collaborated with another professor on a book called *Milton's Madness:* a success in academic circles. But royalties weren't coming. Her lawyer was looking into the wrong done her. She had to come up for tenure next year but there seemed little support among the old guys who ruled the department: her feminism, she said. Already she was sort of planning to leap in another direction: maybe work as an editor. Easier said then done? Or going into business (what?) for herself. Her best friend, this woman called Beth, they were going to see, had *her* own business: interior decorating. Gaining a name as a designer, nobody'd ground her soon. A go-getter, Beth had a birdman's-eye view of *men* and no man was ever going to ever again put his foot on *her* neck. Edna wished she could be as *assertive* ... Beth and Jake were really wonderful: true people of the postmodern world! they didn't believe in sexual loyalty. What'd it have to do with love anyway. They loved each other and wasn't that enough? Edna's voice got higher, more defensive. She went through a red light, nearly killing a man with a dog on his shoulder. Oh, Jake was a little gloomy, kinda plastic. But he would like Beth—she was so *together* ... Beth's and Jake's apartment building was your typical highrise in the flatlands. Typical that is till Edna and Mason got into the elevator and it started moving up. "This doesn't seem to be the same elevator. They must've put a new one in." Mason looked at the buttons: Up. Down. Alarm. All seemed normal till he looked closer: Love. Death. Apple. Q. T. Apple? Q. T.? Underneath Q. T. was this: ("Quiet Tilt.") Halfway between three and four the elevator groaned and stopped. The Love and Death buttons turned red. Disco music came over the intercom. A gloom shook the space: lights dimmed. Then, as though nothing unusual had happened Love and Death went out and the goddamned thing went on to four and stopped like nobody's business. Mason noticed the name plate by the door: J. and B. Marsse. Professor Coddington rang. No response. Mason felt a rising sense of frustration, uncertainty and mistrust. He blinked: a rear-end view...? Juicy...? Twisting. What was, yikes, this, t-this...? Then the door opened and they stepped inside. Nobody was there. Only a giant TV set in the center of the floor. Professor Coddington closed the door behind them. She spoke to the TV set: "Oh, Beth, oh, Jake, forgive me for stopping by like this without calling... Had I known you guys'd gone to bed so early...I—uh...What?" Edna Coddington blushed. "Are you serious, Jake?" She turned to Mason. "He says he's serious." Edna noticed Mason's bewilderment. Mason looked like a stranger in a foreign country trying to avoid speaking to anybody because he doesn't know the language. It was giving him a headache. Stiff legs. He could hardly move. Why was his heart racing so? The professor went to the remote control and turned on the set. Immediately there were fuzzy projections of two human beings: a naked man and a naked woman. Pink, slender, handsome couple. Projected directly from the screen onto the flat surface of the floor. They were on a bed. The image had combat fatigue. Mason rubbed his eyes. They focused. Edna smiled at him. "They want us to play with them. Are you up to an orgy, my good fellow?" Bring on the sodium pentothal? Tenderness perhaps? Pity? He couldn't figure out how to react. Beth looked very appealing but, well, she was all-surface, shimmering pink film...Moments later when Mason climbed atop Beth he felt only the vibrations from the disco music which, he suddenly realized, had followed them into the apartment. When he got his cock into her, it felt as though it were pressed against the seat of a park bench.

Every little hopeless bit helped and was a bird step: even orgasms in strangers who thought you were who you said you were. (Did he really look *that much* like the pictures?) Truth was nothing other than the establishment of trust, agreement—Mason. And here he was the next morning, back over in D.C., on the campus of Howard, that famous Negro university where Mason's grandfather—so he maintained—graduated in 1926. Feeling a hundred and eighty degrees off, he shook hands with Professor, no, no, at Howard it's *Doctor*—I forgot—Doctor Welton Parkson-Ogden, Junior. A dignified, tall, slender man, in a perfectly cut expensive British-made suit, Doctor Parkson-Ogden, flashed his gold tooth at Mason. "Found your way all right, I see. We'll have to run right along, I'm afraid: the turnout is good: the auditorium is full—and that's unusual in the middle of the day, around here." As they walked along one of the crisscrossing paths toward the humanities building, Doctor Parkson-Ogden, Chairman of the English Department, chuckled. "Afterward, we'll take you out to lunch. That's the least we can do. We've reserved a table at a French restaurant down on Pennsylvania Avenue. There'll be twelve of us . . . " The tall man laughed again. "You look, uh, different from the picture on, uh, uh—I forget the title—your book, uh . . . But, of course, very much like the one Cowie sent . . . " Mason assured the professor the jacket picture was taken some years back. Understandable, understandable. The professor who introduced Mason to the packed auditorium had her hair in a Savannah Churchill-upsweep. She came on stage clad in a glittering gold and silver Medici gown. Her introduction had him born in Chicago, author of two novels, an *anthology* of Afro-American slang. Mason thanked her for it anyway. He told the audience he'd read from his most recent novel, but first he wanted to just talk to them. "I'm delighted to be here at Howard, in the Capital of the Home of the Brave, Land of Liberty, Zone of the President, and it gives me special pleasure to tell you that my agency booked me into Howard Johnson's over in College Park so I wouldn't get mugged by any of you mysterious dark people running around over here in D.C." The laughter was sincere—

music: they loved him already: he was early Dick Gregory, late Richard Pryor. Mason had 'em in the sweat of his palm: "I wanna tell you my troubles. You know how it is. Not long ago I realized that this bitch I thought was my muse turned out to be part of myself. Now, don't go getting any funny ideas. Seriously, that's a heavy discovery. My real woman, at the time, an Indian lady—bulletproofed soul with spiritual ventilation—took off not long after. Made me wonder if I smelled bad or something. Had to check my breath. I don't know. Maybe I needed a deeper inspiration, one with a spirit full of cobwebs of the cave. Yet Celt responded to Beale Street Boogie with as much handclapping and footstomping as the best of any of us. She sure could outdance me. And could be into Mozart and Beethoven, too: with as much passion. You don't have to be Jewish to like Levi's. Every girl I brought home before Celt was looked upon with great suspicion, often with contempt. 'Don't bring that little tramp in this house anymore!' 'What her father do?' 'Bring a nice girl home.' I tell you, my mother could be merciless. Maybe Celt was all right 'cause, well hell, nobody could *see* or *hear* her. My mother always did believe silence was golden. Celt then was just the girl for me: the one I should play puppy love with till I got big. Celt was a very active muse: nothing stopped her, in the beginning: midwest bound boxcars full of secret lightning, lithographic surfaces of deep sea classifications, oceans filled with storms. The only problem was: I was dreaming godawful tight *fear* dreams rather than blooming *desire* dreams. Had I been smart I'd have been getting that pussy every night—with my folks right in the next bedroom totally unaware. But my innocence, paste of anxiety, high-minded plans, stood in the way. Celt got pissed. You can imagine: there I was turning her into an untouchable goddess. She wanted to kick my ass. I couldn't stop idolizing her and that was the start of my downfall, folks. 'Before the Flowers of Friendship Faded Friendship Faded.' But Celt didn't go away right away..." and on Mason rambled, then read; then the questions from the audience: "How come your muse had an Irish name and not an African?" "Why was your real woman Indian and not Black?" "Who do you write for: black or white people?" "I read somewhere that Black critics don't respect your work 'cause it ain't militant enough and white critics don't dare say anything about your books 'cause they might offend the Black critics. How you feel about this?" All Mason's answers were as awkward as the sound of a bugle suddenly blown in a quiet reading library. Answering was like trying to launder dirty money. Eh?

Two days later Mason was back in the city then soon up in Bronxville on the campus of Sarah Lawrence. His audience in the big dining room of an old mansion: three shy boys and fifty brash smart sincere cocky innocent girls, the sons and daughters of New England gentility—the children who'd turned their backs on law, medicine and business. Standing before them Mason felt like da Vinci's Last Supper: peeling, water-stained, "conscious" of his own death, badly faded: like the tunnels in Italy: his last stand. Again: he wanted to talk first, read later. "I want to talk with you about the differences between fiction and reality, *real* characters and *fake* people—not because it's cute or literary but because my life *depends* on it. (For me the most important aspects of a work of fiction are: quality of imagination, uniqueness of the *angle* of the author's vision, and the degree to which he/she pushes the language for all it's worth.) You see, I'm in the process of inventing myself—in self-defense, of course. Think of me as a character in a book. I have to win my way, *prove* myself, keep The Narrator on his toes, off my back—treat 'im like a camp dog. No matter how *bad,* morally, I might be I gotta earn your *interest:* if not your sympathy and treasured understanding. My quest is *not* to be Mister Parabola. I needn't tell you I'm not the Invisible Man: yet race—or its absence—remains part of my identity: I am concerned with an encamped deeper sense of who I am, this character that is me. Senghor said: 'We must move beyond Negritude without disowning it.' Soyinka reminded us that 'a tiger does not shout about its tigertude, he jumps.' So I will jump like a tiger. I am approaching this in a binocular sense. My two eyes see two different things; levels of different things. Along with giving up my illusions and losses I denounce (and make public) any interest in the Cyclopian view of reality. The primary responsibility of literature involves creating truth. The text is not just a pretext. I stand before you. I am not the object of the text . . . " Well, he'd lost his audience, but soon moved on to the reading anyway:

" . . . he was still. Hamburger and flies on the formica counter. Big Trailways mobile-tomb out under tree. Restless folks stretching their cramped limbs. Florence Soukhanov ordered onion rings—only, oh, and a Coke. She was now gazing at the flies. Where were his *fries?* Oh, never . . . That pile of mashed cars back on the highway: a forced connection there. He picked up the glass salt shaker and sprinkled the white crystals on the grill-fried pattie while holding the top part of the bun—like a coffin-lid—up. Others at the counter focused on their own. Mister Lascar-face with his wife, Mrs. Goby. And two biddies down at the end. And Miss Willow Goose there eating her cottage cheese off the top of her Diet Spree. Vinegar Joe, on the other side of Florence, dumping stale truck-stop mustard on his hot dog. The Oomph Girl; Aze Simmons—with football shoulders; Max Schmeling with the short-order ribs (sucking the bones); Tan Thunderbolt eating a double-burger; Uncle Joe chomping on Heinz Tomato Ketchup-covered fried chops; Dum-Dora and Chollie-my-Boy in a booth facing two bowls of strawberry and chocolate ice cream covered with pecans, walnuts, whipcream and hot fudge. And, pray-tell, who was that old woman back there at the jukebox, with the electric guitar hung from her shoulder? Fishy situation? To refocus, he peeped Florence. She didn't look like, uh, a little hard-back thing with four short legs and a tiny head jutting out. The hamburger was one of Uncle Billy's old boots from his days as a brigadier general in the Civil War. Fake mustard didn't help. He knew he shoulda been a wheelchair racer—life would've been simpler. (Had they reached Pennsylvania yet? *Ohio?* or could this truck-stop be on some highway up north of, say, Wisconsin?) Florence crunched on her onion rings. He tasted one: making a forced connection between the crispness of the crust and the mushiness of the lily-cute ring ripped from its bulb. Tasted the lard too. *'Phew! Good!'* Florence spoke: "I'm still curious about, well, your *past:* tell me more: confession is good for . . . she laughed; shook her noble head. 'How far—back?' 'First thing you remember?' ' . . . first thing so deep now, like fruit on my mother's table: or the certain way chickens stand on one leg. The shock of seeing the dead chicken about to go into the pot. Death, too, in sparrows. Remember their closed eyes. Hardness of the body: death provides us with life. Playing cowboy, too: death there: guns: defined by grandmother as evil! movies, too, were evil. I remember moments, things, The Impostor and that other guy [meaning *me*] can't touch: a tall neat sky full of sliding birds, for example; I was not exactly a May son, see. I *was* out of breath, thought. The city stank. I wanted to crash at Roosevelt Road and change my identity: go to Paris, start another life. But I was stuck in wet, dark afternoons full of gas fumes and forced connections. Early on they told me: Don't lose any important papers: gave me a social security card, a draft card. If they couldn't trace you to papers, well . . . Officials discovered not only did I not have the proper papers, I had no arms, no head, no legs. Soldiers waiting to corner black kids dancing in the streets as rioters, laughed at the holes in my Broncusi-head. I was a weird example of Art. Didn't matter. I'd learned that *so much depends* on four butterflies waiting quietly on a stem, waving their wings slowly. *I* wanted wings. Sunlight in those days was hazy and if you wanted to feel good you had to make a *forced* connection between fair weather and the unfair climate, between traffic, sky, birds in formation. I was leery of old men in suspenders: they smoked cigars and listened to Lawrence Welk. I wanted *my* wings. Wings of dead chickens didn't cut the mustard! I was also impressed by *good* writing. I learned from it, imitated poets, wrote things like: forgive me dear, I ate the five women you left at the kitchen table. Their clothes were bright. I knew . . . but they were so cool and tasty. Place had no specific meaning. We'd *always* moved. Nomads, we were. You name the place and we lived there: at least briefly. It was nothing to see somebody shot down in the park and the Peter Pan green grass turning Santa Claus red. Mostly I was running; and reading. Wingless, though I had my muse in my corner, I moved as a plumed serpent—though not accepting Lawrence's snake-definition of dark people—across a landscape of hardhats, hobby-horse-riders, serious writers, sluggish traffic, *forced*—. They compared me to *Trout Fishing in America* and *Invisible Man:* running, wingless, not flying. Nobody knew what would happen next. The white fence was the border between the ghetto and the rest of the world. A broken red wheelbarrow rested against it. I watched a movie of a woman taking a shower: one arm raised above her head: she washed under the raised one. Such big hands she had. No figleaf covered her pubic V. I *liked* her. She was not one of those dainty ladies in flimsy dresses coming down Robert Penn Warren-steps. They tended to come down too gracefully, heads erect, wearing flat white hats with tiny knots of flowers stuck to their sides. Or am I thinking of Alan Tate or, gosh, James Agee . . . ? *Save* me! The space behind those ladies was always filled with January blankness. Was it always necessary to make a connection between sky and horizon? On the other hand, scrubwomen wore red headrags and waited in line to vote—sometimes they dropped dead in line: the wait was so long.' He chuckled. Looked at her elegant face. '. . . Enough? *You* asked—' And she shot him a long, clever glance. Then said: 'You still haven't eaten your hamburger, my onion rings are cold, Miss Goose is in the toilet, Vinegar Joe is back on the bus ready to go, Dum-Dora . . .' They went outside under the piss-yellow humid sky. Bus was half loaded. Florence and he were two-dimensional figures against a permanent surface. Be careful in the open. Birds. Space behind them was filled. Clouds: women on bidets cleaning their assholes; guys standing at urinals; Studs Lonigan pulling on his cheap suspenders; Mason himself with drill braced against rubber apron, drilling a hole through connected steel—with shavings spinning out, curling... Back on the road: his head contained a sky as clear and blue as a hangover: trees, in there, shook: thin yellow fingers froze in wind. Florence? Light beat his body. They held hands."

Next, Brooklyn College: he was speaking in a sterile room in Whitehall. His host, a woman with red hair, had given him a modest, friendly introduction. There was wine and cheese for the students at the back of the room. They were sprawled in comfortable plush chairs and on puffy armless couches in a chaotic pattern before him. His "lecture" was about "a hypothetical situation—call it a sketch for the novel of my life" and the relation of "theme" to "form." (He'd taken the BMT over here to Flatbush and written the talk on the subway.) Then, as was his pattern, he ended by reading from published works—this time, poetry, since his host'd told him these students were mostly interested in poetry. At the end one student wanted to know his position on liberation movements in South America, Africa, the Middle East, on "American aggression" in the world, on capitalism generally, on the rights of women. Before Mason could answer another student stood and confronted the string of questions. Would you ask Kinnell or Ashbery *those* questions?" The audience then broke into factions: about half of them on the side of the first questioner, the rest took the other side. And Mason was sort of left standing speechless before them for a moment. Then he ended the squabble by saying: "Listen: no one has *the* answer." One of the two Black students in the room stood. "You notice there're no Black students—except Trixie and myself. It's because The Black Student Union here is staging a protest. We have a long list of objections to the way this university is run. Many Italian and Jewish students have also signed our petitions. We sent word to you last week asking you to join us by *not* speaking here. But I see you chose—" (Mason hadn't received the message). A thin Jewish girl leaped to her feet. She shook a finger at the black boy—who had a face as innocent as a frog's. "Just *wait* a minute!" the girl screamed, "I'm *sick* and tired of this! This man came here *as a poet* to read his poetry . . . " and so it went. Finally, the host stopped them, and whispered to Mason, "Thank you for being patient . . . " Trixie came up and introduced herself. Creamy tan with big dark brown-hazel eyes. "Need a lift back to Manhattan?" Yes and he was grateful. The host thanked her too. In the Renault beside the jean-clad girl, thin as a starving youth in a village in some remote part of India, he asked her if she'd like to stop at a bar he knew on Sheridan Square and have a drink with him. "Just like your generation." Her tone was one of amused cynicism. She was lighting a joint while waiting for a light to change. Something in his marrow-bones jerked. She dragged then passed it to him. He pulled at it: his head was yanked through a knothole. Grass had never done much for him. She parked on Waverly Place and they walked to the Red Lion. She was tough: had a tomboy walk. On the back of her worn leather jacket this: Bed-Sty Hell Cats. When she saw Mason looking she laughed. "Oh, I've had this jacket since high school." After the scotches they went over to Perry where her sister had an apartment. Trixie let herself in with her own key. "I stay here sometimes when I'm not getting along with my boyfriend. Right now he's a pain." The place smelled of catshit. It was dark, even with all the lights on. They undressed without ceremony and got between the crisp greenblue sheets. She stroked his cock to an erection. "I thought you'd have a small one. Is your wife white?" "I'm not married." She had a noble face, the yellow haze of her right eye was nice contrast to the cynical curve of her thin, smooth lips, the hard clean throat. She made him feel deeply uneasy: something was wrong. Why were they *here* like this? Inexpertly she sucked him awhile then straddled him, inserting his cock up into her dry, small quim. His vision improved. He decided to call all bets off: just surrender. Yet...? She rode his bone-hard penis with the kicking and yelping of a vaudeville queen in a cheap obscenario. She kept groaning and hissing, "...you like my pussy?" and when they exchanged positions—with him balanced on the balls of his feet, between the fork-spread of her slender thighs, he threw her long, smooth strokes, spiced, vulgar, smutty, sincere ones too. She grinned up at him with that toughness around the eyes and mouth. "Get that pussy, man!" When they finished she, yes, lighted a classic cigarette and turned toward him, resting on one elbow. He looked at her looking at him. He wanted to do the handsome thing. Be a hundred percent. Bed-Sty Hell Cats? Trixie said, "By the way, man, I peeped your act right away: you're an imposter." She was grinning. "You see, *I know* because I fucked the real dude once: his cock is *bigger*."

Don't ask me why but it was time to approach the Magnan-Rockford Foundation. Mason wrote John Armegurn, Secretary: "...I am back from abroad and am staying at the Gramercy Park. Give me a call as soon as possible. I'm changing banks and want my monthly check to go to the new one, probably Chase-Manhattan. I hope we can make the necessary adjustments by phone. I won't be in New York long and my schedule is hectic." He thought his own hokum pretty damn good. Maybe he wouldn't need any further eyewash, jive or stuffing for the goose. Armegurn had a sharp high-pitched voice and a dry chuckle. He clearly didn't know Mason's so-called Impostor too well because he didn't question Mason's voice. *But* he did insist that Mason come in. "It's easier." A trap? Ambush?

It was Wednesday at three. Mason pretended to check his hectic schedule. "I can see you between ten and eleven tomorrow. How's that for you?" Armegurn stood to shake his head as he approached the desk. His secretary was retreating. "You've changed a bit." He was a handsome, big man, with ashy skin, ashy hair, freckles on his cheeks, even on his lips, thick red hair on the backs of his huge hands. His shake was more than firm: bone crushing. Armegurn's grin was plastic: fixed. "Yesterday, I didn't recognize your voice. But it happens all the time. People change *so* fast. Why, just yesterday, I walked by an old friend—I hadn't seen in two years—on Fifth Avenue. I looked *right* at him and he looked *right* at me. Of course, moments later, we turned and, well... Say, how was France?" And so Mason made small, awkward talk about a France he'd never known. Finally, after watching Mason frantically checking his watch every minute or so, Armegurn said, "I've had Jo Ann type up all the necessary papers for the transfer. All we'll need her to do is insert the bank of your choice and your account number. You sign it then take it out to one of our accounts clerks. They'll probably want to see some I.D. then you're set. Okay?" "Sounds fine." Jo Ann came back when Armegurn buzzed for her then Mason gave her a piece of paper with his Chase account number and the branch address. He stood up and shook with Armegurn again then went out and had a seat while Jo Ann typed. Mason eyed a "battle axe"—his thought, folks, not mine—waiting to see Armegurn who momentarily came out. "Hi, Miss Bambosh—how are ya?" After she'd followed Armegurn into his office Jo Ann, fiftyish and square as a wooden door, said, "She's also a winner." At that moment a trampy-looking young man shot into the office. He grabbed Jo Ann's arm and shouted insanely in her face: "Why is charity so fucking good but expecting mercy and begging are horrible?" then ran out before she could recover—let alone answer. Finally she said, "Every week he comes in here like that. He's a poet. Also one of our prize winners." Her smile was glazed with the pain that comes from being hit below the belt. And she wasn't even an official entry.

A light drizzle in May: the morning smelled of pine: no Sherwood Anderson sky here over Seattle. Two cheery English professors picked him up in a monkeyshit-green Buick station wagon. The airport was the most untrustworthy he'd seen. Had it been constructed to trap him? And *two* weird professors? As they tried to engage him in a discussion of swindling in literature all he could think of was the new smackaroos going into his bank account at Chase. The two guys were drinking buddies. Mason agreed to stop with them for a short one. It was one thirty—the lecture wasn't till nine the next morning. That night: they'd take him to dinner at Professor Melvin Lester Bark's, their "most distinguished (ex-CIA) personage of historical literary scholarship." Bob and Kit, these two, already slightly juiced-eyed, led Mason into a smelly pub on the secret end of North East One Hundred and Twenty-Eighth Street, an old neighborhood bar, their favorite, complete with bar flies, stuck fan in ceiling, unearthly sawdust on floor. Good-Time Charlies, they joked about old ex-agent Bark and his fuddy-duddy fraudulent "historical scholarship." They hadn't been able to get him to even read good Bellow let alone bad Barthelme. On the q.t., his wife was nice though and they were sure the dinner party would go well. Kit, the thinner, darker one, told Mason he'd tried to read one of his novels, but got confused. He couldn't tell what was going on. Mason smiled. Bob, with dimples and a twinkle, said, "I tried too, and I think I missed something." Mason wasn't going to bite. This was a crow-hop. Take me to your leader, boys. That night they picked him up at the campus guest house. He was in the faculty club having a drink. Bark lived on Mercer Island so it would take awhile in the rush hour traffic. An early start was wise. The ferry boat was a twilight-lit sea dragon. After that, a short drive through a damp plush wooded area. Bark was a big man with a pumping handshake and a big smile. Mason didn't catch all the names though he was being told as he gripped one hand after another. A plump light-haired woman with tiny hands. One dark in a low-cut dress with a profusion of pimples all over her chest. A weasel guy. An old poet with yellow teeth and age spots on the backs of his hands. Mason got cornered by the tiny hands-woman. "You have children?" "Yes." "How many?" "About, oh, thirty, maybe forty." She gave him a look. Cocked her head. He could see she felt put on. She started to laugh, decided not to, then walked away. He was sick of these people who always wanted to talk about *their* children. The host had brought up good wine from his secret cellar and many were sampling various ones. Others worked on aperitifs and mixed drinks. Low chatter about deception in the department against subdued Mozart. Plush carpets beneath feet. Indirect lighting. Nothing blue or breezy. Tone: definitely not racy or risque: something almost "old family" British. The dark woman with pimples sat on one side of Mason at dinner and Kit on the other. Kit wanted to know what he thought of detective stories. Was Kit some sort of plotter? Sandra Pirsig, Miss Pimples, wanted to know how long he'd be in Seattle. His mouth was full of mystery steak: he couldn't answer either one. By the time Don Giovanni-Ellis was delivered back to the faculty club he was half drunk and suffering with acute sinusitis. Kit's tail lights finally vanished down the driveway. Mason thought of walking. But, The Impostor might be out there in the shadows! Yet lying down would only increase the congestion, the pain. The villainous damp night air had quickly gotten to him. He turned back. Slept poorly. But the coffee in the morning helped. He had a piece of toast with it. Then it was Sandra Pirsig, this time in a plain sweater and skirt, who came for him. He noticed something suggestive in her eye, a kind of nervous vibration from her body reached his. Funny business. Mason read to three hundred students in a lecture hall then talked half an hour. About? Literary snow jobs, blarney-festerings, writerly deception and the conflict and exchange between these states and the sacred grounds of truth. What else? Hum. Then they took him to lunch and he was, finally, at three-thirty free. Sandra asked him if he wanted to be driven anywhere special. No, he wanted to walk. She thought that interesting and decided to walk with him. She led him down to the shopping area near the university. A pleasant hocus pocus afternoon: an unclear tricky day, and green, green, green and gray, hard gray. The sky was, in part, swollen with dental cement—and sculptures of Presbyterian cows grazing on wet cotton. A mist hung low in the undergrowth as they cut through the park. She kept probing him about himself but his answers were cryptic. Mason tried to unscramble a mental poem buzzing in him but when he succeeded (as she talked on) it turned out to be a woodcut print of—of what? He wasn't sure. Somehow, though, this sadness of moss and lichen along the walkway, appealed to him: nature had declared martial law on civilization. Plush, damp, oozy stretches seemed to pull at his nerve endings. Mrs. Yznaga's seventh grade geography, her talks of the Pacific Northwest, the Olympia National Forest, hadn't prepared him for the sentimental fiddle music nature was coming on with here. Huh? Oh, yes Sandra was saying something about getting together tonight. Oh yes, why not... His flight wasn't till ten in the morning.

He was speaking to a mirage of students from the rotunda of a lecture hall in the Engineering Building on the campus of the University of Colorado at Boulder at four-thirty in the afternoon a few days after leaving Seattle, when he saw in the audience, way at the back, an older woman: Painted Turtle. He hadn't noticed her at first. But when he became aware of her he started tripping over the bumpy surfaces of words on his tongue, choking on double entendres. He became a dying man swallowing a fishbone of language. There was another older person, a man, sitting beside her. The man was snickering, covering his mouth, whispering to Painted Turtle. He'd cock his head toward Mason, listen for a few seconds, then rock with suppressed laughter. Painted Turtle wasn't responding to her companion's jollity. Why was she here and who was the scornful mirth-maker with her? Mason struggled through the talk and the reading then leaped offstage, pushing his way through the unruly crowd of exiting students—against the flow. His heart was apitapat. Not to loose sight of her. Many blonde heads. In a blood curdling frenzy, he knocked the students aside. "*Hay!* What the hell—!" "Mister Lather, ha..." "Get a load of—" But she wasn't there when he got to the top. He was twitchety and hysterical. Frantically, he scanned the remaining people—some of them waiting to ask him questions in private. "May I speak to you a moment?" "Huh?" He brushed the student back and dashed down the aisle. The Turtle had to have gone out this way. "Uh, excuse me: I was wondering if you'd explain—" "In a minute, a minute please!" But *she* wasn't out in the hallway either, nor outside the building. He looked up at the sky. Blue potatoes. Clear as it can get. What bad medicine was this? Some warning? Could she have thought he wouldn't *see* her? He took in a deep breath of the sharp dry Colorado air. "Excuse me, but..." "Yes, yes..." When the students lingering behind finished with him, Mason's host—one of the many kindly old professors of the English Department—led the badly shaken and now muffish "writer" away to the parking lot near Old Main. As they walked Professor Tippoff pointed out the wonders of his campus. Mason hardly heard him. He was jerking his head about: still searching. Then suddenly—on the sidewalk at his feet, these words in blue chalk: *MRF owns Cowie: you're a cow on crutches.* Professor Tippoff: "I apologize for the graffiti. Some student with a laconic message for another. I suppose some things can't be relayed by telephone and sky writing is out of their reach." He chuckled at his own foolproof humor. Professor Tippoff would put him up that night in his elegant old mansion near the hospital just north of Canyon Road. The spring city was atwinkle and, as they drove by the mall, people were strolling in their thin clothes, watching the tightrope walkers, fire-eaters, belly dancers, sword-swallowers, and each other in their endless blondness. Here at the base of the Flatirons perhaps a kind of calmness might be possible, thought Mason. Anyway, in the morning he'd go skiing, for sure. It had to be one of the last possible days. Perhaps the spirit of the Arapahoe and hoodoo itself would protect this native son on the white slopes. He thanked the Tippoffs and set out. Up at Lake Eldora he stood in the lift ticket line behind a woman who turned around and giggling, said, "Beautiful day, isn't it." She introduced herself as Sharon Seeberg.

The fanbelt of time pulled the days weeks months along and everything went smoothly till Mason got his November statement from Chase—one at First Avenue and Twenty-Sixth Street across from Bellevue—which didn't show a MRF deposit. It was now the morning of December eighth and when he went down for coffee at the bar, Sweden, who had no Swedish accent to speak of, handed him a telephone message: "Urgent: call John Armegurn. About your account." The fanbelt? Coffee, moments later, tasted of axle grease and Frankish Morea sewage in Killini... Mason bought the *Times* and returned to the cup. Tricks? Cooler, it hadn't improved. Times: John D. and Catherine T. MacArthur Foundation had announced its new grantees. Mason recognized none of them. Urgent? Steep, sharp winds swept down the Alps of his nerves. Red clouds of fear moved over the baked-blood stillness of his mind. Sahara with a blistering scirroco. What an ungodly excuse for foreshadowing! Perhaps he'd need a new identity to get away... Already the fanbelt was about to snap—or the shit to hit... Mason suddenly got such an uneasy feeling—he felt as though he were being led by three captives into the jungle toward an awful confrontation. Wasn't three a magical number? Maybe only twenty-two was magical. Who knew. Yet he saw himself as a masked figure brought into a village somewhere, perhaps in South America or... God knows where, stripped and forced into an arena of Truth: made to account for his sins, his crimes. Brought before the altar of his family, his children, the women he'd betrayed. And he was supposed to have some kind of message (either in writing or deliverable in some other form) for his executioner—but he couldn't remember where he'd stored it. He was also supposed to drink something called wongo soup before going to the site. He'd failed. Then there was something else about wearing a mask—and, shit, he knew nothing about masks. During this time, too, he kept dreaming of an old man in a red robe but none of it made any sense. Now, Old man Bryn Maur over there, religiously, sipping coffee and reading the *Times,* too. *His* troubles? Any? And there: the retired Lockheed Aircraft guy, Courtlandt, troubles...? And the ex-Commissioner of the Florida Game and Fresh Water Fish Commission retiree, Mister Tredyffrin? The city for him was a troubleless haven? Did *their* coffee taste of the Middle Ages in Greece? of a sewer in Malusi Nquakula? Wasn't it possible to wake to cello and violin, a friendly woman in *Green Pastures*—green emeralds, fire engine-red rubies, cocaine white-diamonds, sapphires, rather than rusty wheelbarrows-without-white-chickens-beside-them and shovels of hardtimes, disap-pointment, corruption? Corruption? "Urgent..." Banjo buggy rubbish! Shouldn't have sold the Polish machine pistol. The bar mirror gave him back his nutmeg face with sleep-puffiness still clinging to its green chrome. The cortex deep in there was tighter. Tensions between the vertebrae and the disc caused a yanking, a painful fear, he'd not before felt. The yin couldn't find the yang and the outer gray area was a disaster zone with screaming, fleeing mobs. Well, he had to face *it.* Back upstairs in his room, expecting the police to break the door in any moment, he phoned Armegurn. And he was listening to Armegurn for a full five minutes before he *heard* what he was saying: "Two hundred fifty eight of our accounts were sublet last week to Gwertzman, Meisnner, Lowell and Associates which is a division of the Kraus-Worner Foundation for the Arts and Sciences. So if your check is late this month this is the reason. Don't worry..." "But—" "You see, Magnan-Rockford *owns* Kraus-Worner. We're just equalizing some of the responsibilities." Mason didn't care for Armegurn's chuckle.

Still in his cellule, about to read himself to sleep, with paperback-fantasies of faraway places, adventures high hopes fears, the telephone rang. Rare. The desk put Brad on. *Ah shit!* "I gotta see you. *Now.*" And when Brad arrived twenty minutes later, Mason—leery—watched his bloodshot leer. His tone was malicious: "I don't feel you treated us right?" "Brad, but we all got the same cut. What'd ya mean?" Face to face—standing. "I read in the *Times* today that you, winner of the Magnan-Rockford prize were back—" "I never left. Wait—" "...in the city. Ha, you know damn well I never believed you: you're as big a crook as I am. I want ten thousand..." *"What?"* "You heard me." "I don't have—" "Don't want to hear *don't haves.*" Mason grinned at his old "friend." Brad was obviously drunk. He smelled bad and looked worse. How had Brad found him? What network of tricks...? Mason considered killing—but killing was not copesettic. A neater way. Stall. The fanbelt was running on its last threads: Brad's death wouldn't prevent the break. Grease-balls and flaws in the scheme. "Okay, Brad. Okay. I need time. Ten thousand is a lot—" "Tomorrow." "Okay, tomorrow." Brad took out a gun. He waved it in Mason's face. "And *no* funny business. Tomorrow at noon. Here." After Brad left Mason went down and got the VW, double-parked it out front; loaded the Selectric, the books, and his clothing in; settled his bill; and drove to the Cozy Inn Motel on Myrtle Avenue in Brooklyn. Who'd ever find him *here?* The room was made of cardboard and the furniture too. In the morning he took out two thousand cash, loaded it in the briefcase then walked over to Flushing Avenue and bought that amount in travellers' checks at Chemical. He'd do this each day at a different bank till he had it all transferred. Also had to close the account at Chase. But how—without risking—well—everything? While eating eggs and bacon and drinking coffee at the counter in Aunt Mary's Kitchen on Lorimer, he plotted his future: sell the VW, the Selectric, get the Chase bread—*if* possible; split. For where? France, of course. Maybe he'd better leave well enough alone. There was only about three thousand in the account: he'd "wisely" taken out most of it each month as soon as the MRF checks cleared. An old rabbi went by. On second thought maybe he'd better not sell the car. But drive to, say, Boston. Leave from there. Or to Canada. Fly from... Yeah. Slow down, think clearly. Gotta stop wearing jeans. Gotta look respectable: that way you won't attract the attention of cops. Three piece suit. Get one. Expensive. And expensive shoes, too. Get a pair. Ace, you're going to make it. Don't even dream of giving up your rightful claim to the chosen name! Dangerous though it may be, you will prevail.

In Nice you can get through the winter. It won't run into you like a boy on a skateboard. At the corner of avenue de Suede and rue Halevy is a bar-pizza joint that sells Sicilienne pizza for twenty-five francs and you can even get dinner there for thirty-eight. If you're feeling rich you can drink at the swank bar of the Negresco Hotel which faces the sea. You might even bump into James Baldwin. The doorman, by the way, is a sight: in his red and blue livery. Out front, erected at a sixty-five degree angle, are the flags of the dominant Western nations. Or if you're feeling like a jock you can walk down the street a couple of blocks to the "Jok Club" at Casino Ruhl. If you are adventuresome you will discover Grand Cafe de Turin down by the Old Place Victoria at Port de Turin and Placé Garibaldi on Jean Jaures just across from the Mercury Theatre and here you can drink the house wine—and it's excellent—all afternoon and not go broke and you can eat shellfish if you like it salty, but eat it that way only in winter. If you get up early and like to have your coffee at one of the cafes then you'll want to find a comfortable one. If the sun is out but it's a wintery day you'll probably sit halfway in the sun and halfway out. Maybe you'll have an espresso or café au lait at one of the cafes on the Cours Saleya— perhaps the one directly across from Echeries de la Mediterranee.

It's good and not expensive. A few flower vendors in the old market area do well on holidays and weekends. Another good cafe for morning coffee is Bar de la Degustation over on the corner of rue du Marché across from the Palais de Justice on rue de Prefecture. There, just beside the entrance of the tiny cafe-bar a fisherman sells his freshly caught fish out of a wobbly old pushcart usually on Thursdays and Fridays. When you buy from him he talks nice to you and wraps your fish quickly in old sheets of *Nice-Matin*. Otherwise he doesn't speak to you but you can sit at one of the tables, with the smell of his fish in your nose, and watch the faces of people rushing by on their way to work or market. You can read your newspaper there otherwise and not watch. If you forget to buy your *Nice-Matin* before you order your coffee there's that little vendor across the way in the shadow of the Palais de Justice. You can make a phone call from there too or get a photocopy made of some legal document you may need to show to the French police.

His hotel room was comfortable and when he opened the east shutters in the morning he got the sun and from midday on he got sunlight through the south window. An old well-maintained hotel, on rue Pastorelli, north side, called Riviera, near Gubernatis. From the window Mason saw neat Square Dominque Durandy in front of the old Biblioteque. On Sunday mornings philatelists gathered here to trade or sell. On rainy days they parked their cars along Pastorelli and while holding umbrellas over their heads carried on business from the trunks. They were each other's best customers. Idle, Mason went over. Fingered timbres of z Republique Francaise: their celebrations. One stamp collector, a handsome young man wearing a bright scarf, seemed to be watching him with unusual interest. Mason glanced back at the guy. Was he an agent of the...?

Mirror was no ordinary reflector: a touch of silver, bed-room dimness, fantasy, illusion, birds in flight, other complications lurked in its illuminations, its "eternal dark-ness." It was a ghost town too. The landscape of screaming. Obsidian in its corners, a river flowed through its center, emptying out into the gulf of its deepest century. Mason might get lost in such a vast ocean. He didn't have both oars in the water anyway. It'd take a chemist to successfully explore the terrain, a levee-expert to stop its flooding. Yet bravely Mason got up, like a sleepwalker, and stood before its silence with strange excitement. Here it was possible to dip into movements of waves deceptively disguised as one's own heartbeat, pulse and spinal nerve-twitch. But would he trust the image . . . ? Well, nobody'd told him he had to confront it. In fact The System might advise against such slander. But he had a plan: he'd look in the old French mirror (with its peeling edges, its mongoose-greased surface) and declare himself visible. At least. Lest he *fall* in. Yes, fully alive. Only the bedside light helped the process. (He hated the ceiling one and never turned it on. Its glare was the slime of eye infection.) He hadn't yet focused on his own reflection but was trying to make out the background: a valley full of vacationers like ants crowded the edge. A red moon. Night had its way. Its sky was no garden of light with mosquito lava and housefly eggs and tiny pupa cups hanging from damp leaves. No, this was a landscape with debris and bathers in a state of metamorphosis. Mason bit his tongue and moved closer for a deeper view. Was this Africa with its delightful myths and mites. Somebody'd scratched a swastika on the parenthesis that was the moon. He felt calm. No green horseflies would buzz near *his* reflection. He was coming to that image slowly. Calmly. Mirror mirror. But wait, wait a minute! There was so much chaos behind the image! Chaos? Who sez? Hundreds of beheaded bodies in doorways and ditches. Where? In doorways and . . . But wait. There weren't any doorways and . . . What kinda rigmarole was this? What was taking him so long? Was somebody running him backwards again? Had his so-called Formula for Clarity been scrambled? Help! Despite himself Mason saw himself. Fine. So he was looking at the, uh ... what was this? *This* wasn't Mason Ellis! Who then? What then? The guy in the mirror was more triangular, Mason himself was closer to the arc of a circle—slightly bent from despair and running. The mirror then might be the intersection of two sets. Leaves in there fell suddenly from winter trees. Clouds crowded the sky. The stranger was nobody he knew. Mason couldn't even identify the creature's race or nationality. And what was he doing? He was holding a forty-five automatic. Aiming it at Mason's chest. What kind of reunion was this? What absolute horseshit this betrayal! The image in the mirror showed no emotion as he shot Mason eight times in the chest. Mason cried out. As he began his descent he recognized the killer: that old mask had fooled him but only for a moment. As he lay on the floor clawing his own blood Mason realized suicide was not the answer.

He was made deeply lonely by the arrival of carnival time in Nice. Too many full moons, too much promise of Spring. Place Messena with its giant cartoon figures of Saint Nick and his nicky helpers, Popeye, Snoopy, Clark Gable, Roy Rogers, were a bit much. The New Moon had him by the balls. Ash Wednesday got his goat. He had the howling Quadragesima blues. Lent let him down. The First Quarter moon drove him mad till the Second Lent. He walked a lot nights now—just for the lights, the carnival spirit ... Hard to imagine himself not followed—or that he wasn't in pursuit ...

She had a clear triangular face. "Do you speak French?" "Un peu." She was an exchange student at the University of Nice. About twenty-one. Knew his name. Was that grounds for celebration or the cue to split. This was in his little cafe on rue du Marché. Barbara Ann Reynolds. Would he come up to the Fac and give a reading? Professeur Jean-Claude Bouffault, one of her professors, she felt sure, would support the idea. Then it was suddenly set for the last week of February. Posters in Old Nice announced the forthcoming event. A week after he'd met Barb, this: at three in the morning the phone rang: It was she. She was weeping Little Orphan Annie-tears. The girl was hysterical. Mason told her to calm. She got louder. Screaming: *"Come and get me!—"* she shouted into the phone. *"He's after me! H-he raped me! I'm, mmmm, l-locked in—"*(she screamed again). And Mason yelled: "Where are you?" only to get this response: *"He's trying to break the door in—"*(and another scream, and—) *"Oh, please, come and get me!"* "What's the address? *"I don't know— I, uh..."* Was this a set-up? For real? A tactic of the Observation Squad? He'd heard about such tactics. If for real, why'd she selected him? Surely she must have friends at the university. He couldn't even call and send the police. Mason pushed the light switch. Light the color of Billy the Kid-gunsmoke filled the room. A crackpot maybe? The feeling and sound of his own heartbeat was that of a scalawag viciously kicking repeatedly—with coldjaw, unbroken pride—a blood-slick fence on a candescent day. But what to do now? Clumsily he stepped into his stiff jeans. The phone rang. Barbara Ann again. "I got away." Gasping. A high ring in the nightwood of her voice. Echo of a sleeper awaking. It dislocated him. Something fishy? Was she another spy after him? She explained that she'd been picked up by the police while running along, God who could remember the boulevard. Maybe Dubouchage. He saw a full moon swinging loosely above her flight. The cops stopping her. Every shadow was too long... When Mason entered the harsh light of the station he knew he was getting in too deeply. He took her away. She was in bad shape: red-eyed. Swollen face: out of focus. Her whole presence warped. The story went this way: she'd been in a bar in rue Droite, the Arab section. Everything was okay for a while with the two American guys and their French friend. Then Jackie went off with the Frenchman leaving her. Well, she and Jackie weren't all that close anyway. But there she was stuck with these two boys she didn't even like. She'd thought the French guy pretty nice. She was drunk. The year the place the season all fell like a landslide down her consciousness. "I made the mistake of trusting that sonofabitch and he raped me." (The other had gone off alone on foot.) She went into convulsive heavings as she talked. Mason drove with no sense of direction. He felt helpless, hurt by her pain. She'd gone willingly to the American's apartment. She did not expect to be raped. She wept. She'd fought him violently. He overpowered her, pinned her down, entered her like a Boy Scout knife. She knew dimly then that no living organism ever wanted to be penetrated. Mason thought about this and its potential.

Lately some woman was turning up in his bed in the night. A chain smoker, he smelled her breath. Could the other hotel guests hear her screams, smell her? Despite himself his fingers seemed always to find the warmth and wetness between her thighs. A hog in armor, he climbed the mountains of her, and tasted the snowflakes falling from her peaks. He fizzled fast though. His heart wasn't in it. Resisting the glow of her red light, he endured her kicking—her yelps. Was she making a movie or something? She huffed and clawed. She squirmed and gagged. Bit his neck. Her toenails dug into his cheeks. "Oh, I'm coming—" His sense of flunkum was complete in minutes. Yet he plowed on: an after-midnight farmer watching buzzards circle against the hazy moon. A cagey "impostor," he hid out in the valley of her chomper. She bit him. *"Ouch!"* "Sorry." Then she whipped out a can of chicken soup...

At times he thought she might be Barbara Ann slipping into his room. He knew she wasn't when one night just before orgasm she said, "Ah, I like foreskin. Bless your mother for not having it taken off. Circumcision is a primitive, barbarian practice: it's symbolic castration with the same intent as clitorectomy. The foreskin which is cut away contains a massive supply of nerve-endings. The elimination of these reduce sexual pleasure—" (*which* sexual pleasure?) "by eighty percent ..." and of course listening to this finale finished the old assertative one. Besides, how could Mason be sure...? Maybe such talk had secret coded intentions.

Mason climbed the darkness, his feet locating steps and at an unlighted door—the only one—he knocked twice. Odd place to hold forth: upstairs over a triperie on rue de Boucherie near rue du Marché. The door opened and Doctor Wongo with bandy legs and protruding teeth seemed to fill it. His thick lips were purple. No extended hand? Lights poured down from irregular ceiling beams. Doctor Wongo made a display of examining the time. His watch sparkled on his wrist. His voice was full of sandblasted rock. "You're two minutes early. Please wait." Wongo closed the door and Mason felt the suction and the uprush of a draft from below. He kicked the railing. A minute and a half later Doctor Wongo came for him. Inside, Mason's eyes burned. The wall to his left contained two windows and between them were wall-hooks and straps for arms and feet. In the right corner: a large metal tub filled with what appeared to be steaming hot water. Doctor Wongo was grinning at Mason's bewilderment. "I'm approved by the World Health Organization, you know... Your problem?" Somehow the question was too clinical with a commercial edge: a red herring. There was detachment here. And mystery. A huge wooden cross graced yet another wall. Blood stains? Yes, but very dry, very old. "Sit down, my son," said the African, "here, on the floor with me; tell me *all* about it." Following Doctor Wongo's lead, Mason sat on one of the large cushions in the middle of the room. Then Mason said, "I see myself trapped in an air-conditioned hotel room somewhere . . . I want to—to . . . Somebody is trying to get a message to me but I'm in a remote part of the world. I'm guilty, like Kafka. The message might have something to do with my release: no separation of body and spirit possible. But I'm not sure . . . My children condemn me. Or did I simply dream that? Or they worship me too much . . . Somehow I'm part of a plot: a scheme: I'm supposed to free a girl held captive. Exactly where, I don't know. I can hear her speak, 'My parents must not know . . . ' Army guns are stacked in my closet. I have no idea how they got there. I keep expecting to be arrested and, uh, I've done nothing. I tell you I've done no wrong!" As Mason spoke Doctor Wongo played with the handcuffs suspended from his belt. Then the doctor spoke: "I can nail you to that—" (indicating the cross) "or there—you can experience The Saint Sebastian Redemptive Method." He gestured toward the straps. "There's another method: you get into a tomb and I close you in: it's called The Martyr Saving Plan. That tub is our little swim: it's The Guilt Absorption Baptism. Downstairs in the cave we have the furnace for severe cases." Doctor Wongo grinned. "It's very hot . . . I'd suggest you take the Saint Sebastian route. Why? Because the arrows are tiny and the sting not so great. The scars vanish quickly. Nail marks from the MSP wouldn't." Mason was suspicious. He knew Doctor Wongo could see his mood. The doctor held up a firm hand. He blew his whistle. "Please. Undress." Mason hesitated, started to speak but Wongo beat him. "You've used up all your rope. The System has very highly developed ways of getting the Right Angle on an Instrument. If you want release from it and yourself you must obey. This is the right place. There's no army guns in my closet: only peace and love. Undress." Stripped, Mason stood before the seated guru. Wongo's face changed as he peered sternly at the emblem branded on Mason's chest. "You poor boy you." Doctor Wongo wagged his head in mock despair. "Take the Saint Sebastian. I firmly recommend it." To rebel along traditional lines? Rubbish! Mason shook his head no. He'd go for the tub. Water. Warmth. Womb stuff. Pleasure? "It's very hot, son. But if that's what you want . . . "

Spring was a gentle wrestler holding the body of Nice in an agonizing embrace. Then he made her kiss the canvas. The sky cleared. Mason's first lecture for IHICE would take place the last week of April, two weeks away, at The American College in Paris. What was this intense windstorm blowing inside? . . . Alpes-Maritimes Agency d'Immobilieres'd located a furnished three room apartment for him up on the old Roman Road, Route de Bellet. He could move in the first of May . . . He'd bought a lemon: a Simca, new and blue and difficult. Parking was a hassle . . . The morning he started driving toward Paris he felt he was in a struggle buggy about to fall apart. Looseness always bothered him. By the time he reached Aix he was cursing himself for not having gotten the Renault. Then just north of the view of Mont Sainte Victoire, as he felt the geometry of Cezanne's landscape, in a BMW speeding South, on the other side, he was sure he saw—would you believe?—Edith Levine: in the passenger seat. The guy driving looked Italian or French. Small world? Mason toyed with the idea of exiting and following her—just to *see* but the next exit was twenty minutes later and by then, well, forget it. He stopped at Arles. The outlying areas, farmland, hadn't changed since that strange, tormented painter cut off his ear here, in, was it 1888. The city itself was strictly tourist: complete with sidewalk cafes, the type with metal chairs and tables. The drawbridge no longer existed but they'd built a replica. The house he briefly shared with that sailor of the South Sea Islands was bombed during Hitler's efforts to construct his own Roman Empire. Roman ruins in the old center. The postman and his wife were not in sight. The lamplighted cafe . . . ? The glare of the lighted billiards table. Mason spent the night here—not wanting to push too hard through the late afternoon and early night: and risk not finding a room. He checked into a hotel called Hotel Malchance. He didn't pay any attention. He was tired. Huge succulent plants lined the stairway up to the second floor where he had a room at the end of the hall. After a shower he lay on the bed. Edith . . . in France? Edith: twenty-one-year-old Jewish Princess from Brooklyn. Calling her a princess was like somebody calling him a nigger. At least Princess was capitalized. Graduated with a bachelor's in sociology from City. She'd irregular, crooked ways even back in sixty-seven: lifting money from his wallet, selling dope to pay back university loans. He always suspected she *sold* a little ass once in a while. Gave away a lot, too. In that car today she was dressed to kill: decked with tons of jewels. A new, upswept hairdo. Back in the old days she was a rags-and-feather hippie. Edith had blown flower petal in cops' faces while dancing around them with other hippies in a mad frenzy of corolla and incantations. She had inbred dignity but she was a fink. Even stole from her analyst. But that wasn't so bad 'cause he stole from her too: a huge waste of her father's money. A chronic liar, she used to fake orgasm—but was unable to let herself *go:* to go meant a loss of control—the fucking abyss, in all its irrecoverable large-capacity garbage bag full of anal-tight *nothingness.* Not coming was a defense: a fortress against the brain-shit of the world. She held back except once when she asked him to spank her. She lay across his lap and he whacked her like her dad used to do: she produced, out of her twat, one drop of perfume—smelled like Evening in Paris or Sunrise in Lower Manhattan. He now closed his eyes. Lying prone. Release. He could see her big cayenne-pink hindquarters now, the curl of light pubic hair there at the crack. When his palm struck the flesh there was bounce-back shudders from the hip flash. These were not hard. Not hard enough for her taste. He? He didn't especially dislike it but it was boring: did nothing for his erection. He never did it again and they grew farther apart sexually: she had her own life, he had his. And they had only some vague thing together. Once at a dance party Edith almost got fucked against her will. She only wanted to flirt but the yellow nigger she was belly rubbing with twirled her away off the dance floor, danced her into a dark room from which she shot distressed and yelping five minutes later. Mason was pissed at her stupidity and that night they fought. But she was a smart cookie: she knew the problems of America and could talk them in scientific terms. Her command of higher math awed Mason. She knew changing birth rates by religion; crime rates by ethnic groups; death rates, income rates, you name it. Medians, scales, variables. She used, in their daily life, the jargon: and after a while Mason felt like he had cabin fever... There was the time her father came over. They'd been together a year. Mason was nervous before his arrival: rare is the white man who accepts the black mate of his daughter. Edith's father, kicked out of the family, now ran a fruit vending business up in the Bronx on Pinkney Avenue for his cousin. The old guy got a lot of colored customers from the Boston Road area ("I *know* colored real well—they buy from me... ") buying his rotten citric "wares"— so said Edith. Maybe Edith was a cold fish and had no integrity but she did write to Mason once while he was in the joint. That was more than he could say for, well, a lot of so-called compassionate friends. When he got out he and Edith had dinner together at Ratner's on First—where the waiters (very old Jewish guys) gave them dirty looks. They *knew.* Her pie had a huge green *dead* fly stuck in its whipped cream. Well, you could say old guys had bad eyesight, but... Such events gave Mason jungle fever. There were times when they were left too long waiting for service in places where the waiters weren't busy. She once said, "New York Jews have some *nerve* hating Black people: a *defenseless* group... after the Jewish experience... " As a child she'd been to Israel with her parents. Her Brooklyn high school teacher "made" her "lecture" on it: the one thing she wanted to say she never said. She went around for weeks telling her friends she was an altruist—not a Jew. Edith was Edith. There was no figleaf covering her crotch: even if she couldn't come. Judaism sort of embarrassed her. And she had no intention of becoming a Christian. She liked Mason because, she said, he was gentle and immoral, beyond sin, beyond crime; existential. Plus he *liked* women. When he fell asleep that night in Arles he found himself not in Van Gogh's house but in Cezanne's: upstairs in the place on the hillside in Aix-en-Provence. Cezanne, in a stained suit—complete with vest—was sitting on a stool, before a canvas. He held his pallet with thumb and fingers of the left hand. His sharp eyes darted from the long, bored body of his son, slouched in a chair, to the half finished painting of him, on the easel. Mason left Cezanne to work. Down the hall and stairway, out into the garden. Skylight was rare here: the trees were thick and close together: it was like having a deliberate roof. He walked peacefully under the shelter.

It might be safe over here to quietly assume his "rightful" identity again. Do a few readings for the bread, which he needed already. Signard, head of the International Humanities Institute for Cultural Exchange's Speakers' Bureau had already expressed interest in response to his, Mason's letter from Nice. Hence this trip... Not likely to bump into hellcat Brad? or agents from MRF?... But surely that woman was *Edith!*

Paris, Paris! IHICE kept a low-profile: entrance in a court-way (not visible from street) of an old apartment building across the street from the famed cemetery called Père Lachaise. After Signard, a quirky little man, gave Mason an advanced check and his itinerary (he'd read at the University of Paris to a class of grad students studying contemporary American fiction) the booking agent walked out onto Avenue Gambetta with Mason and expressed his delight in the beautiful weather. He also told Mason that the university people would wine and dine him either before or after the event. Mason watched him talk. Signard twitched as he reached for Mason's hand. At that moment another man approached. Signard showed signs of recognition, if not delight. The guy looked familiar to Mason. Very! The fact got his fear churning again. Signard made a nervous leap, yanking the two—Mason and the new-arriver—together; meanwhile, forcing their hands together and introducing them at the same time. Mister Familiar's name was Alm Harr Fawond. Arab? But...the American accent? Anyway, the moment lasted less than the time it takes a fly to tune his legs. Then Mason was on his way, with not a second thought.

In search of Richard Wright's ashes, he entered the cemetery's profusion of gravestone and leaf and although he didn't find Wright hidden at the foot of a stairway to vaults, he found the lonely graves of Stein and Modigliani and, yes, Balzac and Roussel and one big, blunt tomb marked simply, "Family Radiguet." Bewildered, he came out at a brisk pace... But Mason wasn't ready for Paris. One bookstore on the Left bank was full of giddy young Americans. Plus he couldn't find his own name (the one, I mean, that he insisted was his) on any spine on the shelves. Pigalle was a flesh hustle that bored him. The lines were too long at the museums. Night life was more expensive than it was worth. He thought of going out to Auvers-sur-Oise to lie down on the bed-springs in the tiny room where Van Gogh died, just to feel, or try to feel, the weight of his own body in that moment. No, there was no good reason to spend a lot of time in

Paris. He'd give the reading, go to dinner with his hosts, then split for Nice.

Back in Nice he moved into the whitewashed apartment. Sold the Trojan Horse—his Simca. Got a Fiat. Felt better. Changed from BNP to Credit Lyonnais. The labyrinthian estate was owned by an Italian family, the Rosatis. The villa itself was a credible altar to the sun overlooking the sea. The owner's villa was up at the northern end of the estate. Downstairs beneath Mason's tiny place lived the Barilis. Madame and Monsieur Barili worked for the Rosatis. Mainly they cared for and puzzled over the sturdy carnations. They also exorcised and harvested the pears, grapes, cherries, plums, olives, in season. Rosati—a frail, tiny old man, his wife, daughter, son-in-law and three grand-children—also worked the land. Being here for Mason was like being in parentheses. Yet—something in Barili's eye. A charm? the look of a spell weaver? Mason felt the eye of a fiend upon him when he passed the fat dark Italian. Surely he was not some diabolical version of The Impostor? That elusive renegade couldn't possibly be *here!* Here was no place for a prince of rogues: Pegasus somehow had connected the earth and heaven. Every day Mason saw sea horses down there flying up out of blue... Yet he couldn't get over the feeling of being a lame duck. Next door? In the big apartment lived five women and two men. Mason saw them going and coming. Their motorbikes parked out in the drive. While taking his garbage down to the roadside one morning he met one of the young women—Monique. Since he'd left coffee brewing on the stove, he invited her up for a cup. Skullduggery? She had dark hair and a shy face. While they drank the bitter brew at his kitchen table they heard the Barilis out in the yard. Some wild smell was in the air. Mason went to the window. Behind him Monique said, "These blood I cannot watch." Mason saw Madame Barili carrying two rabbits by their hind legs. Her husband waited for her by the clothesline where four other—skinned and pink—rabbits were hung by their legs. Monsieur Barili took one of the two rabbits from his wife. Holding it by its hind legs, he quickly, expertly, drove the tip of the blade into the animal's neck—just behind its jaw. Then he stood holding it like that till most of the blood had poured out onto the ground. The other long-eared creatures squirmed and squeaked. Madame Barili, stocky, tough, socked them both on their heads with her fist. They went into shock. Then Monsieur Barili gave his wife the head-end of the still dripping hare. He slit it down the stomach as she held tightly. He then ripped the pelt off as she clung to her end. After that one was hung on the line, she handed him another live one. Mason turned back to Monique. She drained her coffee cup. "I hear the mailman's motorbike." She stood. "Merci. Au revoir." When the postman came up rather than leaving mail in the boxes down by the road he had a package or an express letter. Mason walked down with her. One of the cats, the black and white one, that hung around the estate came from nowhere and rubbed herself against Mason's jeans. The mailman was coming toward them, looking bewildered. "Pardon. Monsieur, s'il vous plaît?" He took the letters and thanked the man. The special delivery was from Schnitzler in London and there was something from Professor Jean Claude Bouffault with the university's return address. Monique was teasing the postman for not bringing her any letters. She told Mason, after the motorbike left the yard, that she had to meet a friend for lunch. This was her day off. What kind of work did she do, where was she from, what were her beliefs, her past? This was not the time, not the place. Eh? Smoke came their way in a sudden gust. He watched her slender body, her shapely bottom as she went toward her Honda parked under the big olive tree at the corner of the yard. . . . Then he went and sat on his doorstep and opened the letter from Schnitzler. He was trying to arrange a lecture/reading tour for Mason in England but probably wouldn't have anyhing finalized till Fall, when the academic year started up again. Bouffault's letter contained an invitation to take part in a detective writers' conference to be held here in Nice at the university. Bouffault explained that he knew Mason wasn't exactly a detective writer but he thought Mason might find the three-day event fun. There would be detective fans and writers from all over.

He returned to Doctor Wongo's studio. A Nigerian woman greeted him, introduced herself as Adaora Okpewho... "Doctor Wongo is in Nigeria on business. May I help you?" Mason didn't think, she could. Yet she was clearly not the sort of person who'd try to cure bad memory or snake bite with calcium tablets. "I came for a body reading." "A body reading's simple. I can give you a body reading. As my ancient mother used to say, 'Him who got text for body way get readers very good'." And Adaora Okpewho laughed a little musical laugh as erasable as sky-writing. Mason immediately trusted her. Emotionally he'd already placed himself in her hands. And he knew she knew it. "Come over where it's warm. You must undress." He followed her past familiar torture-gadgets to the sheet-covered mattress on the floor in a corner. When Mason was lying naked on his back on the mattress Adaora Okpewho bent down placing her knees on a cushion. Here alongside him she looked even larger. He studied her eyes. They possessed the glimmerings of the cud-blurbling of a bad dream. Yet his sense of safety didn't lose its tenure. Her alchemy was working. And she hadn't even touched him—yet. Then she did. Her hands were huge and soft with iron and webbed octaves in their rhythm. They turned him to liquid. Then the reading started. Not with her voice but with the music of her flesh. The first thing she touched was his penis. "This," she whispered, "is your khnemu. The fibrous tissue within is a mask for the shredding pages of Baptist Church bibles. Your legs? One at a time. This one, the left: it is a Pond Cypress pretending to be a hawk giving a monkey a ride across a dark sky—to a place of safety. The right one is a parrot who tells the slaveholder the slaves had a dance while he was away in town. You must *watch* this one. Your eyes are not spies so you can't do it with them. But to return to your legs. They're complex limbs: see this bird-like structure at your knee? It's a mule leading a man. The sound you hear behind the plowing is that of a bullfrog pulling off its jacket. You got femur and patella and fibula and tibia down here: they are all counties in High-on-the-Hog and Getting-the-Better-of-Bossman. Then this thing called coccyx. What can I tell you about it? It's close to the center. And the sacrum is too. Legs are important," said the African woman. "They can be trees every day in the week: milky sap, corky ridges, thorns, twigs, wafer ash, yellow birch. You smell them, taste their sassafras—aromatic, sour sap. Important thing though is this: what the legs connect to." She grinned. And grabbed his cock again. She shook it as she spoke. "This majestic thing is a crab apple one day, a black locust another, a Hercules Club. It has bark. And history. It has fast-moving guys behind it. Nicodemus from Detroit might know more about it than I. Yet, there are times, in the Blues, when the slaveholder gets the better of good old John or Moe or Moses. I'm getting away from—. Never mind. A lot comes from central West. Much from up higher, closer to the sea: Liber Metampsychosis. Ennu. Pu. Teta. So much. I'd take weeks to bend your ear. Ear-tree. And so much that wouldn't fit: everleastingness: kale or collards. Coptic concerns here backed up by all those wonderful tiny Egyptian birds of Thought: facing bowls: or equations: or puzzles." She stopped. "Sorry. I got carried away, chum. Bud. Honey. Pal. I'll start again. Here, your hips are important: and deep inside the sacrum, the femoral artery, cushioned between the hips is the small intestine, the rectum, your bladder. Hum. Birds with tiny feet dance in your liver, your urine... I'm going to move on—up. Your stomach. Ah! this organ pretends to be a fool like a woolly-headed black man in the cotton field who wants to evade a confrontation with the overseer who sees nothing. The stomach is also hooked to a plow. It has John Henry-sweat on it. The stomach is hooked up with the strength of the bear and the wings of the buzzard. It's the organ that makes it possible for you to run faster than a deer. It's against Friday and Monday. Brer Dog and Brer Rabbit ain't got much to do with this organ." She rubbed it gently. "Yours is flat. Butterflies ain't never been in there, I guess. (You wondering why I, a Nigerian, know so much about you, an Afro-American? No? Good. Your body tells me much.) Here—your chest." She tapped it. "Thorns. Silverbells. Here" (she bent, placing her nose within an inch of his ribs) "We're close to the heartbeat. Yours smell of malt and pine nut. Ginger and goat drifting up from below. Ra must have smelled like that. Isis like pears and perch. I hear a herd of Cayuse ponies galloping in there: Your ribcage is a teepee—gift from your tribal ancestors of North America. Your blood is African: it's a storm: 'de wind and de water fightin" (to quote Doctor Hurston). Pectoralis major? The base of your Talking Bones." She sat erect again without removing her hands. "Now your neck. It's the channel: it gets tight when you have to prove yourself the fastest and the best. (Like your grandfather, you're so fast you could go out in the woods, shoot a wild, gaunt boar, run home, put your rifle away, and get back in time to catch the hog before it fell. But this swiftness gives you trouble. Makes you a dangerous over-achiever.) Your throat is subject to infection: be careful. If you have trouble the flower of the magnolia will cure it. Just chew it. Stay away from the Crucifixion thorn. Be careful in Utah or Arizona. In the Peach State beware of the one-legged grave robber and anybody who says he can turn a buffalo around. Now, your head. Your brain is sweet gum. It has a history of tricksterism: it's a dog that saves your life, a rabbit that survives the threat of bullies and tyrants. Your ventricles are black locust." She was rubbing his scalp with the firm tips of her fingers. Your brain stem has the aromatic smell of the sassafras. It protected you from being killed by your mother and eaten by your father. Your cerebellum protects you from the return of vengeful ancestors and enemies: from the dead

generally. Without it you might be stranded in an endless winter between centuries and races. The fluid surrounding your brain is your incense and it is your own hant and spirit. That's right: keep your eyes closed. Concentrate, my son. Keep the hoodoos out. Mojo workers out, too, There's a Two-headed man trying to get inside your epidural space. He has the attractive smell of hemlock. You'll do well to wash your hair with bitter wafer ash ailanthus. Your skull bone is as sturdy as a pyramid and as serious as Zacharias and the Sycamore." Adaora Okpewho stopped. "This is not the end. Your thighs, feet and your rear are left." She shifted her weight and leaned toward the lower part of his body. "Turn over." He obeyed. "Gluteus maximus. This left cheek keeps the memory of your fear of falling: it remembers what you felt as you sailed through the air when your father threw you out the window. It remembers the thud when your grandfather caught you. This other one is a storehouse too: it holds the passion of sin and crime and the whole morality of your life: guilt for the legacy of hunting possum on Sunday; gambling away the family jewels; it keeps the Lord and the Devil from exchanging places. It reminds you you need more faith. It keeps you from becoming a grave robber. It's a mulatto hobo who—"
At this point, Mason and Adaora Okpewho looked toward the door. Somebody had just entered the room. It was Doctor Wongo.

Detection and deception? Possibly. May in Nice was impish: with windswept Terra Amata vibrations beneath its insistent, demanding presence. *Demon* cries! The idea of a conference of detective story writers? Rare in itself. But, well, why not ...? And look: genre people gotta be hipper than, say, all those so-called *serious* types ... even if they carry toy pistols in their briefcases! The first session met at nine in the conference room of the library, on a Monday. Mason stole his way in and sat in a corner at the back. A French scholar was lecturing on Himes's domestic novels: the grotesque and twist-of-fate in his ironic picaresques. *Le reine des pommes* was a killer! A blind man with a pistol could shoot out your reflexes! Grave Digger and Coffin Ed hit like metal file cabinets falling from a sixteenth floor window. The French critic finished and one from Holland lowered the lights and showed them slides as he talked. The jungle was evil? One had to find one's way up a mean, snaky river? or was this a journey into the mind, deep into the unexplored depths of the criminal vegetation-of-human-existence itself? Should the detective take sides with the villain, help him free himself further from the menacing presence of the— undefinable enemy. Tsetse flies might end your life before you could detect even *why* you're here. Crusaders got in the way of the search, the probing. If you're going to throw your lot in with that of the murderer, then you want to be sure to saddle up properly, pack a gun or take spears. Is your curiosity about that obsessed maniac you're searching for just down right morbid? What about your own contradictions. Your fog, your confusion. And there was the possibility of your crew, and the native dancers—who would not escape the brutality, lust and good intentions of the Crusaders. This was years after the Roman conquest and long after the beginning of the exploitation of Africans in Africa. What *kind* of detection is this? Through slide after slide, the Dutchman showed his willingness to explore the farthest terrain of his own evolving process: to search every crevice—even into the nose of a Bahr-el-gazel, in the armpit of a Kano trader, between the rear cheeks of a Basuto. Professor Franz Soethoudt's amazing lecture was a concession, a story, a plot, a line of horses plunging through the desert, carrying riders with muskets. Searching for what? Looking for the cyclical thrust of its own *tale.* . . . The morning session continued in this fashion. Mason went away at noon with a headache.

The next day, more of the same: stolen ponies, shady sandalwood, lost spies, tom-toms, governments in trouble, thoroughbreds in the backs of stolen trucks. But lunch with the detective story writers was different: noisy, cheerful. He didn't really meet anybody: just the surfaces of people. He couldn't detect any reality behind these surfaces. They possessed good faces, even kind ones, and threw off nice music, sweet, tamed voices. There was a Soviet-approved, neo-Tchaikovsky style in some, in others, German organs or French drums. Ladies sipped bitter red San Pellegrino. One, an American, was working on a whodonit about Brumbies being stolen for a meat grinder in a pet food factory. Her friend, a painter, was with her. They both gave Mason the willies: made him want to go on a crusade to save elephants and the dear rhinoceros. After lunch he went for a walk along the sea. Everybody was out. It was hot.

The conference had a lingering effect: he found himself playing detective. Even bought a black cap pistol which he carried strapped to his leg. For days now, Mason went about shooting at shocked people. An old man in a funeral procession at Place de la Beauté swung at him with a walking stick. Mourners filed out of Maria Sine Labe Concerta. They laughed at Mason. He went and bought a *water* pistol. Filled it with *milk*. On rue Foncet, he squirted his first victim: a girl in a yellow dress. She smiled and tried to kiss him but he ran. He settled down at a sidewalk cafe at the corner of rue Miralheti and rue Pairoliere. He was carrying this thing too far. What'd come over him?

They all go over to a hidden beach at the bottom of a steep hill near Monte Carlo. On the way: Mason remembers a dream he had in the night: a tiny woman in large hooped skirts with many sandwiches packed against her belly and groin—held firm by elastic of bloomers—greets him. He reaches for one of her sandwiches and she slaps his hand. She laughs at him. Says: Go suckle the moon! Jean-Pierre is driving insanely fast. Mason's companions are speaking to each other in French. It causes him to want to keep to himself. He wishes he hadn't come. On the beach everybody's like in a Cezanne: nude. Mason and his friends undress. Two fat guys approaching the surf cough and sneeze in each other's face: they seem unaware of the exchange. Mason now is not even conscious of the fact he's a foreigner: everybody who's not pink is brown or tan. Then there's a *very* dark figure coming down the rocky path to the beach. African? Welcome brother! No, not African. Too much *brown* for African. Guy alone. The dark man is coming this way: across the rocks. Carefully. Carrying—what is that? Oh, just a shoulder bag. His white pants are too long. His sandals: loose. Something familiar... Oh, no, shit: it's *Clarence McKay!* Mason staggers to his feet and attempts to split: nowhere to hide ("ran to the rock"...), nowhere... Ten feet from Mason, The Impostor whipped out a giant Smith and Wesson six-shooter and aimed it at Mason. The Impostor pulled the trigger.

There is a tingling breeze coming down from the Alps cutting the fumes from traffic up on the road to Monaco. It's realistic, calm, a friendly day. Mason opens the white wine. Although he's relaxed and enjoying his escape-from-the-bullet-of-guilt, somewhere back there in the glue and glut of his history is a Pony Express rider coming forward, like a bat out of heaven, with an urgent message for him. The word could be anything: that's the problem: it's not clear. From the so-called Impostor? The long awaited news from Himes of Wright, perhaps Dumas? The messenger has heavy saddle-bags. Lots. And the *way—Whew!* Is it news of another divorce, another childbirth? News of being inducted again into the military? Hokum? Word'd come from Schnitzler about the England trip. Soon now. He was arrogant enough to be excited. Meanwhile, enjoy. Wasn't accustomed to all of this nakedness: good though: no puritans here ("we're a Catholic country but we're not very religious"). Yet he was chickenman, chickenman—turning on a spit in a cooker (soon to be . . .) Here on the beach, naked and turning blacker, warmer, happier, smoother, he almost dared to feel *complete:* yet—no way. The wine he'd contributed to the beach party he'd picked up at one of his old favorite caves— Caprioglio right across from Paganini's "home" on rue Saint Reparate. He scans the beach. Such grace and lines: curve of pelvis, tilt of tit, roundness of buttocks, broadness of chest, slope of thigh. Monique was making a "sand castle" with rocks. Well, dislocation is allowed—even in a straight one, ain't it? Ray-monde, intellectual expert on French avant-garde and soon to be shipped to an academy of superior education in Kigali, is spitting out a bitter position pitted against Jean-Pierre's defensive verbal stand on—where'd this conversation come from?—the extent to which France aided the Nazis in exterminating six million Jews. Mason lying prone on his towel with eyes closed beneath sunglasses, picks up maybe eighty percent. Scuff. Jean-Pierre says nobody ever *told* him France handed over the Jews till he saw a movie about it. You were in the streets in sixty-eight like everybody else says Raymonde flinging his shoulder-length dark hair back from where it curled over the left eye—a C-shape concealing the figure eight. Chantal butts in to say the deal they got as a result of sixty-eight protests didn't carry with it the guarantee that anti-semitism would vanish from France. Isabelle sneers: other countries are worse. We do our best: I work every day with the disadvantaged, it's heartbreaking but we at least try. In French. Mason sits up: down the rocky shore Brieuc and Roye are running in all their tiny pinkness with three little female cherubs. A woman with shaved cunt passes going toward the chartreuse tide. He decides to take a dip too. What a cut above Quai Lunel! Monique is already in, a back designed with freckles. How tiny her hands are! In the water he won't have to hear the words he only half understands. That time waiting to cross at rue Desire Neiland the trio of Lycée girls and boys bombarding him with questions in French. How frustrating to have to *be* the dumb foreigner! Selling tickets for charity? You want to hide. And at the entrance to Old Town at Port Fausse on the stairway an old woman asking him *something* as she gestured toward the Cathedrale beyond rue du la Boucherie and Mason's mouth hanging open ... She might have been telling him they were dynamiting in the square and he shouldn't go or that city workers in their blue were no longer trimming hedges into square oblong rows but had now gone wild and were castrating on sight. Why always at stairways? and why did the beggars always approach him: did he look so different? They'd come up with their drugged babies telling him a story he couldn't follow: on the mall at the post office—on stairways! One nearly pushed him down the stairway at rue du Pont Vieux and rue du Collet when he refused her. Another spat on his back. Called him a dirty name. Now entering the sea is like throwing one's nakedness into music made with the feudal stones of a chateau. Even Mason feels it.

Celt-spirit here, pre-Roman slush, plunder, spoils, a Darkness embraced? Gatwick was snow-cold but under a rainstorm of mice-turds. Professor Frank Poole picked him up; delivered him to the Bickenhall, a modest hotel on Gloucester Place near Baker Street. A little twitchy man, Poole left and Mason was glad. He went for a walk in the neighborhood: had fish and chips in a restaurant just over on York. Even Poole was possibly a spy. In front of the liquor store next door an old toothless hag (also a spy?) surrounded by six police dogs, held forth with her begging cup and a cackle. He picked up the *Herald-Tribune* from a vendor at Marylebone Road...Betty Boop wasn't going to come. The hotel wasn't there when he got back. The rules here are gonna keep changing? Wrong street. He caught an Al Pacino flick. Slept restlessly: mam'zels teasing him from shadows of lace. He was writing a novel in which he couldn't figure out the difference between what was real and not: Painted Turtle told him it was 'cause he drank too much. His blood sugar. He needed to see a doctor. He was crazy. He accepted her verdict. There were too many women in his novel, he fucked them all too lightly. He needed a conference on morality with the authorities. He was a sinful beast, a pig—a fink. Then he was on this bus that turns a sharp corner on a mountain road and slides off plunging down into the sun-splashed green valley. How could such a thing happen on such a nice day? Naturally he flies up out of the damned thing—Painted Turtle with him. Locked in an embrace they fall in slow motion to the dry riverbed: "We're going to die." When the crew arrives in a yellow metal bird, he and PT are still alive. The letter he'd sent just the day before to an imaginary person has been returned. The helicopter pilot hands it to him. A gunshot goes off in the valley. Sirens start up. Pilot says, "In French it says Return to sender. Are you the person?" In the morning Mason arrived at King's College at nine and after a brief introduction by flubbering, fumbling stuttering Emeritus Professor of American Literature, Basil Llewellyn Ceconhann, he faced his tiny bunch of enigmatic graduate students keen on some word about Afro-American Lit. His talk was a yellow dog. Later, in Mick's, a coterie of these grads bought him beer and chips and revealed themselves as desperately clinging to the end of the rope of academia. He had a double shot of faith-building scotch in a bar off Oxford where a couple of old neighborhood drunks were making a mutt do tricks in exchange for chips. Harry Schnitzler's left word for him to call. In the morning he was expected at Brixton College and tonight at the Young Vic for a poetry reading. What was IHICE up to? Schnitzler sounded (on the phone) like a nervous twit: "We're mindful, too, of the Fulbright people: they might want you. And ICA..." Anna Birly called at the last minute: she couldn't pick him up as planned. Could he take the tube? Yes. He was only five six minutes from the Baker Street Station. Birly, his host and organizer of the Punk Rock Poetry Festival, was waiting in the flurry. They shook. She was visibly hassled. Punk Rock with added Black attraction: like Miles at rock concerts in the sixties? Not quite. Backstage he sat in the dressing room sipping bourbon from a paper cup. Sebastian, the great Punk Rock poet, was combing his long green hair. It stood out in all directions. His eyelashes were orange. From the corner of his mouth hung a weed. Tamara Polese, in Nazi uniform, was helping Etta Schnabel, lesser-known Punk poet, undress. Etta wanted to read in her birthday suit with a rose sticking out of her cunt. Kicks. Her stuff was Protest: biting. Tamara finished Etta and took the bourbon from Mason. "What's this?" She sipped. Birly, uneasily, answered for him: "Hog piss, honey." The trio called Hot Hips (composed of Sylvie—from France, Cornelia and Punk poet Estelle) went on first. Mason with the others went up and stood behind the curtain to watch. They screamed bloody murder at the audience (young punkies mostly): shook their purple short hair at each turn of each line and beat muscled fists out toward screaming voices: "Wash your mother in blood, rinse your father in the comfort of his own suds..." It gave Mason the chills. How would such an audience receive him? Tamara went on kicking and screaming for war: "I shoot shots from my M-1... put your fuck-finger in my barrel..." then Etta—as a naked belly-dancer—coughed up and hissed a Goethe poem about deals with the devil and Kafka's doomed soul and the end of the West. Thomas Mann was a jerk who moved to L.A. And so it went: Sebastian. Then Mason: slightly nervous but well-received. Politely. And the show ended with straight poet Sven Strom from Sweden, trying to be interesting dangerous exciting but not making it: "...I come bullets into your military-complex asshole! ... " In the morning the slicker went out to Brixton in the rain. Spoke sang cried to a group of scorcheyed West Indians Africans Anglos East Indians Palestinians. Shy and untrusting, these kids were not impressed by the author's so-called "lack of anger." Their highland was a lowland. How could a Black poet write other than *anger*.? What emotional osmosis'd created this freak? At the end one Black kid said "You nigger to the white man, like me. What good you think your sweet verse do to liberate us? You waste your time." The audience cheered. Mason's next stop was at Africa Center, that night. Ironically, there were more English than Africans in the audience. Africans were downstairs in the cozy dimly lighted little bar quietly drinking away their London blues. When the show ended Mason and manager Steven Mackie too went down and started working on a cure for the British funk. Mason went back by way of the tube. A shopping bag had just exploded (people were saying) at one station and mobs were being rerouted out of Marylebone Station to other lines. Two dead, six injured. By ten o'clock news some "terrorist" group would phone in word of responsibility. Revolutionaries? Causes and causes. At a Whitechapel community arts center that night he conducted what is known as a creative writing workshop: eight students. The group normally met at this time—eight—every week to read and discuss their works. Mason was added attraction. Simon, group leader, sat next to Mason and as he analyzed a selection of poems by various members, Simon amened him step by step. One girl wanted to know if Mason believed in love. He said he did. But his poems were *so* depressing. He read a love poem. They said but that's not a love poem. He swore to them he had hope. They laughed and gave him cupcakes. He refused to eat with them. They passed around more photocopies of their own poems. One girl there— Colette—who looked not a bit French, in Mason's opinion, wrote excellent poems about peeling vegetables and discovering the nature of the universe through simple acts like shelling peas or following the journey of a bug along a branch, was also looked upon by the rest with some hesitation. They asked Colette why she didn't write about relevant things. She said but I do. By the end of the workshop Colette was depressed. Along with Simon and a couple of the others, Colette too, Mason walked back to the tube. They all thanked him and shook his hand. That night the King of Illusion-Deceit-Fraudulence-Cheating-Shenanigan-Confidence pulled his own leg in his sleep: trying to center chubby pretty Colette onto the end of his hardon, he experienced a disaster: she turned into a faithful photograph of the Milky Way just as he got it in. It was chewed off by the speed of cubistic light. The Great Bear barked at him with his pants down. He shot for cover. Hid behind General Leclerc in the Square. A couple of old vegetable peddlers started beating him over the head with blette. (Later Colette sent him a batch of her new poems. He saved them till he felt like going up to Terrasse Frederic Nietzsche. Alone he sat on a stone rail at eight in the morning with Nice beneath him. Blue sea. Full stretch. And Bego to the North snow-capped in crisp contrast with the Cimes du Diable. He read her lines: "...you unbutton my shirt/ which is your shirt/ and eat/ the cabbage tips/ of my tits..." She'd signed all her poems with the pen name: Terry Gottlieb.)

Now, Berlin is another story. He was met at the airport by professors Wolfgang Proeschel and Heiner Graf, both Americanists. Had lunch at a student hangout where World War One saddles and spurs hung on hooks from the ceiling over the bar. Eye drift. Amesville was carved right into the wood of the table top where he calmly rested his arms. *He* wasn't alarmed. Already he felt more at ease in Germany than in France: but for the shabby reason everybody spoke his language. Hmmm. Proeschel was round and kindly through thick glasses; Graf was younger and lean with a twisted face holding tiny untrusting eyes. At two he was introduced by Graf to about a hundred students in a classroom on the second floor of the John F. Kennedy-Institut fuer Nordamerikastudien, Freie Universitat. He cleared his throat and said how happy he was. Then: "I once went to a Private Eye for help. I needed him for a novel. He gave me a full report on my problem. It cost a lot. I didn't get my money's worth. I'm talking about writing. So in the end I had to invent the character I paid him to find . . . " and when he finished the questions were intelligent (political, historical, social, reluctantly literary). Mason did his best. That night there was a dinner party at Proeschel's. Mason had only an itsybitsy German: he'd mostly skipped fruehstueck—since the fries were bullets and the steak disguised rawhide. After the party around the dinner he and Heiner went out on the town. Little sneaky-eyed guy turned out to be quite a number. He took Mason in search of the myth of Berlin: the 1930s? A thirst for sekt? for weisswein? A bar called Sloe Gin and Sin (already America, huh!) in the Mitte area. Chilly and damp night. But the little guy knew his way: he led Mason into the indirectly-lit decor of Early Longhair: slender paste-white women in long black dresses wearing Garbo-wide hats with mysterious veils holding ivory cigarette holders in delicate fingers away from the flutter of their own eyelids. Music was Duke's and Whiteman's—not at the same time. Latter-day filmstars millionaires mistresses of bankers or bankers themselves? Mason felt slightly ruffled here: a little too tweedy: mock formality. After the sweetness of the hard liquor and his own cigarettes rubbed him the wrong way he suggested they leave. They were both quite drunk by now. Graf even pissed in the mouth of the alley outside. They fell into a Spanish restaurant and demanded gazpacho and cocido escabeche de pesado—hoping to sober. Night lights showed them the way to filmed cunts: and they gazed at them: Mason was seeing double already—and seeing crazy: a naked man was hanging upside down in a closet: he had a hypo stuck in the base of his spine: for the umpteenth time he fought off Jesus trying to whip him over the head with a blackthorn cane. In Son of Sloe Gin and Sin, Heiner told him to get ahold of himself. He was staggering in respectable places. He saw Melba there: said she was moving to Yoknapatawpha County to avoid the fact that figleaves are shaped like male genitals. But he said they have figs down there! Giggling and staggering together holding each other up in the rain he and Heiner broke their way into a dingy joint where he saw one of his sons—Keith? Arthur? another one whose name . . . ? —a soldier leaving with a German woman. Oh, my oh my, thought Mason! Party time! But the young American soldier and his—date? girlfriend?—"companion" walked right by him as though he were a stain on the carpet: despite the fact that Mason cried out: "*Keith*! I love you! I'm your father!" But no dice. And Mason and Heiner held each other up as they stumbled past the reception desk from which Mason snatched a big antique vase (with hand-painted ladies in a garden along its central swell). Roses stuffed in it. Hmmm. Under street lights he cackled till he fell in the gutter—but he didn't lose the flowers. Heiner helped him up and Mason saw this woman in mink coming walking with her poodle. As he approached her with the vase she lost faith in humanity and ran. Immediately he turned and bumped into a girl perhaps eighteen: he rammed the vase into her chest. she automatically wrapped her arms around it and laughed. She got the joke. And he and Heiner continued to follow the flute sounds of some Pied Piper. After Heiner vomited in the gutter and on the fender of a VW he started blabbering about Spanish food again. A place called Castell de Ferro. They stopped a taxi. Mason told the driver: "Take me to my mother's place. It's on Drexel." Heiner punched him lightly. "No, no. Pal, we not—listen we're in Barcelona. Didn't you *know* . . . ?" "No," said Mason. "I don't want to go to Drexel. Take us to *my* place in the Village. Edith'll cook something for us. Even if she's asleep she'll get up. You'll like her, Cowie." "My name's not Cowie." "Okay. Okay." The driver said, "Which hotel?" Heiner's pronunciation was good even through the haze. The driver delivered them and they managed to pay him—twice. But it wasn't the right hotel. Across the street a bunch of people stood huddled together in a plastic tube waiting for the bus. Then it happened. Blam! Mason's eardrums refused to take the sound. It was the end of the earth. The people in the tube flew to pieces—arms, heads, legs. A flash. It wasn't anything but a movie: couldn't be real. Must be watching TV. Yet... there was something different about this movie. He could *smell* it. They stumbled across the street through jammed traffic!... didn't notice people running crazily from the scene. Mason touched a bloody arm on the hood of a parked car just outside the bus-stop area. Is that a *real* arm? The fingers were cold. But, Jez, uh, the damned thing *felt* real. Where was Heiner? There: squatting over—what was that?—a dead horse? No, an old man, probably: too much blood to tell. Sharp smell of burning plastic. Gelignite? Screaming from a gathering mob of stick-like figures dangling against darkness and the profusion of glittering pin-points. And approaching sirens. Gotta wake up. Just force yourself up out of it. Now there was pushing. Who'd he been with? German guy. What's his name? Mason fell. Feet lifted over him. It took ten years to get on his knees—the ground was ice cold—and to crawl from pavement to snow-covered dog-shit smeared grass. There he climbed to his wobbly feet at the edge of the mob. It seemed to him that something was really happening. Was he on a train being searched by Feds? If not then why was that rumbling going on beneath his feet? Perhaps some hanky-panky on the part of MRF? He heard 'em up there in the dark even now: geese flying overhead. Bright red and white lights flashing. Cops. Medics. He stumbled back into bluer shadows. Wasn't that Edith there at the edge of the crowd—dressed as Kitty in *Gunsmoke*? Without a coat... Mason touched the wetness on his beard. Held his hand out under a beam of light coming through fractured tree limbs: blood. It was warm blood and his... He felt his teeth. Big one right in front on the left was loose. Ah, Holy Kabbala! Cable Cab Calloway! He was losing his grip. With his tongue's tip he held the big chopper in place.

Heiner Graf wiped the blood from Mason's face. An irreducible self looked out of Mason up at the Taurus one above him. If this were the world in microcosm Mason wanted nothing to do with it. "Come! Off to the Potsdamer! We have a train to catch!" Mason lifted himself to an elbow. Bettle lava had his tongue glued to his mouth roof. Despite the slat stone and sting of the winter night, Mason was sweating rutabagas. And where were they going? He felt a blazing need for Wongo's galaxy of advice. This insane journey was driving him bananas. Who was this grief-stricken maniac pulling at his arm? Hadn't they just swam the Spree all the way to a fruit barge anchored near the Reichstag and the Friedrichstrasse. And hadn't he fallen into a soot-covered barrel of coal covered with kerosene-smelling snow. And who was it that saved this Taurus clown from his own skullduggery when a bunch of workers at the Anhalter Bahnhof wanted to nail him to a fence beneath a billboard that said, "Shop at The Karstadt!" Then wasn't it just hours ago that they'd gone to the bloody railroad anyway and hadn't they travelled some distance. And got mixed up with a bunch of strikers and beaten by the police in front of a factory gate in north Berlin. And it couldn't have been too long ago that this same man led him along the aisle of a devil-out-of-hell S-Bahn car filled with people as stunned and stiff as figures in an Ernst Fritsch or a Cesar Klein. They were all armed with cubist costumes. So why go anywhere else? What was the point. Mason didn't want to get up. Something, perhaps his left knee, was frozen. An asteroid churned in his lower stomach. He felt the lunar blues. Yet Graf pulled him up and leaned him against a car that looked like a middle-aged nude by Grosz. This had to be a frame-up. Else why had he seen Florence Soukhanov, a fictional character of his own making, in a coffee shop on Potsdamer Strasse spying on him from behind a crisp copy of *Der Sturm*. And why had he been unable to convince Graf that she was a spy for Painted Turtle. Graf claimed he'd never heard of Painted Turtle. He also denied knowing Little Sally Walker too. But Mason knew something was fishy about this whole situation. It wasn't just his well-justified paranoia. As Mason attempted to sink like a wet noodle, Graf held him up. "Care to dance?" "Not funny," Graf said. "We'll miss the train. If we're going to do this thing right we should go all the way. You haven't seen the winter bathers at the Wannsee Standbad. I must take you to the grave sites too. Look! There's a cop coming. Let's move! Can you walk?" They were on a one-way street.

Reality was not just a portrait in pastels: especially not this November, in this city. Among these strangers he thought he recognized—sober the next morning—were Nietzsche; and Gauguin posing as Lucifer and yes, that detective guy whose name turned out to be—according to Roy Seidel Ota, fence supreme—Andrei Gorbatchev, a Russian spy. Mason took the city tour of West, not East. *This* was Yalta's legacy? This and that half-remembered explosion last night. Anyway, the newspaper had a full story this morning and the waiter told him it was the work of a neo-Nazi group. No RAF fluff. The tour guide had a morbid sense of humor but his English was spotless. He joked about Hess in his cell costing taxpayers thousands: the most expensive prisoner in the world. Mason's memory: Angels with dirty faces live fast and die young. They were approaching The Wall. Its grimness and scars were especially sharp in November dreariness and chill. Checkpoint Charlie and its guardhouse were bleak. Lonely. Ah, snail-paced winter held frozen any sense of, ah, the thrill of victory the agony of defeat or was it... Surrounded by porcelain silver gold and glass Mason watched the alien yet known world with mistrust with awesome respect. He was dying to light a Camel. At the end of the tour he strolled at dusk on the mall people-watching. Zaftig women in furs, the Porky Pig-men in business suits and top coats. Charmed strollers of Old Frutz's chic veneer... Durchreise and the interchic! A gaze at secret frosty reminders of the hysteria of bygone. Where? Was he hearing whispers of the death camps and the death packed earth already?

When the bus stopped at Keiser damm Bismarck near the Zoological Gardens for a stop light, about twenty young men in black leather jackets rushed in front of it. Like figures out of an Elizabethan tragedy, they chanted blood. Mason watched three of them beat at the metal and glass of the door. The tour guide was scared. The boys started rocking the bus. A couple of women tourists screamed. An old man stood and shook his cane at the window, shouting in British English to the boys: "Get away, you scoundrels! Go campaign your Nazi propaganda in hell where you belong!" The boys shouted German back at him. Neither could hear the other. Mason cringed. The tour guide forced the old man back to his seat. "Just be calm." Two or three of the boys now had lighted torches and were shouting threats of fire bombing the bus if the driver didn't open up. Suddenly the light changed to green, the Marquis de Sade's good eye. Mason felt the bus lunge. The boys went crazy. Some of them were hurt. The guide ordered the driver to stop. He slammed on the brakes. A woman standing in the aisle fell. The guide pulled the lever that opens the door. It opened. The torch bearers stormed up into the bus, followed by some of the others. Meanwhile, the sirens of police started up in the distance. The boys grabbed the bus driver, Mason, two women, the Englishman, and marched them out. The captives were roughly pushed into an alley and herded along the narrow paved darkness till they came to a building with an iron sliding-door. One boy was bleeding badly. Mason could hear the honking and bitching of traffic back there where the stopped bus now caused a jam. Police sirens were closer. Mason felt enraged. But the knife at his throat kept him quiet. He figured the way things were going lately he had to quickly do something aggressive or he'd lose not only what little identity he had left but his entire existence. The kidnappers knocked them along a long dark corridor till they reached an elevator. They were kicked and shoved onto it. The leather-jackets, six or seven of them, crowded on too. They were nervously chattering away, barking at each other, snapping orders to Mason and the others. It was minutes before one, then another, switched to English. Their English was excellent. When they were all finally locked in a dimly lighted room far beneath the earth, the leather-jackets slapped the women for whimpering which only made them cry harder. The Englishman got a knee in the balls when he tried to defend the ladies. Mason was taken to a separate room, one the size of a closet. A single uncovered bulb hung from the ceiling. The two young men who'd led him there smiled at him. "I'm Franz." "I'm Alfred. We know you Americans like to use first names. We know your name already: Right?" "No." "Oh, yes we do." "Oh, no you don't." "Oh, yes we do." Franz, a red-faced youth with a preppy haircut, punched Mason in the nose. "We said yes we do." Mason swung at the guy but Alfred blocked the effort and drove a serious-business fist into Mason's guts. Mason folded, holding the area with the delicate and passionate concern one might give to an exotic, newly captured bird. Outside, in the larger room he heard the sounds of brutality, hysterical outbursts, and the small whimperings of grim diffidence and taciturnity. While Franz and Alfred quietly but intensely discussed some urgent matter, Mason entertained himself with a song he'd sung as a small child when he was the seeker rather than the hunted: Three pound of beans/ Three pounds of greens/ Who not ready holler queens./ Strawberry chocolate vanilla pie/ Who not ready holler I. I'm not ready. Ran to the rock. What an indecent moment, full of obscene god-forsaken torment. Alfred squatted before Mason. "My friend, you are now going to tell us all about the Magnan Rockford Foundation. Okay? Ready?" Mason grunted. Franz kicked Mason's thigh. "Start from the beginning." "We have ways of getting you to talk," Alfred assured Mason. He had broken teeth, yellowed from too many cigarettes. He was lighting one now. He blew the smoke in Mason's face. It made him want one too. Mason smelled the cigarette smoke but he also smelled another kind of smoke. Smoke was coming in under the door. Franz and Alfred too were aware of it. In German, Franz said he'd go to see what was going on. Alfred handed Mason the cigarette. "Unfortunately, this may be your last fag. Enjoy. You see we plan to break you of many habits. Smoking may be one of them. A lot depends on you. Our mission has started in Berlin, the hottest place—politically speaking—in the western world. Unlike in Hitler's dream for the future, we plan to include the likes of you. The Magnan-Rockford Foundation doesn't know it, but it's going to help us, the way Ford helped Hitler. We have plans here in Berlin you wouldn't believe. On your little precious tour I'm sure you saw some of our targets. Among them, that Jewish Community Center on Fasanenstrasse, is going to speak to the world for us." Mason inhaled. He let the smoke out in Alfred's face. At this moment all hell broke loose the door was kicked in and torrents of smoke poured in. Men in fireproof suits, wearing gas masks stood ten deep at the door holding machine guns. In German, Alfred and Mason were told to surrender. They put up their hands.

Everything changed. On the plane to Frankfurt he lighted a Camel. Holding it by its hind legs he watched the hair along the hump sizzle: its smell, a fresh skid mark. "Turkish & Domestic Blend." The city on the back was hot and dry: just the place to be: down through clouds: a glimpse of the vast metropolis. Settled in, he took the train out to Mainz and arrived at eleven sharp. Professor Rudolf Semler gave him a warm but brief intro and the students in the typical German fashion rapped their desks with approval. Hating the taste of a recently smoked Coffin Nail he climbed up. But it was better than Alfred's smoke in his face. Hungover, the would-be decided to try to merge his personal disaster with its desolation and psychic gangplanks from Georgia to Chicago and from the inner coils of his longing to Be-Somebody-Safe to their—or what he imagined to be their Black Forest, their old-woman-roasting-children-in-the-oven, Tristan and Isolde and their stained glass-fear of the same *unknown* he feared. Dreamer! Mason dared trust a blind connection: It was as insane as dumbass engineers of say a spermbank scheme—the gimmick of a nut with the smell of Hitler's asshole coming from the lower depths of the throat. These bright-eyed undergraduates? connect to *his* mysteries? What shape could they put to the incongruous rubbish merged in this voice-filled presence? Perfection can never be deliberate!... Think about it: his crazy sea his gentle ladies fanning themselves his maze of one-night-stands his quickies his harsh knife-warfare-life behind the walls of Attica his, praytellblasted Celt! Could they see their own secrets through him and see through him? How about the crushed and cursed desperate enterprise of that night's rush to the isolated trainyard as a connective tissue in the action? Should they? And this deeper question (even halfway admitted to himself) of scathed name, of forged identity with its built-in layer upon layer of the genuine the unreal the sort-of-authentic, the honest geocentric force of the gray area—what of all this? What of this complex, plumed and damned quest to . . . well, *you* know the story! I don't cast the first stone, mind you. Well, at least he hadn't stumbled going up on the stage to face three or four hundred faces. Here in this tiny city where the printing press had its beginning, Mason wanted so much to leave an imprint: to inform with form, to push a verbal text beyond a pretext. What could he on the other hand take away with him? That ancient sound of the press's grinding and the hard stone of germanic faith . . .? He tried everything: forced connections, exchange and conflict, the secret design, you name it. You gotta give him a bit of credit I guess: he *did* reach these inheritors of another kind of difficult history without telling them about his ancestors of West Africa and the Middle Passage and the pit. And the centuries. What he said was, at best, symbolic: the plan was this: survive and try to survive without too much humiliation and graceless-ness. Nietzsche was right on at least one point: writers wrote to conceal. The possible reality of the effort? Mason's good intentions were not writerly, folks. He wanted out from under. He spoke a convincing game. Hark! Whatcha do wid dat? Had Mason's fear tipped the scales—now that he was insanely sure his game'd been peeped, at least by me—or would he swing the other way toward arrogance and defiance, toward graceless combat with shadows armed-to-the-teeth with expert weaponry? You're close enough: Ask *him*. Mason, step forward, my son: *speak!*

"...then he opened the closest door and went in. Blitz-krieg! Suddenly he was at sea...Commander of his own vessel, his guest was Captain William Robinson from the Hope-well. Robinson suspected a bunko-game? Gag on him... as they fried the fat in gabby Gaelic, Clay Potter listened to Robinson's tale of entrapment in a circus of battleships two days out of London a year ago...Clay then had his tale of woe: here on the Celt-Prodigal he'd been lucky to still have his head on his shoulders since the mates were restless and surely plotting something horrible...Clay'd delivered those classifiers to their destination where, heck, they were probably still scraping bird shit and slime and the petrified bone-dust of woodchat's from the pottery found at the bottom of the sea. A bronze bucket, the classifiers told Captain Clay, had been found near the coast of Liberia. Cap'n Potter went on: 'They found the remains of Shine near there, too.' Robinson hadn't heard of Shine but knew legends the slave traders'd brought back... Potter advised him to read a recent book: *The Memoirs of Madame Rose Marie Butler*

Williams, Grand Queen of the Best-Time-in-Town-Bar-and-Hotel on Butler Street. It was full of sensational and historical information given her by sailors... Robinson was visibly getting sleepy from the sweet wine. Potter walked with him to his cabin. They shook. After leaving his guest Potter, assuming he was still in control, returned to his cabin. His first mate was there. Captain Clay Potter had another story for Robinson in the morning. This, faithful reader, was the breakfast-table tale Robinson got: 'My first mate was in a gumbo frenzy. Sir, he said, shaking like Clarence Snow in a Shirley Temple icky-flick, w-w-we, uh, a-ain't no longer at sea! (*Christ,* Jesus as a Hollywood *coon* of the 1930s?—*Come on!* Some jinx on Latino vibes!) *What in the devil do you mean, man—speak up?* We are moving, uh, across *land,* uh, Sir. Nonsense! I shouted in his—. Uh, Sir, come take, uh, look, Sir. I followed him to my trusty porthole. He stood respectfully aside, waiting with the jitters for—. My clay-lined porthole didn't lie. Mirror, mirror. By jimmydecricket, my First Mate was on target, was not just a fragment, a stooge, a yoyo. We *were* moving across *land*! But, I cried, we don't have no wheels—how can this be! Together me and my sidekick trotted up on deck and dashed toward the bow to discover a team of oxen under their oxbows. I needed oxygen—no, an oxygen-*tent*! Chicago, New York, Attica, Air Force, no place was *like* this! The oxen were dragging my honey through mud. Her skirts—filthy. I shouted to Jesus: Gib me my periscope! You Dumbbell! I snatched it from his claw. Through it I saw far into the future: my success—critical acclaim, money, position, travel, the works. Looks like a form of civilization, I murmured, as I looked through the magic glass beyond the foreshadowing to the background: of trees and huts and dark people in grass skirts carrying on their heads buckets of Amesville fertilizer, baskets of excellent clocks, sacks of wild oats, netted-bundles of pome-granates, Cadillac parts, boxes of turtles packed in ice, and Cross Damon's crash at Roosevelt Road. Resigned, I whimpered. Where'd we get the oxen? Mates had 'em down dare in de hole, Sir: in case uv ah 'mergency. I cleared my bellyaching-throat.

Jesus whined. But, Sir, there should be another sea or at least a lake or a river, Sir, up ahead—beyond that batch of celt trees and curoi mountains. I hoped he was right as I wondered about the inconsistency of his speech: was this spic putting *me* on? Speak! Oh, well. I hope you're right, Mister Jesus. I had no Annie Oakley off the floater, so I returned to the submerged discomfort of my cabin. I took out my best maps: of the unknown worlds; spread them on my children's faces (I heard them whimpering under there with many axes to grind). There was the famous Blue Arrow the Fall River the Mary Lake the Grand Lake the Shadow Mountain the Green Ridge the Stillwater the Emerald Lake the Rainbow Curve the Crystal Lake the Lawn Lake the Odessa Lake the Thunder Bay the Fish Creek the Dream Forest the Spruce Lake the Baron Lake the Sad Lake the Telephone Route the Well-Entrance, I'll-Be-Damned County, Nymph River, Jungle Jim Cove, the Scenic Peak, the Junction of Highway Fifty-five and Sixty-six next to Deer Meadow and the Snake River. No celt tricks. It was all there all clear but where could I place my *x*? I wanted to be able to say, 'I am here!' I certainly wasn't anywhere near old pal Billy of Chicago, a sailor who taught me to sail, Blue-jersey Jerk, Jack Tar, Siwash, nor near Paradise or Ponderosa or Granby or Bluebird or Billy Barnacle, nor Sandbeach or Bonaparte's or Iceland's Second Winter or Skua or Razorbill or Puffin or Little Auk or Nightjar or Pinewood or Sea Crab, or Buttermilk Bottom, or Swab-jockey Point, or Corinth, or Lyons or the Egyptian picnic area nor the Bearded-Tit section of Water Dog Falls or South Side or Beaver-Nice or Antique Creek or Avant-Garde River or Clarenceberg Heights of Zedtwitz Star or Moca Ridge or Gwen Falls or Mafia Meadow or Ala or Nipson Womb or Zimm Lake or—hell, all those places were back a ways. Likely I was not any longer on the map. (Maybe I'd accidentally given my best maps to Cap'n Robinson.) Nope: no longer on the—up here beyond the frame of the C-shaped map. I looked at the table top where the map ended. Doesn't look like much: Just a table top. I sniffed a rat and avoided using the back of my left hand to wipe away the tear running down my right cheek.' "

What else is new: he was horny! As he moved on he noticed the petrified landscape closely frigid under its mineral snow from the heated train window. And the Mainz professors waved goodbye to him from the sternly rooted old platform. Lunch with them in the campus restaurant hadn't been bad: but he was still hungry. Who said food was a substitute for Dancing in the Dark? Mason's response to the deepness of his cravings was a wire-cable spinning fast from the winch deep in the forecastle of his stomach: a tricked Pavlovian dog unable to salivate. With wings he could fly into the arms of romance but those shabby inherited gadgets were things of the past: he was no pretty flycatcher with a red breast although he did sport a rather brown tail. Tale? Back in the city: Frankfurt blinked its new facade so persistently that it was difficult to glimpse the buried gemstones, crusts and relics of its ancient temperament and pulse: in the hotel room he was restless—too restless to even jackoff. That night he'd speak at the University of Frankfurt, *but*. Like a politician on the trail he'd give them a pep talk, a slap on the back and pull their leg. He turned on the radio: Chopin's Mazurka in C Minor, Opus Thirty-three, Number Four. Switched it off. He had all afternoon. Shit. Why didn't they plan these things better? He went out. Outside in front he leaned into a taxi and asked the driver in an honest and unemotional voice if he knew a whorehouse. Sure. Mason got in. The cabbie drove fast. Took Mason to a residential area. Stopped. "Hokay." The house was respectable, quiet. But Mason made the driver wait till he was sure—of what he wasn't quite sure. Then when the man at the door invited him in Mason turned and signaled to the cabbie who hit the gas. Here the game was simple: since Mason was the trick he had to sit at the bar and watch the porno flick while surveying the "girls." The gentleman who'd let him in took his coat then served as bartender and made him a scotch. He struck a match to a fresh Camel. Soundtrack to the flick was funny: Uh ah uf oh ooooh yes guud agh! I'm coming! and the stupid inevitable withdrawal at the point of orgasm: to say see guys I did it I'm a big boy, see! It wasn't a busy night: that was clear. Young woman in a black satin evening gown on the stool next to him. Others over on the couch. One down the bar. Black Satin with dark hair had a certain *pull*. She wasn't sipping real liquor he could tell. But her cigarette was real. He knew she knew he was shy or pretending to be. She finally turned to him. "You interested in sex?" He was. She told him it'd cost him seventy deutschmarks for a face to face fuck. Fancier action cost more. This wasn't highway robbery, so... On the way upstairs the intercom gave the fireworks of Tchaikovsky. Her name she said was Musa. His was Vincent Van Gogh. She laughed. Well, getting to a point earns a gold star. In the room she put out her Peter Stuyvesant. "Come." She led him to the wash basin, unzipped his pants, fished around inside his underwear for his cock, pulled it out. She clinically inspected his organ. She wet the soap. As she washed his cock with soothing warm water and gentle strokes she wanted to know if he was American. Yes. Was he from California. Yes. Why not. He gave her a silkscreen picture of his charming past. He unzipped her dress on request and gave her the bread also on request. Musa, naked, pushed her stomach out. "I got this disgusting belly. See." She'd been holding it in inside her satin. "Isn't it disgusting?" It was. But her arms were thin, so were her thighs. She had a pretty face too. But that belly was the pits. This Musa had earnest little dimples behind her knees. He had a semi-erection despite her dispassionate touch: wild broncos galloped along his scalp, down the veins of his thighs. He was trying to remember where this damned *washing* ritual had happened before, as he got into bed with Musa. *Ah! Voila!* Professor Sandra Pirsig in Seattle—she'd done that. Imagine that! He didn't imagine her performance had been for the purpose of detached inspection. Pirsig did it, he thought, to give him pleasure. What an egomaniac! To dawdle before his shrine!? Who's to say Pirsig wasn't a secret health conscious nut. Herpes epidemic, ya know. Negative reinforcement—or positive? Remember? They got together on his last night. He didn't especially *like* her: her manner was abrupt, she talked big city-fast, was frantic and smoked too much: when he kissed her her breath tasted of lye and metal. For every Camel he lighted she smoked six Salems. Not in English, she taught philosophy and shared with him this: "I'm working on Kant." He grunted his brittle interest and she went no further. Pirsig had bad skin: yellowish. She suffered some sort of affliction which claimed every inch of her body: face too. "Nerves, says my doctor." Her hair was the color of a marmot's pelt. As she drove he sensed—feared?—he might have to *deal* with her: he *was* horny. But—. In the motel's parking lot sitting in the car, Pirsig told him her life story: she'd been a bright girl who'd grown up in Manhattan where she attended Spence. Smart as a whip she went to Harvard with honors while others her age were still in high. She earned a Bachelor of Arts then took her doctorate at Yale. Her father was a psychiatrist with a famous practice on Fifth and Eighty-second and her mother, before her younger brother was born, was a nurse. When she finished she bluntly asked: "You want to fuck?" In the room she did the warm-water wash routine over the face-bowl. He tried not to focus on the pimples on her face chest arms thighs. ". . . he said they'll go away but'll probably leave perma-nent scars." Now his erection wasn't all that terrific. It didn't help that she made a lot of lunatic noise while they fucked: she reminded him of a bad porno flick. Also while humping away with her he imagined her inflammation oozing onto his own skin and causing—certainly by morning—eruptions he'd be stuck with for life. As she flailed and screamed Mason couldn't figure why he was riveted to such a crazy act, such self-destruction. He'd die in an acne shitstorm! Pumping away in this casuality of an exclusive, guarded childhood of sharp-talk, corrosive, savvy, money and tedia, Mason remembered the crowded sadness in his own childhood of meanness. The memory swam up through his motion. After the act, she started on his Camels. All the Salems gone. "I try to stay with filters but I really prefer a *real* cigarette." Now the talk was of her bad marriage. Hubby intended to be a professor too but ended up dropping out of Harvard in the first year of grad school. She buckled down to her studies and he went off searching for dope in Bangladesh Uruguay Malaysia Fiji and

Malagasy. Last she heard he was sane again and running a Half-Way House in Boston. After the marriage she wrote her first *real* book: *Women and Logic in the Nineteenth Century*. Her dissertation, *The Feminist Challenge to The Age of Reason*, remained unpublished. She said her biggest problem as an intellectual woman was loneliness and an inability to find a "decent" man. Trapped by her smartness, her profession, her only friends were women, other feminists. Mason was sleepy. Finally when she shut up and sleep came it was restless. She kept tossing and getting up to piss and smoke, waking him time and again. Once when he was snoring she shook him violently and asked him to blow his nose—even handed him a tissue. Jez.

Now here in Frankfurt after getting his cock washed he was led by it to the bed. Musa sat him down on the sagging side and squatted before him holding a condom. *Whhhhhat?* This wasn't in the deal! "No." "Yes, is necessary. Is good to prevent disease." "But I—" "Cost you another thirty-five deutsch-marks to leave it off." (She'd already put the seventy in her little purse.) His erection lost some of its headiness. Some sexual sendoff! Mason decided not to give in. She went ahead with the pre-wet membranous sheath. Cold and distracting. Harnessed, he didn't feel up to foreplay one tiny bit. Musa got on the bed and opened her thighs. Yet somehow even with the rubber wall between them the tango was intense and sweet with calm ballet-motions strangely mixed in. He made better deeper wider richer contact here than with tannic Pirsig. When finished Musa encouraged him to come again for a mere twenty more. No thanks my dear fraulein. When they returned to the bar downstairs three other men were there watching the tangle, slipping-and-sliding on the screen. In the back seat of the taxi, he felt unsatisfied, slightly depressed. A sense of futility took him.

At a certain point he paid the cabbie. Night air was biting cold. Suddenly he was in a bright winter crowd in some shopping center or a mall.

Herr Bend, a writer of perverse novels, handed Mason an autographed copy of his latest. "They made me sign a contract at gunpoint for this one." He laughed so hard he turned into a Grosz-face in *Widmung an Oskar Panizza*: blasphemy was oozing out of his skin , red as burned crosses. "Let's be on our way. We'll be late for The Event." Mason, pretending he remembered, slapped Herr Bend's shoulder. "I'll saddle up my sorraia. Did you come in your usual Kindl-Brauerei truck? Why'd you haul those barrels around? What's in 'em?" "Never mind. I'm doing research for my next." Mason left the tip and the waiter, as lively as a Mendelsohn composition, thanked him as they stood. Outside on the bustling plaza a couple of giggling guys rushed up to them and playfully punched both in the mouth. Herr Bend's nose started bleeding. Mason tried to kick one of the jokers as they fled. He checked himself for broken bones. The taxi ride over to The Oyster had its merits: traffic was orderly, efficient. A crew was shooting a film in the dark park. Herr Bend kept slapping Mason's knee. "Fritz Rasp? No. I think he died. Valeska Gert? No more proletarians around?" Mason sneezed: "Was Brecht a communist? *Kuhle Wampe*." But before the dirty writer could answer they were out. Herr Bend slipped immediately on a banana peeling. He slid toward The Oyster's brick wall and banged his head on the metal door as he fell, loosing his bleached wig. The Event had already started. Theatre was fun? But wait this was not German theatre: not *De Bettler* not *Die Wandlung* not the ghost-prisoners of *Hölle Weg Erde* climbing the narrow stairway from hell up to an unpromising earth. This, yes yes, was still hell: red hot and grimy. This was

Rock. And weren't those people up there on the stage the same ones he'd performed with in London? The stage was crowded: musicians with yellow or green hair played instruments that released swine-grunts and bat-farts and ... Yes, that *was* the great Sebastian! He'd changed the color of his hair to a blazing red with streaks of yellow. He was shouting above the voices of Silvia, Cornelia and Estelle, creaming the audience: "Give me your weak, your hungry, your poor/ I'll make gunpowder out of them!/ Lend me your ear: I'll bite it off/ and stick a firecracker up your asshole!/" Sylvia was screaming one long streak of Munch-pain. At the end of it she spat blood: "I shit on the mysterious silhouettes/ of your limited warfare-bombs! I crap on your stockpiles!/" And, just like at the Young Vic, Tamara Polese, still in her Nazi uniform, was running about the stage shouting her own mean verse and swinging the butt of her rifle at everybody in sight. She knocked Cornelia's teeth out and stuck the barrel of her rifle up naked-Etta Schnabel's cunt and pulled the trigger. Etta flew all over the place, pieces of her hit the ceiling and dripped down on those still singing and dancing. Then a team of police officers entered the theatre from a side door. Mason and Herr Band leaped up. But they didn't move in time to avoid the nightsticks. Mason's head was bashed in and everything went black. When he came to he was in the back of a lighted speeding van. His head was cradled on Tamara's lap. She was stroking his bloody forehead. "Who's driving and where're we going?" "Ssssh. Don't talk." The van was crowded. Where was Herr Bend? "He died for a noble cause. It was better," Tamara whispered, "than going by way of ulcers or diarrhea or colitis or a ruptured thyroid." Mason felt his swollen joints: felt like he'd fallen down a ski slope with teethgrinding intensity. He felt the humiliation of the hotel doorman demoted to toilet attendant: long live Murnau! A couple of feet away, Sylvia and Estelle were trying to put the pieces of Etta Schnabel back together. Cornelia was resting in Sebastian's arms. She was grumpy. Said she felt depressed. Hadn't had a bowel movement in days. Had a urinary tract infection. Strep throat was surely coming next. Sebastian, bleeding from the ears, tried to soothe her. She said her muscles were too tight. Mason suddenly became conscious of his own tense muscles. Somebody up in the cab was stuttering. Mason's tension headache was paralyzing. Whiplash and arthritis had a good grip on him. Tamara said, "At least you're not on your way up some Fritz Lang-stair-way of Death. Okay Doctor Mabuse? You can trust all of us. We'll take your blood pressure, tell you if you have irregular heartbeat, flutters, palpitations. Your hands are cold. Where we're going you can let blind men count your money. We're gonna make a whole new world safe for the swinging moods of a new self emerging from the old one."

This was hectic ego work. The train along the Rhine took Mason's vermin-breath and held it somewhere inside. Snow covered hibernating vineyards and the torrid castles up the hillsides matched his own desperate frost... Then he arrived at the dreamy (deceptively quiet?) little city of Aachen... In the night he slept through the gunfire of his own plot: Clarence Mckay was after him, and this time, jack, with cannons and machine guns! Mason couldn't find a rock to hide behind. In his hasty flight he bumped into William Carlos Williams, on a beach somewhere. Bill grabbed the shaking man by his shoulders and spat these words into his face: "Nine-tenths of our lives is well forgotten in the living. Of the part that is remembered, the most had better not be told.../ We always try to hide the secret of our lives from the general stare. What I believe to be the hidden core of my life will not easily be deciphered." Doc's speech only made matters worse. Despite Mason's respect for the poet. His plot still had him in a fit. It wasn't simply that he was not achieving what Public Enemy "told him to do, he hadn't even yet embarked on the discovery of the basis for his complex identity. Well, he might be able to fly again but he'd have to swim, like Shine, to Greece, to find parts of the puzzle, then, surely to Africa for the other parts. France wasn't enough. England? Forget slavery. Germany was as useless as his "false" past. And, hell, he had to do something about his own paranoia! Everybody wasn't an enemy!... He lost himself in a network of beach rocks. True, he wasn't driven to avenge himself any longer. No need. Since leaving the states he knew he'd changed. His needs were now different. How? Well, he got up from sleep. But it didn't make any difference. He sat in the dark and looked into a patchy bed of lights from beyond the Gaestehaus window. One had to become Somebody or Nobody. Odysseus? Since arriving in Europe hadn't he reached a murky point? He couldn't go back. He was now assigned by desperation and the sense of urgency he felt always to go on, to discover the Whole Picture. The parts were everywhere. That was too bad. Their discovery though was his only hope of building a Self firm enough to withstand the threat of "The Other." The Other? One was driven for reasons other than one's shortcomings, one's mirror. The more he thought of it the more convinced he was that Africa would offer a way in. Why not Italy and Greece, too. Anyway, keep moving! He made up his mind to plunge, to swim... Without turning on the bedside light, Mason began work on his novel-in-progress. In the morning at the Technische Hochschule he wanted to give those bright German kids the best prose he could produce. The quality of his life depended on it. It was no longer just the blank page he had to face:

"... He was born in, I think, red-dirt Georgia, grew up, maybe, in hog-butcher Chicago, had many thick-headed problems in elementary and high and was a hardcore dropout... got into trouble in the Air Force... He's got something against all of us: was busted for possession... served time in

Attica from 1977 to 1978; while there he was betrayed by a guy who claimed to be...this other so-called writer was receiving grant money due him, the *real* writer...the Foundation had gained a reputation for giving such awards to 'people of talent and accomplishment' who had not been widely recognized for their professional efforts...Victim he surely was...It's true he'd been a fart and a troublemaker from day one, he'd fathered—in and out of unholy wedlock—possibly as many as fifty kids, certainly a minimum of thirty-five...Before going into the joint he'd come through, so they say, many failed marriages... Though there were those who protested his right to everything, even his birth, he insisted he was born December thirty-first, 1936 in Georgia at Grady with wristband number 105847 clamped tightly to his little red arm...He was taken home to six-o-seven McGrader Street, South East, by his parents...so how did he find himself years later in Amesville, ready one fine day to step down from a John Deere and set out to reclaim his identity?... Well, parole ended: that was certainly a factor plus a private detective in New York had agreed to find the culprit...But, Jez, it was like coming out of amnesia with a sudden cold memory of endless dark tunnels of the past...Walking away from that tractor, he looked up at the pancake in the Sherwood Anderson sky and took a Saroyan-breath, exhaled it...Minimum wage was chicken, no birdshit...He stepped through freshly turned earth till he gained a road then the highway...Beat his blunt toetips on concrete...He stopped in the city of Amesville for a cup of coffee...A yellow-white cat with one green eye, one blue, leaped onto his lap...He rested his elbows on the red-dotted plastic tablecloth...Cat refused a sip of the brew...Clock on wall reminded him of something: what was it: gave him an awful feeling of anxiety... clocks were always running: warning you of the thing you didn't want: that magnetic force: hands without fingers: radium into visible light...He had to move on: it was urgent...He though the cat was...he set her down...He didn't have much faith in his luck to thumb a ride so he began walking...His mudfrog, a birthmark on his right forearm, itched horribly... Ass still sore from the tractor seat... He stopped to rest under a tree: turned out to be Joyce Kilmer's... Quick! a train was coming along the tracks only a few feet from the tree... Was he dreaming? A woman was tied to the tracks where another set crossed... He got to her in time: untied her and threw himself and her into the ditch as the iron beast shot by... she was nutmeg color: a dark beauty and spoke in a musical and mysterious voice... said she was from a reservation in New Mexico, had worked the canteen circuit, made movies, danced professionally, hung out with gangsters, but was now seeking a new life... She told him her name was Painted Turtle... He was heading for New York and she, well, she'd go there just as soon as she'd go anywhere... "

A barrage of bullets swept the room. Mason hit the floor and crawled under a table. Munich was not a safe place. He'd been talking to an old friend, Lilia Pant, when the violence struck. Leaves fell from winter trees. It snowed upside-down. Knucklebones broke in butterfly lava. Gangsters were moving in. Who would have thought the gambling room (called The Wheel) at the Greta Garbo Entertainment Palace would become the scene of buffoons of death? Pant hit the floor too. Some folks ran. A barracuda fell from the wall and got stuck on Marlene Dietrich's head as she too fled the madness. The air felt like that of a Prussian boarding school. Except at the moment nobody was much for bedside-baroque-chatter. Gunsmoke seeped into wool cotton and silk. Screaming and crying competed with drum rolls and bells. A stranger under the table with them said, "It's just carnival time coming early. Somebody thinks it's February." Another, who introduced himself stiffly and drunkly as Eichberger-the-Calan, spoke: "If we crawl slowly, being sure to stay under the tables, we can make it to the Faust-

Mephisto Room where they're showing an erotic film of Otto and Lucie against a yellow sky. They're supposed to be immoralists who've escaped the Russian October Revolution. Lots of finger-fucking." Mason figured he had nothing to lose so he was the first to follow this Rasputin. Lilia trailed him. They were snails with scales moving along the surfaces of the soggy orange rug. Rasputin's big ass waved in front of Mason's reluctant face. He held his head sideways. He could still hear shouting and fists smashing into wine glasses and Peter Lorre-lips. In the Faust-Mephisto Room the three escapees stood and blinked. Mason's sugar-coated eyes saw an orgy at its peak. Geese were flying up out of flesh. One man was dancing with a bullhorn hanging from the crack of his ass. Intestines were scattered around the floor. Expressive ladies and unrelenting men were deeply engaged in a daisy-chain of sixty-nine action. Projected on the wall was an on-going series of scenes depicting Otto and Lucie in goggle-eyed combat: frosty steam lifted skyward from their action. Lilia Pant groaned. "Here we go again!" Mason laughed with her. Six sailors emerged from a torpedo and joined the carnival. One waved to the camera. An expressive lady grabbed his left thigh. "Oh, Chief Mack-Verand! You're back!" He took off his mask just as Lilia fainted in Mason's bruised arms. Rasputin said, "Oh, my dear!" Back in The Wheel the gunfire stopped. Mason could hear the official counting of the dead.

Early December sky over Catania was filled with a calmness in casual contrast to the chaotic life below. (The day before, Mason'd driven his Fiat up onto one of the giant white ships of the Tirrenia line at Genova; he'd paced the upper deck while gangs of Italian kids, lovebirds, old folks and crew, also restlessly wandered about: a long tiresome voyage; older passengers sprawled before the TV set in the lounge absorbed in artificial light. This thing—il dio, il re, l'eroe! The food was horrible. Fearing he might throw up he stood at the rear watching a crazy flock of gray gulls flapping in the ship's wake which, in its splitting of the sea skin, turned up fish they fed on... When he woke in the morning he was sick, truly. Claustrophobia in his narrow private space got to him. He was sure the room was bugged. Why hadn't they simply arrested him? How much more rope would they give? They docked at Palermo and in line he drove the Fiat off into the honking, busy city. Famished. He went to a restaurant a truck driver he'd met in the lounge recommended. This guy was from Napoli and knew his way around. Here he pigged out on lasagne verdi al forno and two big bottles of vino. Stuffed, warm and a little tight, he drove that long green stretch through plush countryside to Catania.) The sky, as I said, was serene. Below: one way streets that didn't make sense: insane intersections crammed with cars and people crossing in every direction with no direction. Madness! Whistle-blowing traffic cops who made no sense either. It was dusk. Lighted shops. Packs of teenage boys intent on their desperate enterprises (one tried to open Mason's door at a stop)! It took an hour to find the damned hotel—instructions had been so poor. Hotel Pericolo: the perfect secret of the sunny southern tip of Italy! A warning—? In the hotel room he took a shower and while doing so the phone rang. Wet, he answered. Professor Carlina Momachino wanted to know if he'd arrived and if all was well. Well how?... That night Mason had dinner with the Momachinos: polla alla cacciatora. A childless happy couple: she, a specialist in American fiction, he a specialist in marble. He looked like a palm tree with arms and she was this little dainty thing all motion and flutter with painted nails and pointed toes. Signor Vito Momachino drove him back. Exhausted, he went to sleep and while there found himself in this strange market place called Albano (wait, hay, this wasn't Italy, whhha...) off some place called Gran Via to the, uh, right and another way, Casa Christino; and passing showcase glass seeing himself (just like some prison mugshot of himself) and here an old man was pushing his way through the crowd carrying a poster with some squabble about some government official whose identity was in question but there was a caption about the Union of the Democratic Center or the Centrists or was it the Left. Boy oh boy. Then this young dark guy—he could have been Italian or Spanish or even French— came knocking his way through—pushing aside two chubby senoras with yellow straw baskets, knocking over stalls crammed with cheap leather colorful cotton radiant metal glazed plastic painted glass and the guy, a hisser, tugged at Mason's sleeve, speaking in what sounded like Spanish or maybe Italian all the while flashing a wrist of Bulovas and all Mason could think was, Take me to your padrino. You from Morocco? And the watch-pusher said he was Pocoraba or Ernesto or Piazza but it didn't matter; in a nearby cafe they ordered government approved vino blanco. Now you don't want coca leaves, right. You got cash. When can you get it. Senor Aristides Rayo Barojas you see. Very formal. And suddenly they were at the entrance of a cluster of dilapidated chartreuse apartment buildings. Across the street for no reason: a fancy hacienda surrounded by kidney-brown debris and a vacant lot of broken bottles and gun shells. Before Pocoroba knocked on wood he kindly requested five hundred— not lire—but pesetas! Mason vaguely suspected he was some-where in Spain: again, after... Mason unhanded the bread and waited. His moneybelt itched worse than a mudhound. A servant came and led them to Barojas: through tall dark hallways with pictures of thieves generals ancestors fingering the handles of swords, guys with chins stuck out, dudes with waxed mustaches curled up to a fine finish. It all *felt* like black lace. The languid summer outside hadn't ever reached this depth. The watch-pusher and Mason waited in a canary-yellow room lined with gold-painted Nineteenth Century volumes nobody'd touched in fifty years. A rotund gentleman in a smoking jacket entered. "I am Senor Barojas." He didn't offer his hand. "May I help you?" Mason realized he didn't know why he was here. Barojas obviously sensing the confusion spoke again: "Don't be shy. I have the documents ready. Do you have the money?" But the dream he woke on was of Edith in New York and he had an erection straining up through it—her?—then one thing led to another and he knew he had to lecture at nine at, what was this place, Universita di Catania, section: Facolta di Lettere e Filosofia, Cattedra di Letteratura. He sat on the side of his bed waiting for the right moment to stand. Why had a player in such a casual ancient moment come back tugging at him with her big-girl erotic self. A light changed in him: brilliant green.

A gas bomb, they said, started the fire in Misterbianco. Just for the ride, Mason went out in the jeep with Vito, a shy man in a red plastic jacket. Vito was a new inspector for the Catania fire department. "Go see the flames," Carlina had said, tossing her dark shoulder-length hair back from her left eye and giving Mason one of those serious-blank Modigliani looks. On the way to Misterbianco Vito said it had to be the work of either a crazy arsonist or a revolutionary. It'd started at the Guglielmo Vanvitelli, a food processing plant, and, according to the voice on the phone from Misterbianco (where there was no fire department), the nearby hillside, trees and grass were burning away rapidly. Vito'd called for help from coastal Contana Rossa and Paterno, slightly inland to the north. As they approached, Mason saw the smoke drawing the village of Livorno as it looked on July 12, 1884, against a red chalk and terra verde sky. "Holy Galileo!" Vito slapped his own cheek. The yellow-orange flames were leaping furiously up the hill, higher than the cypresses, leaving a blue-gray ash in their wake, Mason and Vito jumped down from the jeep before it stopped moving. An old rusty fire-truck with *Paterno* painted clumsily on its left door was parked about fifty feet from the food plant. Several men, working one hose, were fighting the flames and smoke there but nothing was being done about the spreading. Beyond the cypresses was an orange grove. It would be next—and soon. Mason looked into Vito's excited eyes. "What'd you do *now*?" Vito didn't answer: he ran back to the jeep and snatched his telephone and began shouting in Italian into it. Mason wished he was on the Titanic, going down slowly. Rowing a mean boat. Or how about being at the Battle of the Amazons. Or at the Resurrection or at the Descent from the Cross. Where one *was* counted, every moment. Maybe being the Snake in the Apple Tree was a good role. But here? Watching a fire. Well, there was always Mardi Gras. He watched a woman with a Medusa face running from the plant toward Vito. Then beyond her, he noticed for the first time about fifty workers, mostly women, on the northeast side of the building, watching it burn. One man in the crowd seemed to be playing blind man's bluff. Suddenly a horse appeared on the burning hillside, stopped, gave the fire a skeptical look, then ran off—toward Mason. Something wild in Mason turned him into a seventeenth-century general as he leaped upon the galloping thick-footed Calabrese. It was white with black spots. Mason held on by its mane and gave the right pressure (with his thighs) to slow its pace. Luckily, it wasn't a wild trotter breaking out of some sepia and wash landscape. Its lines were as graceful as Venetian quill strokes. Vito was shouting and gesturing to Mason as the horse reared. Medusa too was shouting at Mason. Several people from the crowd came running down to the jeep. The horse kept trying to dislodge its rider by rearing and dancing around in the plush blue grass. Two police cars and two more fire trucks arrived just as four thick-set Venetian horses, straight out of the Iron Age, appeared on the same hillside where Calabrese first paused to inspect the heat. Everybody now, except the fire fighters, had come down from the food plant. They were watching Mason's effort to hold his own: some cheered him on, others angrily shook their fists at him. One man, who looked like Pope Gregory III, tried to catch the horse by its neck. Another yanked at Mason's right leg till his shoe came off. This one had a Caligula-look. As the cops approached with drawn pistols, Mason fell from his perch into a soggy spot in the grass. Did he think he was a figure in Beckmann's *Carnival* triptych: in solemn pursuit of a sexual posture? Vito helped him up. So did two policemen. In Italian, the one with the frog-head asked for his identity paper. Meanwhile, Calabrese ran off to join the Venetians. As Mason brushed at the wet seat of his jeans, he glanced over his shoulder in time to see Calabrese lead the Venetians down the other side of the hill, like paper figures dropping into a manila envelope. They side-stepped the fire with the heavy grace of Degas ballet dancers dislocated in Bartolomeo's *Assumption of the Virgin*. Mason handed frog his passport. "Come si chiama?" frog asked as he flipped the pages of the passport. His companion, meanwhile, was speaking to Vito: "Chi è quest'uomo?" Then Vito explained in Italian that Mason was a writer visiting the university in Catania. Yet, in minutes, despite Vito's protest, the officers had Mason in handcuffs. They gagged him and tied his legs together, too. He struggled like a Tintoretto figure. The crowd had become a mob. Fist fights broke out. The firemen continued to fight the flames. One, under orders from the police, turned the hose on the crowd. Mason was thrown in the back seat of a police car. The horse returned, running through the burned grass, up past the food plant. Something with huge wings flew overhead, causing a momentary shadow to cover the chaos. Mason spat phlegm on the seat. His nose rested on a spot that smelled of semen and sweat. As he was driven away, he heard Vito shouting after the car. One cop sat in back with Mason. In the front, Mason was aware of a woman's voice and the voice of the cop driving. The woman was called Priscilla. The cop beside Mason said, "Da dove viene?" When they arrived at the police station in Catania, the cops went for an officer who spoke English. He was plump with pendulous breasts. He seemed happy as he spoke this distant tongue: " . . . you will be charged with arson," he told Mason. Priscilla'd come into the station with them. She got slapped on the ass several times by cops just passing the reception desk where Mason stood still in handcuffs. His legs now though were free. He wished he were back in 1920, in bed with Jeanne Hébuterne, soothing her, giving her a reason

to live. Mason's rage was met with a slap across the face. He kept
telling them they had the wrong man. Breasts laughed at him as
the officer at the reception desk, with Mason's passport spread
before him, booked the Afro-American for arson. How much
injustice could one endure. Moments later, Mason was pushed
into an interrogation room. Bats hung upside-down from the
ceiling. A couple of men in armor hung out in one corner playing
cards. A portrait of Mario Buggelli was tacked to the wall
alongside a reprint of Beata Matrex. Mason almost wept on sight
of it: what lovely African lust lingered beneath its intentions! He
was forced down into a hard wooden chair. Four or five cops
surrounded him. Breasts held Mason's bearded chin in the palm
of his hand. Then he spat in his face. Mason blinked: while his
eyes were closed he saw Abraham travelling toward the Promised
Land. Then the door behind him opened and somebody said the
name Vito Momachino. His wife, the professor, they said, was
with him.

Professor Rosa Bartoli had reserved a room for him at the
Argentina in Florence. Why'd he felt so safe lately? was it
possible The Impostor was *no*where. Mason drove north,
pushing his luck, enjoying winter warmth. The nefarious trickster
arrived at suppertime. In the lobby the TV showed a cartoon of a
woman belly-dancing and doing a strip. Tease? She wasn't
fooling! She ended her act with only her reflexes X-rayed.
Hanging from the construction site of her body was a placard
with this message: "... Egli la aspetta." He felt yucky hungry
horny and free—no lecture till Monday and it was only Friday.
Determined not to fall for any rigmarole of false clues, a hateful
vendetta of his own mind, he was a masoned wall of faith. Self-
confidence was his middle name. No pun. Concreteness could be
seen all over historic Florence, as he walked. He looked into the

facade of the city: workers in stone had made it a towering monument to something he reluctantly understood. Well, even *he* was beginning to realize the real subject of his story wasn't this damned quest he'd thought he was on. He stuttered angrily realizing it: "I'll b-b-be d-d-damned!" He pulled out a Camel and struck a match to it. Wasn't he really playing the ultimate pinball machine of luck and trying (even with a false name) to be himself. Don't answer that. A true freemason? or just an ex-apple cart urchin adrift in a string-of-lucky breaks. He slept then got up and went out: daylight was a silicon blessing. Was Eye *really* watching him? or was it just his paranoia? Free as he felt he still felt trapped. Yet he went forth: into the chapels churches cloisters galleries fortresses gardens and like a good winter wanderer, scanned the squares—crossed and recrossed Ponte Vecchio finding the people more interesting than the whatnots the tourist-trap jewelry the sexy manikins. Lotta girls with slender brown legs. After doing the Uffizi he went to Dante's house: went down on his hopeless knees before it and burned a candle for five minutes. Passersby thought him a fool. He felt like he was fucking in public. Relentlessly he explored the Medici Chapel, seeing the way Michelangelo left the marble to speak of itself as marble, and moved on to Piazza della Signori. Museum floors were hard. Inside Museo Nazionale the dreamer of bird-seeds became aware of the hugeness of his new hunger (seemingly endless, right). He'd already focused one slanted eye on a ristorante boasting tripe in the Florentine manner. As he made a scientific investigation of the menu, a kid snatched a purse from an old woman and split on his bike. Mason whispered to himself, you are not a moralist. As he wandered he vaguely thought about Monday: his lecture wouldn't be just another narcissistic rug-cutting act. Then he got his tripe: in a tomato sauce: it was good.

The seven-headed, fire-breathing dragon that now faced Mason did not promise to be just or moral. It was midnight and somehow he hadn't gotten very far: hadn't he been trying to cross Piazza Saint Giovanni since noon? Had time caved in on him? Sunlight at one point—now a full moon. Some impious rite of ... *"The horror! The horror!"* Had he been going around in circles since mid-day. Hadn't Bartoli been with him. The taste of sparkling silverware and the soave they'd drunk at lunch was still in his mouth. The Duomo sat there like a giant toad with semidivine intentions. Sentimental boys and girls giggled in the shadows of its facade. What'd set him off? Bartoli's question: "Are you for *real?*" American words crowded with fresco-saints in silver and gold! As the beast roared, the kids went on with their mockery of his disorientation. Or were they laughing at the past: at, say, daisies in chalcedony or precious stones around the neck of one of the Medici women. Mason stumbled about the piazza, unable to decide which way to go. Too many variables! Too many directions! And, jokingly, hadn't he admitted to Rosa Bartoli, "Yes, you're right, I'm *not* the person I claim to be," but wasn't it clear in his face that he was putting her on. He was talking to himself now: "She gained my confidence then betrayed me: promised not to tell *any*body: yet she went off, leaving me blind drunk—or stoned?—to reveal my secret to the world. *Curse* her! *Aliosha!* I was once a boy who believed in *everybody!* I trusted. I had confidence!" The kids snickered. Mason swung his fist at the moon. He howled and barked, then fell to his knees, slobbering. No dignity? Everything that rises will converge. The winds blew. One could always fly home! Or die, after an uneventful, passive, stupid life! Okay. So, he'd gone along with Rosa. He'd played the game. A lunch game: "Yes, you're right: I'm not who you *think* I am. I'm the Hunter Gracchus. I'm ... I'm *lost!"*

But soon he *really* got lost. The streets didn't make sense. He'd followed his own "logic"—along a certain alley then suddenly the cobblestones spread in a concentric pattern. This was a circle, a circle of mysteriously gloomy buildings (museums? churches?) casting mid-morning shadows into the half where he had now stopped, puzzled, unwilling to retreat or go on. He fingered a folded lottery ticket in his pocket. Straight across the circle, on the stairway of one of the larger structures, was the figure of a person. Man or woman? At this distance, he couldn't tell. Nobody else in sight. Mason started out toward the person. Hesitantly. Halfway across the circle he was able to see that the person was male. Or seemed so... When Mason was within ten feet of the unusually still figure he felt a slight murmur of the heart. Then the man flung his cape back, whipped out a sword, and flung it toward Mason. The thing clanged on the stone before him, only inches from his toes. Mason strained through his sunglasses trying to focus the face. It *was* a face. Yet something was wrong. The face wore a mask. Rubber? Deer skin? Did it matter? "This is a private matter," the stranger said. The voice was gentle, almost sweet. "Pick it up." Mason hesitated. Why should he? Although he felt compelled to obey without understanding why, he continued to stare at the figure and didn't move. The sword-carrier then jerked another sword from beneath his cape and flashed it in steep sunlight coming down through marble arches. The order came again, this time more forcefully: "I *said* pick it up!" *Who* was this, *what* was this? One of his beloved friends coming back into his life with dramatic humor? A son, a disguised daughter? John Armegurn serving as a hit man? or perhaps Mister Berdseid? No. It was only when the strange swordsman started rushing down the stairway, leaping, skipping, with his sword-tip pointed directly at Mason, that Mason picked up the weapon at his feet, and stumbled back, trying to escape. But the caped-figure advanced too quickly and Mason was obliged to defend himself. He flung wildly and awkwardly—lashing out at his opponent. The dashing figure propped the fist of his left hand on his hip and with sword and body he made unmistakable gestures of invitation. Mason, still retreating, stumbled on the cobbles. The swordsman continued to rush him, to feint—expertly. Mason's foil was dangling. He kept swinging it back and forth before him to keep the saberman off. Then Mason fell on the wet stone and found the tip of the other's sword pushing against the skin of his neck. The victor spoke gently: "I have a contract for you to sign. Either you sign it or I kill you." As he spoke he dug the paper from a pocket beneath his cape. He dropped it on Mason's chest. "You may read it first." The first thing Mason noticed about the official-looking document was its letterhead: Magnan-Rockford Foundation. The swordsman meanwhile pitched a Bic down to the ground at Mason's left. Mason made an effort to read the damned thing. He couldn't concentrate. *"Sign it!"* The tip of the sword dug deeper into Mason's throat. "But—" *"Sign!"* He signed *Mason Ellis*. The moment he wrote the name he realized his mistake. But it was too late.

Mason was up—as he rapped to students of Florence. "*My* Apple, as they say, was not theirs: I smelled whisky on breaths. Gwen, my oldest sister, my mother too, wrote to me rarely. I was alone: in isolation: as though in a country where I didn't know the language. Casual affairs clung to me like fish-smell in the beard. Appletrees nowhere in sight. I screwed married women on kitchen floors: pale fire, pale leeway: possessed with keys to their own dark places these women went mad, on their knees before broken or drunk husbands, clutching Lower East-side yellow rent-stubs and smearing their red, red blood on Flea Market and Klein's furniture. They stayed hidden in First Avenue-deadness even when there was a Way Out. Their Deadness was equal to my own. And of course there were the young women so different from the older, married ones. How different? They were not shut-in damsels waiting to be serenaded below their windows. No eighty-miles-per-hour jerk was going to climb the vines of their castle-wall to get an axle-grease-coated finger on the elastic of their Bloomingdale-bloomers. My concern was also still Chicago: for the boogie-woogie oobop-shebam girl with sweat under her arms. They were doing the Twist, the Pony, the Cakewalk, the Superman—a dance *I* invented. The pill later did not rhyme with castle. Such a rich history: I'll never know how I spaced-out in Amesville on a John Deere, up to my nose in wet cowshit: I couldn't even see that Cezanne's *Portrait of Henri Gasquest* wasn't really Rod Steiger posing. Although gnatcatchers and beetrappers were after my sanity from the start, I turned out to be Somebody. Wesley could have, too, but he had no *need*. I took issue with the ache of my own body. Rather than leaning against my own death or ecstasy, I—Pokerface, Boston Blacky, Wild Dick, Holy Joe, Fingers, Mister Zilch—discovered Stein's American space and in that terrain sweated my way along the floor (ground, desert) of an orgy of heavy laughter, dry tongues; voiceless friction, dry areas, yellow eyes, red skin, sharp fingernails; breasts uneven and staccato teethprints in shoulders and necks; climbed into frowns, broke my way through polka-dot shame and awkward, uh, long sentences, twisted rhythm. In other words, I made *direct* contact. I pried open and entered salient spirits: slept well while growling, yodeling and chewing sounds surrounded me: as confusing as that scene where Florence played a bonyleg-squaw shielding the infants as the braves sent arrows into General George Armstrong Custer. She must be *twice* my age, eh? Never mind . . . Had I been the pilot of a two-engine I might have gotten a *wider* view of Stein's American space: from the aircraft I might have watched the wavers below wave at my waving propellers—might have thrown artful kisses to those poor suckers stuck to the terra cotta: those Goldilocks, Big Bens, Fatsos, Molls, Babyfaces, all of 'em! Innocence fun-crushed by tangy sadness, eh? From up there, *ohboy* . . . the shadow of my craft bewitching the pink earth with its purple shadow: tits for mountains. I might have looked, from on high, into my own darkness, my potshots, my wild guesses, my calls, this bamblustercated fear, my own—: not for perception or higher wisdom but for the oceans, seas, deserts, cities beyond Celt, that were surely in there. Know what I mean? But, like everybody else, I was stuck by gravity to the spongy earth: in birth action death. Framed. So by the time I first drifted to The Apple—with unreliable Celt just above my head—I needed quick solutions: to the mystery of married women; Deadness; being spaced-out; the problem of wild oats; unfaithful muses; the elusiveness of Stein's space; orgies; but more particularly I wanted a formula to solve the problem of the inherent muddle inevitably found at the bottom of, in the final stitch of, any given perspective. This was not to say: the world, history, couldn't be changed. People made it all up: it could be remade. But how, when and where. I played a lot of angles: for lack of an answer I got together a gang of shadows and captured the black angels, let them down into the slow waters of my own bad eyesight: Albert Ryder was back there riding a white horse against the dawn. The angels were supposed to protect: yet they could not prevent dancing devils from lynching my father at daybreak. I found pieces of my mother's flesh and hair in my bowl of soup. I tore open the chest of history and hundreds of years of blood, gall, acid, crossed-wires, frazzled brain tissue, broken promises, disremembrances, killings galore, starvations, diseases rampant as—. It all poured out. Too much for the normal eye. Terrible: sentimental, romantic. I'll never escape. Times when the hard, cold precise word, thing, refuses to make your point. Poor Amygism. I tried once being the king. Prayed for goodness but kept doing all the wrong things. Love? I gave up: it was hopeless. Wore a shabby beard, carried a tall staff—befitting my rank, spoke to everybody I met about the possible solutions to perspectives, and, uh, about other matters, too. I'm getting long-winded. Don't want to bamboozle you. It's just that I'm still sorta... Never mind... "

He was in the bank when everything went out of focus. Next in line, he never got his American Express Travellers Cheques cashed. The floor turned slightly. Pictures reproduced from works by Raphael and Pinturicchio in silver frames behind the counter slid sideways. Mason felt as transparent as a metalpoint on blue handmade paper. His panic was reflected in the eyes of the clerks and other customers. The guard was the first to cry out. He was an old man who fished in his holster for his pistol without luck. The tilt continued for . . . who could tell how long. Time itself left the space. The ceiling cracked, slightly. "Che cos'è?" "*Oh* no!" "Oh *no!*" Was the ancient city of Florence being *bombed?* Mason found himself huddled in a corner with the others. A man who was probably the bank manager started shouting for everybody to go to the basement but nobody made it. Why? Six men with ski masks came in with submachine guns. They shot the guard then told everybody else to make like they were praying to Dante or God or David or Michelangelo himself. They all got their hands up. Although Mason was funny at times, this time he wasn't shaking like Willy Best as he held his hands above his head. His eyes didn't buck. His teeth didn't chatter. The floor beneath them continued to rumble. Five gunmen aimed their guns on the clerks and the manager. One took care of Mason and the other customers and potential customers. He kept talking to them in a Bogart voice, which sounded pretty funny in Italian. An old woman among them fell to her knees and started praying to Lazarus and a fifteenth century Tuscan pilgrim Mason had never heard of. The floor cracked as the clerks filled two canvas sacks with lire at gunpoint. When they finished, the plate-glass window facing the via D. Corso flew to smithereens! Mason couldn't help wondering if some nasty streak of bad luck was following him. He sort of wished he was sitting at a sidewalk cafe enjoying a glass of wine with Italo Calvino . . . When the police arrived, minutes after the robbers fled in their oxydized gray Fiat, the bank—as all of Florence—was still shaking like a drunk the-morning-after.

The bed in his room at the Argentina was lumpy. Sleep difficult. He was beginning to fear sleep anyway: it held too much danger. Yet he had no choice: the asymmetrical shot of a runner—himself?—(no longer a swimmer)... What mocking sound out there? Bats in the...? Nightmare alley... Hay, w-wait!... wasn't that an old Bogart-Eddie... No, you're thinking of *The Wagons Roll at Night*. Go to sleep, tough guy. You've made your own bed of nails. He who lurks in the company of hyped-up cons, charmed thieves, rejected marks, the damned in flight from search warrants, outlaws with golden arms, carpet-baggers, elastic molls, addicts who wheeze, killers in Little Caesar-shoes, forbearers in search of big money, Cagney-dudes turned Camus-sharp, Studs Lonigan dupes, wild-side-walkers, dudes in Houdini-getups whispering farewell my lovely, and ex-skateboard freaks with butterflies tattooed on their proletarian buttocks, cannot expect to soar in unsentenced clean flight with restful sober falcons. Maltese? No, no... sleep. Your days will become indistinguishable. You thought you were like a gray boy, could grow up and marry a Vassar girl, settle down on Moby-Dick, your yacht, out there...? Pull—*pull* harder: conflict is connecting with yang and exchange is tangled into yin. Thought you smarter than Invisible Man, joker! You pastoral cowboy on the run! Will you run to faith or with facts? The priest will hand you over to cops. Vice versa: if Gary Cooper or Wayne don't get you first at gunpoint, gunslinger. What was that noise—out there... in, i-in, uh, the hall... Public Enemy ain't here now, bud, to spoon feed ya. For crysake! Clean up your act—grow up! Pity: you can't turn to anything 'cause you don't believe: oh, you remember hearing about the Black Madonna in Poland? if you were a God-fearing Christian you'd be able to trot with your guitar or harmonica up the Jazna Gora at Pauline and sink to your holy knees before the icon and beg forgiveness or go to the Holy Grail or... oh, hell, forget it. You think Mexico or South America the answer. How can you be sure you're not being observed right now, that Schnitzler and Signard and Armegurn are not all connected? Maybe you should've never left the ghetto,

swindler: might've been better to marry your secret design or, yeah, how about the first grownup woman to take your skinny butt to bed: remember Mabel Study? Presser with thick arms, fried hair, red eyes with yellow rims: rusty feet, huge sagging mammary glands: and when those hard black thighs opened on that two-bit hotel bedroom you smelled her machine's steam lift to befuddle your face. Yet your youth and inexperience and, bygolly, your teenage hardon, led the way. Mentally maybe you never left that plateau! Did you leave that episode baptized in her steam? You humped away at her hardness till you couldn't hump anymore. Then you knew she went home to her dingy house full of ill-conceived hungry children. You on the other hand threw your "proud" head back and went in search of ... of what? ... to have married her: a sturdy life of brainrot to protect you from this gruesome plight. Nobody knew your name then. Nobody knows it now. Native son? Naw. You remember Defoe—ha! "My true name is so well known ... that it is not to be expected I should set my name on the account of my family to this work ...
It is enough to tell you ... the name Moll Flanders so you may give me leave to go under that name till I dare own who I have been, as well as who I am ... " You're now on a roller-coaster to the ... May as well: O picaro! You devilish old Lazarillo de Tormes! Huh? God protects the victims ... ?

... Cooler up here—after a good two hundred and fifty tunnels: Hem at seventeen was abed here back when the Universite Degli Studi di Milano was a hospital. As in Catania, the school was right in the city—Old Town, actually. His hotel: seven minutes' walk away. Professor Ina Bulletti, who'd just had a cancer operation, emitted a sense of vast humility. Her handshake was like walking in rain on a sunny day. She must have been sixty. "I met you once in the states but that was years ago. You wouldn't remember... " Her smile was self-effacing. "Your work will be the subject of a whole chapter in a book I'm writing." They finished their coffee and went across the street with its old street-car tracks toward the university. It was midafternoon and people were going back to work. She led him into the courtyard then along the walkway to the Instituto di Lingua and Litteratura Inglese e Letturatura. She was chairman of that outfit. As she rapped about the author he felt a strange twitch: wanted to turn himself by voodoo or hype or hip or volcanic faith into a snail safely housed inside a Prince Albert tin at the bottom of the last ditch on the outskirts of the last cockfight with wagerers screaming, shouting, calling through cocaine-thick voices for more blood. Keep close to the action. She gave him an upbeat introduction. Mason started off talking about his early influences—mentioned Vittorini, bridged this with the French thing, connected to Toomer's magical rendering of soft, lingering shadows, the dew and dusk, morning mist and mulattoes, sweetness of a land without Spring snow. His language was like stepping nervously in fine grained cowboy boots made by Santa Rosa 1906. He hooked this whole romantic mood to Claude's hectic, joyful exploration of nightlife in Harlem and gave them the wonderful details of that ol' banjo strummer rambling mentally and physically about Marseilles. The whole so-called lecture was a merry-go-round of egocentric, brash jive with references that some of them caught only because they were students of Bulletti. This stuff was sculptured language; cryptic skip-system junk; pretzels; jigsaw hunks. After the show the "champ" got a big hand then went to the toilet where he did *not* find a message from headquarters scrawled on the booth wall. A Nazi symbol, yes, but no word from Control. Although Professor Bulletti took him to Santa Maria delle Grazie to see those cracked and faded figures, it made him feel like a bleeding tunnel through a stone mountain.

He was spacing—not quite sure where he was: was this Zocalo and was he feeding the stupid pigeons peanuts—? Never mind: it was lonely being a fugitive. Had somebody slipped a different name into his little blue book? Say, Jack Verbb or Geechee McKee or Gauz Gazabo or Heavy Hebe or— Cut it out. He'd come through more tunnels, he knew. Italy? It had to be: then why this feeling of Mexico City—chatter, tinsel, beeps, rumble, screech. Gringo negro on the run! If only the Templo Mayor de Tenochtitlan were there to hide in, lie still in. You must have a bad, bad hangover: this is *Italy! Italy I said!* Sure, sure. And I'm on my way to the Empire of Genova, right. Correct. Roger. Check. One thing he needed was time. There was a cactus taste in his sour mouth just beneath the whim of scotch. The tavern smelled faintly of kerosene. He missed his Monet Fall surfaces, the Mediterranean: though it wasn't far. Finally, he saw the road sign: Pisa. Took exit. Tried to hold up the falling structure with all he had. Crowds of tourists cackled at his effort as he gave up, crawling to safety as the edifice tumbled. But it wasn't Pisa that he wanted was it. No, that Empire. Back in his vehicle he turned on the radio to try to short circuit the circle of his flapping fangs. The radio, in English, said, "Hi. I'm still your friend. Keep on trucking." It turned out to be an American rock star making it big in Italy. Then there was an American punk star singing an interesting hit full of pals and gals guys and girls dudes and dames. It made him laugh till tears.

In Genova and totally a victim of vertigo Mason flapped his wings and threw his voice against an auditorium ceiling. If he could make his whirling voice *true,* being in brackets wouldn't matter: swastika and cross both could exist within the confinement of a triangle. He read: "He felt his heart had been cut out. He could still feel a draft where holes had been driven into his head. He was Still Life with Holes. Hard of hearing, he didn't listen to Florence whispering, the pineapple and chocolate lap of her bitter tongue. The flesh of his body seemed all he had—at the moment. His enemies—unclean spirits—tied him down and searched through, back far into, his cave, up into the flue of his flamed mind, down through his Coca Cola-cold blood, in the shoestrings and telephone wires of his being. They cut sharply not only along the flesh but deeper into the fanged bone. Devils! No yolk, no jelly! Only the ashes of an ancient West African village, a teepee pole, the scarred boots of an Irishman, the apron of an Irishwoman. He smiled. Alone in himself, things howled at him in the mineral night. First snow, through gray heat: he could almost see a white bank glowing in fog. Flakes wide apart. Black limbs of emotional trees with Springtime pink blossoms. He hoped for renewal, a kind of life, to unseat the lame-duck. Florence held him but not closely, not with feeling, with enjoyment. She also held a large bunch of artificial flowers. Going deeper into himself he found a jazzhall full of brass: nobody'd ever robbed *this* place: decked with scarred, juice-stained, tough furniture. But walking in the city—for him, as he remembered it now while lying in bed—was a comfort, a distraction: in front of an antique shop on a narrow cobbled street an old woman—Celt in disguise?—with a mullet-face wearing a tartan fumbled at the window of a bar he was about to enter. She couldn't see in there: wasn't wearing her specs. Flaccidly pretending to be seriously involved in life, she touched her tam-o-shanter gingerly then pulled her fifty-year-old dress unstuck from her girdle; found her rhinestone glasses then looked through her luster at the imitation figures moving around: he was one. A full silty sky was clamped firmly overhead. It was carnival time in these streets. Confetti floated from high windows. He looked into the woman's alarmist-eyes: they were paste and gem quartz: salmon tongue, spotted. She aimed her best eye at a big tree by the cathedral: it was just a way to avoid the piercing and derailing eye of Mason. What did he *want?* The state of his mind: noise. He liked it: it made him want to go to the center of the carnival, dream there, as though inside the delicate fluttering heartbeat of a nuclear holocaust: he'd ride a ferris wheel—oiled by faith and politics. He'd drink pig-tea from a wooden creosote-dipped cup, dip horse-snuff: it was always the same when he tried to reconnect with lost Celt or to find the root of C or the siren or Kangaroo Eye or Wind Voice or Chiro or—: they were each so distinct; interfaces yet interchangeable.

He got through the Genova episode somehow without remembering it: he did it well and nobody knew he wasn't there. At Hotel Cosimo near the opera house. A message from Professor Pauliani Poggi: "If you're up to it, my husband and I'd enjoy having you come to dinner tonight. Just buzz when you arrive . . . " Dinner went so smoothly he hardly noticed he *was* there. And the lecture the next morning took care of itself: despite his strange hard-to-follow reference to conquistadores raping the beJesus out of Indians and to Cortes and hidden eyes and what was meant to be a joke about the wallpaper in his hotel room (" . . . of the glittering sword planted in the neck of a defiant black bull—repeated eight thousand tiny times all around him on the wall . . . "). Mason didn't let his bat-infested head spoil things. Although he'd gotten on well with pure Pauliani and guarded Gino, answered student questions and shaken hands with the faculty, he left with wild birds riding his back and monkeys clinging to his legs. He even stopped to rest, on his return to Nice, in a tree: a leafless old black tree. Demented goblins and unfortunate old women (referred to as toothless witches) danced in dank moonlight below. Mules and goats dressed in formal attire paid their moist respects to . . . Mason almost escaped the beauty of their strangeness when he was about to be dragged before a firing squad to be shot for imitating a . . . But at the last minute he was needed to fill a vacancy in a gigantic choir. Yet he didn't know the Medieval song they were ready to unearth.

February was the aftermath of magic. Noel and le jour de l'an had gone so-so for a lonely loner. Now it was Carnival time again. On the day before somber Lent began they all went to Luceram for the *real* traditional feast and festival. It was a little-known event Jean-Pierre knew ("in some parts of France these medieval ceremonies still take place . . . ") and he led them there. In the Alps-Maritimes near the Italian border the village charmed Mason on sight: filled him with tin-glazed happiness . . . Shivering, they entered the restaurant facing the village center. It was just after noon and the place was crowded with peasants and other workers seated around long closely arranged tables. These old men and women and children and young people were having a ball: loud boisterous talk; knives, forks, spoons, clicked against bowls. Lots of lip-smacking enjoyment! Coughing! Sudden outbursts of traditional songs! Hand-clapping. Jokes! Back-slapping. All in that great warm darkness of this tiny restaurant where two old women shuffled about serving everybody endless wine and bowls of steaming hot guts, spicy livers, thick kidneys— cooked together in a massive stew—and served in crude clay bowls with—believe me!—old hot-water cornbread (just like they make in the South!). Mason sat squeezed between Monique and Jean-Pierre. He guzzled down the table wine and nearly choked himself on the strong innards. Up front at one of the long tables by the door a furious political argument broke out between two farmers. Within ten minutes the guys calmed down and were embracing and kissing each other's cheeks. Then a rock sailed through the front window. A boy swept the glass behind the door and everybody went on eating and drinking and talking and laughing. Then one gray old blue-clad farmer toasted Monique's beauty and handed her his glass to properly share the salute since she didn't have one in hand. That's how she became the Queen of the Feast and ceremoniously got the shared-cup going around the room. Everybody took a sip and the whole place eventually burst into song. Mason, not knowing the French lyrics, only pretended to sing. From where they sat they could see through the front windows the festivities increasing in the square. A group of youths and a couple of older men were stuffing the King. As fists beat on wooden tables for more wine and bowls were filled for the fourth and fifth times, Mason saw the awesome effigy being erected on a pole at the center of a pile of twigs, paper, boxes, branches, and old planks. The clowns were gathering around the King. It wasn't till Mason and his friends were ready to rejoin the festival that he noticed, carved into the table top at his right, this: Zizi/Nobody. *Nobody?* Wasn't that an English word? Just a passing curio. Then they went out, thanking the waitresses on the way. The dancing'd already started: they joined the gyrating maypole-line as it wobbled and giggled and bumped its way around the King. Already the sun had dropped behind the hills and somebody struck a big match to the rubbish. Smoke zigzagged up from the little spark. Smoke-smell quickly filled the square. Dancers danced harder to keep warm. The fire wasn't much yet. Kids from shadows were still throwing snowballs at those in the square. Dancers now were ideal targets but took it good-naturedly. Mason got bopped on the head once or twice. Monique got one in the eye—which caused her to stop for a few moments: the snowballs were like fishbones in delicious fish. In ten minutes or so it was dark and the flames were leaping taller than men. The King's trousers began to crackle and the smell of burning rags whirled about the dancers. When his crotch burned away the clowns and dancers and spectators all cheered. Snowball-throwers too came out of shadows and clapped. From here on out it was all joy and hysterics: everybody went apeshit when the King was consumed to the neck and had only a head left to offer. When the head fell all holy hell broke loose and the dancing and clowning, like the tiger chasing Little Black Sambo around the tree, turned them to butter: everybody was wiped out, spent . . .

How did he get into a red rooster suit? Couldn't remember. Must have been three in the morning and festivities were still up. Shrove Tuesday? Nice? He'd lost track of who was who: Jean-Paul was possibly that stupid ibex dancing with a gazelle. The gazelle? Perhaps Chantal! or Monique! Thousands, it seemed, were moving, jumping, dancing, shouting, to music— which was loud, brassy, headache-causer. Night sky at Place Messina was a turkey turned upside down full of Old Norse noise and bursting up in it were trees—Catalpa Paluownia Horse-Chestnut—in full bloom. His mood was *curved* and his senses out of focus, yet he continued to flap his big wings. He beat them with a lusty power. Mason did the Camel Walk, he strutted, he pranced, he got behind the gazelle and said, *"Cocka-doodle-doo!"* She responded with a squeak. Looking over her shoulder, she hissed and cried out these words, *"I'm Asahel!* Solomon *sang* for me! You're crude! Don't *touch* me!"* Mason didn't take the rebuff too hard: he went after a wild ass—called The Onager. It looked like a donkey, with thin, thin legs. But he couldn't catch *it.* Its love for freedom was too great! Weren't there any *hens* around? There *was* a camel and *Gauguin* had come back from the South Seas! Mason was sweating myrrh resin. He wanted to rest, but where—at Place Messina—do you go. (The spirit of carnival didn't provide seats other than those paid for.) Roosters needed to rest when defeated. Besides, whoever said a rooster could mount anything other than a chicken? Answer me that. So poor Mason found himself sitting on the curb between two wine-drinkers with tin cups, just to rest. While there, he hummed then sang. They laughed at his accent, his voice, his bad French. Then joined him. He loved them for this: thought they probably didn't deserve his love. The vocal burst went out: "Amazing grace, how sweet the sound,/ That saved a wretch like me,/ I once was lost, but now I'm found,/ Was blind but now I see." The others, his friends, danced on. They were happy, he was not. When "Amazing Grace" ended he threw himself stupidly into another song with them: "Run sinners, run,/ Run sinners, run, run,/ Run sinners,/ Won't you run?/ Cause you house is on fire,/ Cause you house is on fire,/ On fire ... " One guy, an Arab, leaned over and whispered in Mason's ear: "This song is like the wall of Jericho, the Wall of Tell Beit Mirsim!" Mason gave him a dumb grin. From his retreat he could see his friends still cutting loose. There was Christ in the Garden of Olives. He was a little out of character: pretending to be A Still-Life with Fan. And The Fat-tailed Sheep, trying to become a sacrifice, was digging her nose in the hide of the mule. The mule, clearly, gave every sign of cautious approval: this donkey belonged to King David and was proud of its ancestry—which went back to Ezekiel and the people of Togarmah. Mason, dazed, was impressed. He climbed to his feet as a float, escaped from a day-time parade, started moving in the circular pattern around Place Messina. It was lighted like a star fallen from some larger-than-life acacia-bearing Saint-John's-bread-tree! On the float, punk rock stars were strumming, crying, shouting. A stripper ate candlesticks as they worked out. Mason fell over Japanese Symbolist, Yellow Christs, Breton Girls, Old Women of Arles, clowns from Martinique, tough guys dressed as Nudes, Easels, Seasides, in his effort to reach the moving float. He *recognized* among them friends up there! Through his own particular haze, he cried, he shouted, *"Cocka-doodle-do!"* Literally, he *barked* it! He trotted behind the float. The winos trailed him. So did the cops. The spectators (mostly old folks) in the review-stands around the plaza cackled, enjoying what they (apparently) believed to be a *planned* part of mardi gras. When a spotted dog started following Mason, snapping at his heels, Mason stopped. Turned. Stooped. And *bit* the animal on the neck! Man's best friend skipped off yelping like a hyrax that lost the cow trail! Stumbling, fumbling and falling in the shadow of Sebastian, Tamara Polese, Etta Schnabel and the group Hot Hips, Mason finally grabbed the tail-end of the float. But fell on his face, clutching crepe-paper! The chicken feathers against his skin felt like rat-tails.

Mason drove down to San Remo to buy himself an Italian suit, a belt, a new shoulder bag. Going back he picked up the hitchhiker at Ventimiglia. The boy's sign said: "Nice." André-something spoke only French; was returning home after attending his grandfather's funeral in Rome. He'd hitched this far in two days. Their conversation of course was difficult. But Mason thought he understood the boy to say that his poppa left to a museum the family replicas of ancient Frankish icons and purity-symbols. As they approached the toll-gate at San Isidore, André made it clear he wanted to exit here. Sporadic shelling behind his eyes? Mason was relieved. He took the old narrow road up through the hills. When he got there the villa was quiet. Afternoon shadows lay to the west of its trees. Somebody had stuck a Telex message from Schnitzler in his door crack.

Greece in the middle of April? Driving into Athens from the airport was hectic in crazy laneless rush-hour traffic. Hotel Corinth on Safokleous and Klisthenous became a place of sleeplessness. In Greece Mason could go searching darkly and secretly for ... for answers? ... Morning light was a gift from the gods. Before noon he was drinking scotch on a roof top: the only customer in the restaurant till a group of noisy men and women came in around noon chattering away in English. All had Greek accents except one. Yellow Eyes was surely American. The guys certainly had talent for supporting roles ... Later, Mason wandered around as the shops began opening. Saturday night shoppers were out. He was observer, spectator—not participant. He felt no different from what he'd always felt ... The next morning Mason was at the National Museum trying to provoke Cycladic. From her stern place as mother goddess and model for modern sculpture she refused to respond. Mason was unworthy? Insulted, he rushed on. Goddess Hygieia? She would not heal him. Her mission was set—as fixed as his. Kikori too didn't even consider responding from her Fourth Century B.C. perch in the Temple of Artemis. He beat at her stone. A guard threatened to arrest him. He shook the guard's hand off his arm. Then Mason met his lover: that beastly deadly ungodly unworldly feathered creature (with lice under her wings): Sepulchral, the sad-faced holder of the death-crying lyre. O Siren! *His* lost wings . . . ? No, it wasn't that simple: something more complex. He moved silently through the gravestones. No smells here. Burning hair? Fried pig ears—as odor? Nothing of the sort. Tar? Dyed leather / Perfume? The feel of the tongue against okra? This was a more elusive—cerebral—reality. He looked suspiciously at the black figure found at Antikytera. That shipwreck rang a bell. Then the comic mask of a slave found near Dipylon in the second century B.C., hit a raw nerve. The answer surely was not that: it was part of the problem. And there she was again: the winged one with her bird feet and woman breasts! Mason slapped her. No blood dripped from her eye. Her primitive lyre didn't bang to the marble floor. He kissed her. She did not respond. He arrived in a remote gallery just in time to help Aphrodite in a vicious struggle with Pan: she had her sandal raised threateningly against him as he tugged at her arm. A shorter figure, he was a mean fucker. But it was hard to know exactly what the cupid figure—on Aphrodite's shoulder grasping one of Pan's horns—meant. A cupidic bridge between . . . He moved on, still with confidence: nobody else was around except for an occasional guard. Unusual. Soon there was Hermes carrying a lamb. Mason felt the Roman weight of it. Picasso's man with goat? To slaughter? Surely part of the answer was hidden there, in the slit down the belly, in the expert removal of the testicles? Music for every occasion: the kythera with seven strings. Seven and one? Play please. Bronze cymbals he thought surely served to reach into the classic depths beneath, say, jazz: sacrifice: aulos; funeral: anlos; drama: lyra (solo). The more removed from earthly concerns the more permanent in their stone and static insistence were the resistant figures. Even mortals sat as dead weight on thrones of, say, six hundred-thirty

B.C., like Egyptian gods. But they were goddesses weren't they? "Heroized." Mason touched the rims of their blunt eyelids. The gesture was sexual. Yes? Sexual and moody. In the geometric period he missed whatever clues were hidden in the duck the horse the... Even his spiritual forefather: Satyr was useless, in a way: his music did not give the bird woman the rhythm she needed to fly! Something was deadly wrong in their relationship. With his flute strapped to his head—allowing freedom for both hands—he was still not the receiver of total benefits. Mason stroked her bronze skull. She smiled. Ah! (...*and* he knew the brain changed when the body was turned upside-down: in the fourth stage they turned the figures, inverted the models in a kiln and fired them, causing the quick wax to melt... but there were five stages!) If this museum was a cool sanctuary then Kabeiroi near Thebes in the sixth century was even more so: Mason scratched under her wings. Griffins nearby cackled. A bird-snake of Argos said, "Polly wanta..." It was at this point that he realized he wasn't going to get the answers—the way he wanted them—here! On the way out, out of friendliness, he scratched the belly of the pregnant toad-person.

He woke in a furious sweat. Leaped out of bed. The signing of that contract? hadn't he begun the long surrender of the Self? in signing that MRF agreement—to God knows what—in the name *Ellis* hadn't he in effect ended his own potential? He would go on, wouldn't he: vanishing and resurfacing alternately till he achieved his identity or disappeared forever. Then the dream cleared. He'd been trapped on a tribal set. Surrounded by strangers, he was told to pee into a clay pot. He hesitated. Was there some deep authority in hesitation? No. It was simply that the Self did not vanish quite so fast if one paused before... Passively, he pissed in the pot. A scientist in a handsome lion's skin took the pot into sunlight and examined the liquid. In ten minutes he returned with his report. "This man, rough, and in need of revision, better focus, cutting, pasting, more action and less telling, is faced with a monumental decision. In his urine the sign of his desperation is clear." The village chief stood and placed a firm hand on Mason's shoulder. "My son, you are about to discover how to pull it all together. Do not—" but here the dreamer gives up the...

Who formulates the questions? It's noon and Mason's at Restaurant Europa. His table is on the sidewalk. The wine is simple Domestica. The moussaka is two or three days old—made with stale potatoes. Better to have ordered the shish kebob or lamb and potatoes? Hardly. He is stuck with his bad decision. He sits, drinking too fast, and watches the old prostitutes hustling on the mall: this is a particularly sleezy area—Omonia Square—where drunks or young boys can—and do—pick up fat, run-down whores for two to three hundred drachmas. It is lunch time and the whores are not having much luck. Mason watches their pacing with something like interest. Their bodies are swollen like the bellies of toads. He cannot level a question against their presence. Their comic and frantic movements—back and forth—give him no usable clue. Across the mall at another restaurant sit five Greek men drinking beer. By one they are singing Greek songs and toasting each other with more suds. Mason broods. Then pays seven hundred drachmas for his awful lunch. He wanders about the streets. He is not feeling drunk or spaced when he realizes that his shoulder bag has been snatched. He's walking along Stadiou toward the Sintagma when these two kids hit him and a third one grabs his bag. Mason responds like Bat Man: kicking and punching in reflex time. The one with the bag is running. Mason takes off after him. Bumping into side-walkers, peddlers, hawkers. He leaps over a table (where a man's having after-lunch coffee) to avoid a cluster of people at a narrow point. The kid's tiny and fast: he's taking the street *and* the side—even leaping cars. Mason's losing ground. He feels his age. Then he sees the boy run into a woman: she falls, the kid falls. A crowd gathers. Mason's bag is on the ground in the scramble. When he gets there—elbowing his way through— he dives for his bag. Gets it. The woman is shouting in American English at the boy. She calls him a little snot, an asshole, a rude son-of-a-bitch. She is helped up by two Greek men. A woman hands her her purse. She bangs the boy over the head with it. The boy is looking for a way to exit through the thicket of bodies. She whacks him again. Mason grabs him. A cop pushes his way through the crowd. Mason explains what has happened. The cop takes the boy by the ear and marches him away. Everybody laughs. Then Mason realizes that the American woman is Yellow Eyes.

She had a Greek name: Melina Karamanlis. They went to a cafe just a block away on Georgiou; ordered Dymphe, a decent Volos blanc sec. She told him she remembered him from the rooftop restaurant. As it turned out she knew his name. It gave him a funny feeling about her. She was a journalist, a film critic, here visiting her sister, Sophia Papadopoulos who was married to Nikos. Sophia was American too; Nikos, no. Melina was interested in the avant garde theatre and had come to this work through friends in New York. He had mixed feelings about her pretty smile. She *was* pretty: very. Although she presently lived and worked in Albuquerque—and liked it—she was a *born* New Yorker. She had the accent down. Gestures too. She seemed delighted to meet a fiction writer whose work she'd read. "Normally," she said, "I read Joyce Carol Oates, ye know, but

I'm happy to say, I'm also interested in what *other* people are doing." Impulsively and cheerily she invited him to dinner at her sister's. He hesitated. She tickled his funnybone: "I promise you *I* won't do the cooking: my brother-in-law is a genius in the kitchen. You'll get a sample of real Greek home-cooking." She was obviously impressed to learn he was here to lecture next week at the university. She'd bring all the relatives she could round up. He didn't especially like her joke. Just before she left Melina said the boy who angered her so by knocking her down might actually turn out to be a blessing in disguise and a catalyst. Mason didn't respond and didn't know how to translate that. He was expected at seven-thirty that night. She gave him the address. The taxi driver would know. She then took his hand and shook it. She swished off leaving a whiff of Mycenean Rose—if there's such a thing. Why'd he get himself into these jams? Did he really expect to find any part of the puzzle there tonight? Or was he just looking for an angle on another piece of leg? He now felt keenly alone: on the way back he smoked his last coffin nail, courtesy R.J. Reynolds. Made a mental note to replenish. He parked the Ford in the underground lot beneath the hotel. Went up. In the lobby there was a Neolithic female figure with winged-arms lifted as though conducting lobby traffic. Holy red mullet! He gave her a close inspection. Something deadly in her stance. He couldn't quite put his finger on what it was though. Anyway, all through dinner he'd found difficulty refraining from staring at Nikos' eye-patch: around its edge there seemed to be a rim of light: it was like being on a dark street and gazing at the closed window to a lighted room. Nikos and Sophia were a handsome couple! She was jaunty and talkative. The chicken and rice with garlic sauce earned an A-plus. Conversation was mundane: ranging from Onassis and Jackie, Maria Callas, the island Skorpios to Jason's state of mind as he was about to set forth from Volos in search of the Golden Fleece.

He read from his novel-in-progress: "...Florence Souk-hanov watched him from the ground.... He was shinnying up a flagpole at sunrise in this strange gawdawful mid-western town near the bus stop.... Her view: he was a bug in orange light.... What is he trying to *see?*... What'd he *hope* to see?... Soukhanov felt a little embarrassed waiting down there for him.... At the top he looked in all directions: with grinding, plodding attention, he applied his vision.... After twenty-eight minutes of focusing he came down.... Soukhanov wanted to know what he saw. 'Goldfinches and flunkies clustered at a distance.' He caught his galloping breath by its throat. 'I saw seven-thirty light through wet trees. I strained. I was disap-pointed. Originally I went up to try to catch sight of The Impostor's tracks. I got interested in other forms of deception. I tried to detect the real from the unreal.... I wanted a view of all the connections: forced or otherwise.... I saw The Impostor traveling in foreign countries: he discovered there was nobody in the foreground: everybody except he knew how to talk.... He went to public baths under skies juxtaposed with the complicated architecture of clouds pretending to be maternity wards or white guys in blackface.... Everything from up there was deception.... I felt assigned to the crazyhouse of Black Letters: oddball'... " He stopped. Then told them he wanted to try the whole thing all over again—from a different angle. They were confused enough to care. He started again: " 'I was disappointed. It wasn't so much that I was trying to track down The Impostor—although I tried to spot him, *too*—... I wanted a view of all the connections, forced and otherwise. Ya know? What can you make of a ringing church bell, a bra in a puddle of water by a yellow school bus filled with tiny faces, in a bloody parking lot—behind the parish? or a guy who looked like you-know-who grabbing his bloody chest, torn open by history... or those slugs down on the poolside: I knew they didn't add up or connect. But out beyond the horizon I dug farm workers in disguises working fields and there was a tree shading a cabin—I'm sure The Impostor hid there—and maybe the dude stroking his sideburns or the straw boss hidden under his straw hat was *he*. It was like viewing one of those vast romantic landscapes on which many tiny communities can be seen in hectic activity. There was even a gunfight between a very dramatic stud and a law-and-order man. The stud or stuntman vomited ketchup and died theatrically—on a hillside. I knew he wasn't The Impostor: his action was, well, too unenterprising. The hoers, diggers, planters, though, might have been real moneybags, pepless pimps, bellringers, addicts, fans of his. I couldn't tell. Crazy? No, I'm okay. Even the sheepherder herding a flock on the hillside where the gunfight took place, was not exactly who he pretended to be: he looked California but was Jersey under his front. . . . A forest growing dark; just from tires lifting along a road; a figure stepped from a cabin and rang a cowbell; beyond, in the brush and undergrowth, a fire blazed; Kenneth Patchen herding seahorses; hooded lynchers riding out-of-sight of his anger; and there was a cubistic arrangement of The Impostor—as Moca—galloping on a silly donkey with sword raised; and Celt—just an illusion?—juggling an impressive circle of frosty infant bodies. . . . I saw a lot—a lot was confusing: The Impostor trying on a cowboy hat in the jungles of Mali; I saw myself holding The Impostor by the throat, trying to force him to confess his betrayal of my purity, my Truth, my place as a Human Being; saw him dancing with snakemen around the victims of "justice" in a valley before a cave-entrance; the smell of human flesh reached me up there; saw him go among a group that looked like university students and I'm sure he told them lies—as though it were sixty-six, sixty-seven, sixty-eight when every serious Black writer had to be Malcolm X or Martin Luther King or Eldridge Cleaver before such groups. *Lies?* Which lies? Later lies. Up there, my dear Florence, I smelled Art farted on; my tongue got caught on the inside of my own lower and upper borders. My gums ached. I tried to gauge myself for shock— disruption. The flag was not up its pole: I was. I felt insecure up there but mine was composed of deceptive fat, loose skin, crooked noses, dirty ears: all so difficult to touch—certainly not sensuous or sexual. My hard-frown-of-concentration on attempting to come down that pole, finally, was like the downward pressure of an airplane beginning to descend in an emergency landing. . . . ' "

Now, he drove toward Volos and stopped at the Bay of Kolpas. A priest sitting at a table under an old tree at bayside didn't look up as Mason slammed his car door. Two mothers with children who'd by chance met on the road were exchanging words. Hazy day. He looked carefully: there were no winged sea creatures out there in the water. He crossed the street to Restaurant Pemba and sat at an outside table. The waiter came out and Mason got up and went in with him to take a look at the available fish on ice. He selected three different types. While they were being grilled the waiter brought him a bottle of Dymphe. He poured some into the glass while Mason gazed at the priest across the street. Maybe the guy wasn't a real priest but some kind of plant. After lunch Mason got a bright idea. In the back seat of the car he took off his jeans and put on his swimming trunks. He had the radio on while doing this: American pop music. He locked the car and stuck the key into his tiny pocket. Tipping down the rock path he noticed a group of about eleven people sitting in a rough circle at the water's edge. They were eating and drinking and laughing and talking. A couple of kids played near them. Scuffed fishing boats were anchored farther down the coast—a few smaller ones along here had been pulled up onto the sand. Mason looked back. The priest was watching. Him? Mason flapped around in the water. Two from the beach party came in. The man said to Mason, "Bless the Bay of Kolpas. She is warm!" He took up a handful of water and kissed it with a big smacking sound. Mason laughed. The woman was infected by his laughter and laughed too. They wanted to know if he was from North Africa. When he said America they laughed. (How did he like Greece? Very well, of course. The man introduced himself as Elias Vouliagmenis and the woman was Helena Moutsopoulou. They spoke English as naturally as drinking water. Another member of the party came in. She swam smoothly as soon as she was in deep enough then went on by them. "How long will you be in Volos?" Mason shrugged. "In that case, you *must* come to a party we're having tonight," Elias said while slapping Mason on the shoulder. "It's perfect! You arrived today? Which hotel? No hotel—yet? In that case, perhaps..." The woman who'd swum by was now returning. Mason was trying to explain that he'd planned to go on to Larissa when Elias interrupted to introduce Zizi Kifissias, a painter. Mason shook Zizi's hand. She was a handsome woman. Presently two other guys joined them—obviously curious about Mason. They too shook his hand. Names: Pavlos Kallethea and David Pangrati. They were quick to say that they were co-directors of an artists' cooperative first established in Athens but recently extended to Volos. What did he do. Well, wouldn't you know, he was a writer. That suited them fine. They shook his hand again. Helena was now swimming out as far as she dared. Zizi had her head cocked at a forty-five degree angle away from Mason and was watching him out of the sides of her eyes. Was that mistrust? Mason noticed there were still others back there in the half broken circle on the sand talking and drinking wine. When they all went back to the sand Mason met the others: Christos Papadopoulos and Stefanos Georga and Costas Massalias and Mariella Tricoupi and Alexander Papadiamantopoulou—all painters or sculptors associated with Pavlos' and David's gallery. Mason began to relax. Even if he were at the center of some sort of scheme, if The System was seeking and gaining its revenge on him, he could not believe these pleasant Greek people were part of any plot to bring him to "justice" or to trap him, use him, push him further into a complex Buckeye-Nameless plot. Nobody'd held up a card and asked him to describe what he saw. Nobody'd asked him to try hard to remember his name. The real one? Any name. Pick a name.

Name your name. So he relaxed. The moment he did, something that had been festering in the back of his mind broke, and the clear puss poured out: that name, it now made sense: Alm Harr Fawond was Alan Henri Ferrand. Think, Mason! And realizing this his heart and brain shrunk. Should he just wait for the machinery to close around him. Surely he could. But this was crazy. He refused to believe himself a Pynchon yoyo or an Ellison dancing Sambo paper doll.... Somebody was speaking to him and he wasn't paying attention. Something about giving a couple of them a lift in his car. Sure, of course. "Besides, you can get first-hand directions...." Dazed with anal-fear and with Zizi beside him smelling of salt-water he began to doubt his ability to ever become free of this elusive and massive plot. He also for the first time doubted his ability to be himself. What was Zizi saying? "...and we call our villa Princess Aliki. No reason other than it sounds good. It's just a name. You'll be surprised—"

It was a mellow September afternoon. As Mason drove toward the entrance of the estate he saw an archway. At its curved top—at first—the words were not clear. Moments later they were. Four-thirty slanted sunlight accented them: Villa Princess Aliki. Across these somebody'd driven a brush stroke of black paint. Using the same brush, the person'd painted—on the wooden board—this: Home of The Brave Willow Plantation. Owners: Bobby Joe and Miss Lindy Belle Sommerfield. Zizi, Christos and Helena broke into star-spangled laughter at the sight. Mason was bewildered. "Straight ahead," they directed. He followed the curving driveway till he came to the house. "What was *that* all about?" He was serious. "You'll see." The other two cars were already parked in front of the grand pillared stairway to the enormous doors, which were opened. Mason, as they got out, noticed a man in the yard covering long tables with white table cloths. Inside the foyer Mason got the impression he was in a fifty-room mansion. A man who was obviously a servant came up the hallway from the back. Zizi told Mason he was Plato. "He'll show you your room." Plato led Mason up a winding staircase and along a corridor past a series of closed doors. As Plato was opening the room he wanted Mason to occupy, David Pangrati popped up from around a corner. "Hello. I see you found your way. Good, good. Just make yourself at home." He went in with Plato and Mason. "What size are you?" "Size?" "Never mind," said Pangrati, "I can tell. Hagnon will bring your dinner clothes up. Once a week we do a different period. It's really sort of ironic that you're our guest on a night when we've planned to do pre-Civil War Mississippi." "What?" "Oh, it's fun! You'll love it! Wait till you *see* yourself! I got the idea last year when I was in the states. Had a show at the University of Mississippi." Mariella and Pavlos came in. In Greek they discussed Mason's probable sizes in shirt, jacket and trousers. Then they all left except Pangrati who took a tiny, live spotted bull snake from his pocket. "It's only seven," he said. "What?" The time he meant. "Oh. What's *that?*" "It's my uta. It looks like a chicken flying upside-down in a Chagall but it's really not. I use it as a model for my fresco. You won't find *him* in the Blue Guide." His chuckle was snagged on the blue fence of a cemetery gate. Mason cheered up: "If I had a lyre, I'd charm your damned pet!" Pangrati's laughter beat its wings against the wallpaper which was a birthday party scene of floating lovers kissing repeatedly eight thousand times against a background of handpainted blue silk dresses, glazed stoneware, in a living room where sky and earth met in the name of Oceanus. Green violinists provided soft music seeping along the baseboards. Mason dimly realized Pangrati still was talking: " . . . Need anything just . . . Hagnon . . . gardener . . . His wife, Medea . . . " Mason felt suddenly very ill. His stomach was a cosmos of burned pine and rubber. " . . . Ciao!"

Night. In the sitting room they were delighted when Mason appeared. He looked great in his tux! He'd brought down with him an armful of things he forgot he had: gifts from Painted Turtle: a few porcupine quills, a beaded necklace, a rawhide vest, a sacred headdress, some smoked meat. Having found these items in his suitcase, he now presented them to his hosts. "Just a little token of my appreciation of your hospitality!" They all ooed and laughed nervously. His stomach ache was now joined by a killer-headache. As they fussed over the gifts, he dropped onto the couch like a sack of frostbitten sweet potatoes! *"Quick!"* somebody shouted, *"he's ill!"* When he came back to consciousness—an hour later?—it was time for the outdoor events. On the way out, through his fog he heard, "What shall we *call* you?" "Just call me Mister Nobody!" Odysseus? They laughed. He laughed and slapped their backs with the gentleness of pink and green in the *Equestrienne* of 1931. Rock-cut benches lined the yard. Mason clicked his champagne glass against other precious glass. Many of the women—some he hadn't seen before—wore long white or yellow off-the-shoulder hooped evening gowns. Little children hid under some of them. Dogs under others. Perhaps snakes? doctors? A couple held above their heads an unneeded parasol. A horse-drawn carriage waited in the driveway. Necklaces and bracelets and rings glittered all over the place. The night smelled of snake-skin and mossy wood, of vaporous flowers and Nijinsky's socks, of white lilac! Mason heard banjo music. A small group of musicians under a tree were doing their best to carve tones of hillbilly refinement. A couple of piglets turned on spits over a bricked-in fire under moonlight. Dining tables were arranged in rows. Mason sipped his champagne in the hope that it would turn him into a prancing antelope. He had plans for this night: for him it was like being a personified ship entering a narrow passage formed by two blissful, nameless islands covered with white ash and volcanic lava. His expectations were high! Some of the guests were beginning to dance under the lights: patriarchs and ladies! Pavlos like some figure rising naked from the sea, cutting a jig on the rough black grass! Where'd all the *kids* come from? Brats all over the place—boxing, pissing, giggling, rolling in the music. Pavlos stopped and came to Mason. "Won't *you* dance?" "With you? Why not?" And as their heels dug new scars into the faces of gods and demons long in the dust, Pavlos told him how last month they'd done eighteenth-century Russia. Helena then interrupted, *"Now, now, tut tut:* two men dancing together! *You* come to me, Mister Bobby Joe Sommerfield! I'm yo little ol sweety pie, Miss Lindy Belle."* Her accent was so funny Mason fell to the ground in uncontrollable laughter. But his perplexity was still safely at arm's length: veni vidi vici! vogue la galere! tout comprendre c'est tout pardonner! truditur dies die! The pungent smell of pig whirled as Mason later danced with Helena, then some other woman. Mister Nobody stomped the grass till half the lights burned out. Sunlight was winking through the branches of evergreen when he realized he was already asleep though still moving. But how'd he get *moccasins* on his feet? He'd surely started out with *black* dress shoes!

... Where? This stuff on his face. The woman next to him? Black smudges on her cheeks. He rested his head and reconstructed. Yes. Something—not long ago—had hit him like a brick between the eyes: he'd awakened and saw a woman in bed next to him. On each shoulder blade there was about a thirteen inch oblong scar: as though powerful wings had long ago been severed from her. He refused to connect this to anything. She was still asleep: that breathing was unfakable. Elias had fallen in the duck pond. Laughter. Except by then he was Jed the Red Neck. Mariella turned out to be Rebecca of Jacksonville who was a virgin at thirty. Helena, as Miss Lindy Belle, got pretty vulgar after midnight: she danced nude in moonlight. Pangrati, insisting his name was Big Papa, eventually did a jig. He also played "Skip to My Lou" on his harmonica. The musicians grew weary and after grinding their way through "So Long It's Been Good to Know You," six times, they gave up and went off. He'd fallen asleep with a jingle swinging in his nerves: "Railroad, steamboat,/ River and canoe;/ Lost my true love,/ What shall I do." And the dream: a snatch of it: strange how one was sort of native yet not exactly in the vernacular. Verna, ho! Had somebody played a washboard. Was it Hagnon, I mean, Sonny Boy. Surely a hooped skirt lost its cloth and the huge puffy bloomers beneath the wire-ribs seemed to blossom like a giant night flower. Who was Baby Jane. Pretty face—but she'd come later. Real name he never caught. No matter. Susy Mae. Mary Alice. Bo. Big Boy. All masks for Achilles. Phoibos. Zeus. Meidias. Lysias. Dionysos. Despite the unrealness he had to admit they had real imagination. And he as Blackface Hermes (as Zizi called him at the end of dinner with a toast) was up and all along cheered. One woman very much out of place (who he later learned was Vietnamese) came to the fancy dress party wearing a serious oriental mask: it was antelope skin meant to look like human. Her black hair hung to her spine. She was terrifying: the tiny eyes peeked through the slits like rat eyes: desperate and on the run. Wasn't it Pavlos who'd said her real face was completely destroyed by the explosion of a booby-trap. Or was she a figment in or beyond a recent dream. But the woman now beside him? Zizi. Moonlight and memory: no help now. One thing was clear though: he was not just drifting: the design was terrifying in its connections.

The Larissa interlude was lost and worthless—he was now in Kalambaka at the Divani and it was morning. Meeting those two mountain climbers, Seymour (with his pot gut and Slavonic-thunder-god face) and William (a classic Centaur) last night at Cafe Zeus was a lucky break. Mason trusted the calmness of their eyes. Seymour, drunk by ten, sang Leadbelly: "Green corn, come along Cholly!" He was good. Feeling chipper, Mason gave him a voodoo warning, "You sprinkle goofy dust around my bed/ You might wake up and find your own self dead." The point: in the morning (this one) they were going to climb to the untouched, secret cave of an ancient monk called Hecrate, Knower of All Truth. Legend had it he'd left (in some form *other* than writing) a "text" which addressed itself to the problems of the soul's relationship to the body and the body's to the group of other bodies beyond itself. Mason was not getting his hopes up but he was *damned* sure interested.... (Late yesterday, on arriving in Kalambaka, he'd followed his nose and driven up a road through the Meteora Rocks because those ancient hermits might've held part of the question if not the answer. He parked near Varlaam Monastery: a giant eagle's nest perched at the top of a peak. On a swing-bridge a group of German tourists were being conned by a Hindu maker-of-little-wood-images of Ereshkigal. Mason looked up through the monastic aura and saw, from the embankment, a delivery man loading a satchel of goods for the monks. He watched the guy wheel it over on a pully. The bundle reached a tiny opened window. Hands jutted out but rather than capturing the supplies upset them: meat and milk, eggs and bread, turned into birds with broken wings. Mason uncrossed himself and moved on, deciding against entry. At nearby Monastery Hagios Stephanos he cornered a nun and told her his name. She said, "So?" He whispered, "Be in love and you will be happy. Be mysterious." He knew she was wise to him when she responded: "You are a relief in bad wood: esoteric, sarcastic. Go cast yourself in *Tamanu*." Three alarmed nuns approached them and stopped a few feet away. Carpenters in the background were hammering on the facade of a nun's dwelling. He turned and ran. Driving down: no time for sentimental reflection. All experience was a smooth swift surface. Really? The fourteenth century couldn't be trusted! He was sure now there was no difference between the Garden of Eden and Hell. After a few drinks down in the town he sped back up and parked on the road near Monastery of Metamorphosis. The dusk-sky was a traffic jam of old cars with their headlights on. Mason didn't expect the *real* Transfiguration. Nor any help from the monks. But he was surprised! He was led to the Charnel House of skulls and thigh bones. The guard told him to take his time. Once the door was closed, Mason sat on the floor and picked up a dusty skull. He placed his ear to the thing. It spoke: "Do not eat of the turpentine tree." He put it down and took up another. It too spoke: "Do not trust the cult of the gods." He lifted yet another to his ear. Its message: "Father Divine is the supplier and satisfier of every good desire." After listening to eighty-eight cryptic messages similar to the first three, Mason gave up. On the way out he left a donation of a hundred bucks. From there, he stumbled on through farther gloom to baroque icons. He tried to kiss them through the glass, he placed his ear to the cases: nothing! In the museum a shabby man who said he was from Phigaleia wouldn't leave Mason alone. He kept explaining Truth and Reality. According to him both had been documented in the ninth and twelfth and thirteenth and fourteenth centuries. Mason finally gave in. "But what about *transfiguration?*" A group of tourists came in with a guide and scattered the man's response. The guide said, "The manuscripts in this room were restored after the war with money from the Magnan-Rockford Foundation in America.")

Mason, Seymour and William went up in the jeep. The air was fresh, clean, even sweet. Sky was a honeymoon, a tapestry of fauves gaiety! In the climb, Mason was in the middle. Just in case. Progress was slow. Inch by inch. They stepped upward, testing rocks that looked like underwater roots, fuzzy rocks, slick ones. Mason didn't dare look back nor down. His hands reached, alternately, for a bright forest of flowers and a

grove of weeping spruce. One way to *transform* the harshness!
He kept reaching! When he thought he was grasping leaves of
hemlock, his fingers curved around steep stonerock. Then,
unbelievably, they made it! And what a *grand* view! There was
Varlaam over there—and in this direction—there was Hagios
Stephanos! Then they turned and entered the cave. Mason was
still in the middle. He held his breath: an old habit left over from
early childhood, perhaps infancy. Darkness. The three men
stood together in darkness. Strangers. Nervously, Seymour
cracked the first corny joke. Then Mason said, "There are thirty-
eight types of ants in Jerusalem." William snickered then spoke:
"The Royal Poinciana is the most flamboyant tree in the world."
Mason said, "I'll *buy* that!" Seymour then clicked on his
flashlight. "No!" hissed William, "Let's wait for night vision!"
Mason's night-vision had already come. He saw the full contents
of the cave the second before the light went on: there was nothing
but dust, dust, dust—*and* dust!

He drove through the mountains and small villages and
towns up to Delphi. Herds of goats got in the road but
Mason was patient. He arrived at mid-afternoon. Hazy,
hot, pretty. Nobody here rolled out a red carpet: he wasn't
expecting to meet a man named Menekrates nor one called
Dionysos. Mason was alone. His heart beat too fast as though
something was about to happen. He was afraid. He threw his
luggage on the bed and went down for a drink. For a change: gin
and tonic. Finished, he walked: tourism up the ass. But cute. Real
gentle: not mean to strangers. And cheap drinkable wine, he later
discovered, in an effort to avoid getting drunk: Athos—made by
monks. A tremor of fear swept through him. He saw double.
Closed his eyes. . . . In the night while struggling with a griffin
then a sphinx he was awakened by the gawdawful cry of some

beast in its struggle to escape wooden walls—which woke all the dogs and the barking went on till dawn. Mason sweated it out in the air-conditioned dark. Was this damnable hotel *below* the earth! . . . A relief when first light came. It was on the hillside site of the classical past, the archaic stones, that he stumbled and cut his hand on the wing of a shredding woman-lion. Caught in a brief morning shower, he found the stadium at the top nevertheless. Above and below were the winding slopes and nerve-system of Parnassos. Before the Oracle he had spread himself on the ground. Unaware that he was not alone he kissed the earth. A little girl giggled. Mason leaped to his feet. Stumbling over a sudden line of peasants trudging up the narrow path with sheep and goats under their arms, he dashed down through their ranks. The smell of blood lifted behind him through the trees toward the iron clouds. Below, he saw the tourists' buses arriving. Apollo's shrine was the bone structure of a dinosaur, below: its hymn was not in honor of Chicago. No sanctuary for Mason here? Mason paused before the guardian of the Temple. His body did not suddenly merge with his soul, nor separate. The sky was clearing as he drove up to Arahova—only ten minutes up from Delphi. He poked around this village of weavers looking at the tapestries. In one dingy shop he spotted a table cloth with an interesting design: at its center there was an elusive cunt-shaped structure. While the clerk was trying to pressure him into buying the thing he picked it up for a closer look at the paradigm. It changed before his eyes: an old T-Model Ford was smashed into a huge rock at the edge of a cliff. That was it. Maybe he was still back there drunk as Blackface Hermes or needed to push on to Glarentza fast. Something was going wrong with his eyes; his mind perhaps. Was the boulder meant to reveal something? He put the damned thing down. He turned to leave the shop. The clerk held him by the shoulder. Pleading. Mason looked back at the cloth: the center had changed again: this time to a fat cow on a table in a speakeasy. Beneath the circular picture was the word "Oxford." When Mason got back to his car a little boy leaped from it and ran. A woman stuck her head out of an apartment window overhead and called, "Herakles!" As he drove back it became increasingly clear that the separation of body and spirit was going to remain a problem. Oneness was lost somewhere back there in the ruins. May as well move on, buddy. Make the best of it. Unless, uh, unless you're ready to search in the remote depths of Africa.... But for the moment live with the erosion. You have no choice. You don't have to be deterministic to dislike the present tense.

They'd gotten his signature on a document, threw women in his path, plotted God knows what else. Delphi was not safe. They must be here too. Behind every stone. The thought made *his* search seem so innocent, so childish. He tried to write. Florence Soukhanov wouldn't come. He felt like a slightly porous opaque clay pot fired at low heat. Think, Mason, think. What is your true name? Buster Brown. No. Think, boy, think. I know it's not Mason. I'm not Ellis. Can't they see I've given up? Why won't they call their dogs off? Get off my back. Mason was drunk in his room. A young man on his terrace across the way was watching Mason pace. Mason pulled the drapes across the sliding doors. Even that guy was probably one of them. His chuckle was a mad cackle. "A Cowie man. A hit artist." No, if they wanted me dead they could've knocked me off long ago. *They want to use me.* But *how* and *why?* And for how long? He smoked and sipped scotch and continued to pace.... Fell asleep on the floor. In one alcoholic dream he was a writer on a lecture tour. Nobody knew his name. He couldn't remember it either. Every town and city he stopped in had announced his coming but with some embarrassment. They hadn't known what to call him.

Leaving. Leaving was difficult—and a relief. Early in the morning he drove from Delphi. Thinking about Greece: there was *something* you could hear in the music and taste in the food. Then, an old man jumped in front of Mason's rented car—apparently trying to get killed. He was hysterical. A death in the family? He demanded Mason drive him to Clovino. Mason opened the door for the smelly old guy who chattered away in Greek the whole distance—which took a half hour. At Clovino the desperate man leaped out and dashed down a dirt road toward a cluster of shanty houses. Mason drove over to Clovino Beach and parked in the lot of a beach front restaurant. He had a coffee and gazed at the sea. His goal was to reach Olympia by nightfall. He had to step on it: yet a sluggish sadness gripped him. Hard to push. What would he find useful at Olympia? This was not just tourism you know; pieces to the puzzle were supposedly here. Surely. Anyway, he drove onto the ferry at Andrirrion, disembarked at Rion, drove through the bustling city of Patras. He held his breath: almost all the way to Killini. He felt a bone-rattling chill as he drove past Hotel Glarentza. *Name* sake? The red carpet? No way. He drove down to the beach and parked. He couldn't feel anything of "himself" here. He might as well have been in Watertown, South Dakota or Watertown, Wisconsin or Watertown, New York or Watertown, Massachusetts. People were coming off the boat from Italy as he ate fried fish at one of the beach front restaurants: American backpackers and Germans; also Greeks returning from holiday in Italy. It was frustrating to Mason that nobody greeted him. Him? Shouldn't he have been automatically declared the prodigal son returned from chaos?... His arrival at Olympia was equally uneventful. The band was not waiting. The ruins though were worth it: step by step. But the next day he left and stopped at Khora. Men at cafes eyed him with that careful scrutiny you know about. Wall scrawlings here as everywhere before: KKE on the one hand and PASOK on the other. Then he found in the Mycenaean ruins of Pylos the Linear C Script on eight clay pots locked in late-Helladic silence. And Nestor's Palace itself was no match! He celebrated the find by buying a good bottle of Villitas and finding a park with drunks on a bench and sharing the wine with them. Even this disappointed him; they didn't warm up to Mason. He moved on. Here he ate octopus in olive oil and felt sorry for himself. In fact he *stuffed* himself. He was thankful that sleep that night in a plastic Kalamata hotel, was not memorable. In the morning he set out for Mistra—up through the mountains: roadside vendors beckoned in attempts to sell pine-cone baskets and honey. Herds of goats frequently blocked the road. Mason was patient. That Linear C Script kept pressing in on his consciousness but he resisted assigning it a place in the puzzle; it might not fit—exactly. In any case it was too soon. Mistra: a medieval hill city with few ruins. Didn't matter though. The sought-after connections were not necessarily in the ruins: in fact, they might be more persistently in the *living* presence, the people, the spirit of the people. If he were a "product" of the West—and this was the "cradle" of the West, then . . . well, add two and two. Do you get Africa? or the doorway from Africa . . . ? *He* got Sparta as the next step in the chain of possibility: nothing much there: he of course did check the skimpy ruins but found only the dust from boys driving their motorbikes around the grounds. . . . Time to move on to Tolon! There one could give up and just relax. . . . Not worry. . . . At Tolon Mason parked on the beach. Walking down to the hotel he was bombarded by word-messages: Beach Skiing Lessons! Rent Pedalos! Take a Sea Cruise! Boats for Rent! Each one was like a left hook in the right eye. The spirit here was seedy. It made Mason feel shabby. He checked into Hotel Coronis but didn't like it and moved right away next door to Hotel Knossos. Not much better. He went back down to the beach. A group of vacationing French mignonnes sunning themselves on the beach and smoking Panamanian noir. . . . He gave in to a Camel and turned his lust toward the sea. Rented a motor boat and headed for one of the islets. Already windy and cold. Half way there he lost faith in his mission, but pushed on anyway. He landed, turned the motor off and climbed the rocky path. In a clearing at the top was a tent.

Pull here? Yes. Mason went to the tent, looked in: a man with a beard sat yoga-still, arms crossed. He was covered by a leather garment. A woman sat next to him in the same manner. The man didn't focus on Mason. The woman did and she spoke: "I could love perhaps any single male individual among, say, seventy-five-percent of the men on earth. You are one. Also there is this: you are no longer in parentheses: you are in brackets: falling upside-down in an effort to be a union of two sets. Rain and snow coming your way. No stationary front. Your given name is not exactly a subset. Let my advice sink calmly: do not let your visibility be reduced by smoke. That is all. Go." She closed her eyes. . . . That night Mason tossed and jerked—struggled to separate a swastika from the infinity sign then the whole mess got tangled up with the Christian cross. Having decided the swastika was a hunk of cheddar cheese and the two circles were pots of poison the situation became even more dangerous and para-doxical: he had to keep them separate at all cost. Then around three he heard the fishermen starting up their motors. He went out on the terrace. Half moon lighted the bobbing boats. He looked toward the islet he'd visited. Hovering above it was the lighted arc of a circle. The moon reflected? No. Part of the sun? No. ". . . do not let your visibility be reduced by smoke." He went in and got his cigarettes. He realized he must not get carried away at these intersections.

Greece was winding down. He stood in the center of the circular theatre at Epidauros with raised arms—hearing the cheering of thousands seated on the stone benches. They loved him. That love became his bridge. It nourished him. Blackface Hermes the clown was happy! Celt CuRoi should see him now! A group of American tourists arrived and jolted him out of his itinerant glory. He then jogged around the place. He bought a basket of figs from a peasant and drove on. . . . At the walled city of Tiryns, the one Homer wrote about, he met a stone worker who was hiding in the shadow of an archway. Mason squatted with him and chewed the fat. They agreed that there were thirty-three million, three-hundred-and-forty-thousand people in Thailand and eight million, eight-hundred-and-sixty thousand in Ghana. They agreed on many other important points. The guy had stone dust in his woolly red hair. Mason liked his leathery skin and sharp rat-eyes. But agreeable masons and the ruins of walled cities had their limits. . . . As Mason drove toward Corinth he remembered that that old stone cutter back there in Tiryns indeed had connections back in Twenty-five hundred B.C. . . . On the way back to Athens, Blackface Hermes stopped at Sounion. The sky was ice. He climbed a path to the Temple to Poseidon. Vanity. All was vanity. Tourists since way-back-when had chiseled their "glorious" names into the stone foundation of the restored structure. The *insistence* of it! (bringing one's own chisel and mallet up was a bit much)! And wouldn't you know it: Byron too had left a sign of his own desperate arrogance and insecurity. Graffito was a chisel. . . .

In no time he was back in Athens. The minute after he checked into the King George he was out exploring. At a cafe, workers were singing rebetika songs. A couple of tough young men started dancing. Beer was spilled. Mason finished his Robola and squeezed out just as a table loaded with octopus, macaroni, keftedes, souvlaki, pastitsio, mousaka and fetta was accidentally knocked over. The bartender got his hatchet. . . . At a sidewalk cafe, in shadows, he heard a violent argument: The Greek War of Independence was not over! Yes, yes it was! Ecclesiastical hymns somewhere in the dense background chopped by traffic noise. . . . Mason restlessly moved on.

He became a dolphin in the sea of Greece. What bullshit! Yes—
Mason reached out now to the Hellenistic Koine and felt the click
of the testament inside his own mouth: one exslave knew another
exslave. Stress was right. The Benaki? It was the next morning—
and he hadn't understood what'd happened to the night. He got
the drift of ancient wealth—before the Akritic cycle. Turk rule.
Then in the park he was dazed by a man balancing chairs and
bottles in a high fortress on his own head. Nothing toppled. . . . A
snatch of conversation: "My cousin in Chicago got the niggers to
hassle. We still got the Turks. It's all the same." His erection woke
him—when he didn't even know he was asleep. He opened the
anthology. George Seferis: "The stranger and the enemy, we have
seen him in the mirror." Mason wandered the night market
around Sofokleous and Klistohenous and Athinas: veal was
glossy, so was lamb; whole skinned pigs hung upside-down from
iron hooks. Tripe bloomed under glass. Each black olive emitted
one glowing cuticle. Plush tomatoes winked their red lights.
Dates in brown profusion, soft as plastic wood. Then the dried
fish with its salt-covered skin. Crates. Boxes. Cries. Crowds
under electric bulbs. While asleep—again—Mason was in great
distress. There was no place to sleep. Dream within a dream? He
entered a furniture store to buy a bed. Decided to test the
mattress on one. It was comfortable. He slept. Then something
woke him. He jumped up, greatly alarmed: he'd to get to the
party. Everybody was surely already there. He'd probably missed
everything. Painted Turtle would be there. He knew if he tried to
penetrate her his thing would turn to paper, fold up. It was
raining. Where was Athens? Which city was this? . . . He got in his
rented car. He had to decide between driving up a washed out dirt
road and getting stuck or missing the party.

Word came from Signard in Paris that Africa was all set but Mason wasn't. He was caught in a Nice maze: he'd gone again for guilt-treatments to Doctor Wongo. While enduring the Saint Sabastian Redemption Method his mudfrog had gotten ruptured. It was like this: Mason saw the arrow coming. It was coming for a long, long time. He knew where it would hit. It was the kind of experience seemingly without end that suddenly ended with flash and shock and pain between his eyes. Then Mason found himself chewing on some woman's ear till the cows came home to roost. Life these days was crazy and rough. With some of his Arab friends he went to a party in the foreigners' ghetto, L'Ariane, east of Nice, where pretty sober-looking dudes were into some terrible actions and plots. Lights were blue and low. The music was out of Cairo then Syria then Algeria. Mason loved the strangeness of it, the smell of yellow candles and green incense. Conversation? Not heavy: "...and it's like zat nowadays, I tell you...." ""Z places 'ere 'ave changed!..." This was the night Mason met Habib Imed Maherssi, the gentleman who decided to get all of Mason's books published in Arabic. First, Maherssi would urge a friend of his in Morocco to write a big story about him for the biggest newspaper in the country. Then, *hey,* look out...! Mason was eating dinner with Habib and Hassan and Baraka at a couscous joint in Old Nice when the kitchen blew up. They were lucky. They got out with only their hair, faces and mouths filled with plaster and smoke and ash and dust from the ceiling—which was falling down around them.... Then there was the trip to Musee National to see the Chagalls with Chantal and Monique. The guards (according to Chantal) thought Mason was Arab. Mason joked about it: "Should've brought my Arab friends with me..." But Chantal wasn't amused. Mason went away from Chantal here, lost himself in the museum: it became a place of unfolding possibility. Moons and cows and plush pink underwater plants and shimmering fabrics and trembling virginal couples floating near the edge of space turned him around, pulled him under their spell. Put him on an insane spin up through mountain roads of canvas, down through sea-level pathways of suicide-fears. A mermaid's scaly skin rubbed against his naked arm. Mason stepped up into the canvas and entered the home of an old rabbi. The rabbi's daughter was a plump girl in a flaky strawberry red nightgown with plump virginal breasts and hips. Her bridegroom waited in the doorway, trembling with expectation. "Who are you?" asked the rabbi. "I am Haze, I am." An alarmed group of monks entered the cottage. They too wanted to know what the hell this *devil* wanted. Why was he here? They threatened to send a messenger to the king if he didn't spill. Moon-eyed cows gazed in through the windows. "I am here," Mason said, "because I feel a sense of *kinship:* which I suspect you deny." "He's an impostor!" shouted one of the monks. The others raised voices of agreement. The rabbi's daughter bravely went to Mason's side. She leaned against him. Everyone in the room was horrified. The virgin spoke: "You all know me as Edith. I welcome this stranger to my father's house. He will break bread with us. Are *we* not *all* the children of the same plant shoot, the same husk?" Before they could answer, bells (with an inner echo of water-music) sounded from the nearby cathedral. Shooing the monks out, Edith left Mason and embraced her father, saying, "Time is a river without banks." It was late when Mason left, a bit dazed from sweet red wine but feeling as energetic as a licensed jester. He flew up into night blackness with its purple doorways dislodged from houses too soggy to stay hinged to the earth. When he tried to hold a bridge down, he discovered the weight of his body wasn't sufficient: it floated up, carrying with it smelly and hazy, gray green pink blue farm animals; and escapees from carousels and classified catalogues. He found himself on the banks of the Seine. The Eiffel Tower had fallen into the river. But this wasn't Nice! A fisherman came along and offered to share a bowl of red fish with him. They sat together, legs dangling over the edge of the embankment, and ate together in silence. Their images were reflected in the gray water. Then suddenly there was Chantal shaking him. *"Hay!"* he said. *"Okay!"* Was he trying to *avoid* Africa? Naw. Leaving Chantal to her own flight, her own wedding of separate words, he went to be alone: at Bar de la Degustation. Free here in his world of silence, he brooded. White and blue emergency van shot by with the half dead body of yet another old person. Mason's own soul was wrapped so thinly in wax paper he was sorta glad this S.O.S. amities was available. Maybe he'd have one day to thank his lucky moons and the nuns of the infirmiers. A man walked by carrying a crucifixion with a black bird nailed to it. But this whole moment was still some kinda circus: and Mason was diving, diving, diving straight down into a blue *depth* without a net. . . . Well, cheer up, buddy. Life is full of vivid harmony, jagged lines, forebodings, floats and twisted fiddles. Rereading the letter from Signard, Mason drained the last bitter drop of coffee from his cup. So, what the hell, he'd go to Africa! He sat there watching the people go by: Daphnis and Chloe, girls in jeans and red French cowgirl boots and those ones in black stockings and mid-thigh long skirts, boys in too-large punk double-breasted plaid suits, old ladies with humped backs, little blue-clad men carrying shopping bags. Yes, in Africa he'd be able to climb onto the back of a butterfly and fly to larva heaven. Or turn himself into a desert spiny swift and dart across the rock of the universe! or get involved with a revolutionary group and become an international hero. He could *surely* find Tarzan and wipe *him* out for ever; feed him fruit flies and spray his tree-house with the processed blood of a dimetrodon. Africa's insistent sun would include Mason soon, as wind moving along city pavement includes all the shadows and leaves and cigarette butts, as it whips the debris into a haystack between two buildings. He'd be a gray-eyed crow in Africa: He'd keep his wings clean and he'd fly! . . . The day before he left, a manila envelope arrived from Signard. It contained a brief note and a sealed envelope addressed to somebody called Chief Q. Tee. Mason read the note: "Please kindly deliver this when you arrive in Monrovia. Be careful with it: if its contents leak you may find your health in danger. Your tour in Africa is dependent on your carrying this envelope safely to its addressee. Thank you. Have a safe and rewarding trip!"

Had Mason lost something in Ghana? Myth and mystery loomed in the drums, pots, musical instruments, terracotta heads, funeral relics, linguists staffs. Mason looked at a figurine with large eyes, thick nose, wide mouth: in each eye: motion of cow and countdown. A whip-lash little man with a fixed grin, Makola drove Mason through unfocused shanty town: rows of bleak, unpainted huts along the restless coast. Lean women with fat babies on their long hips; others with huge bundles on their heads, grandmothers tending community fires dancing in beds of rock. May winds came in from the Sea of Guinea bringing with them the sea-side smell of garbage. They parked. Went into a hut. This was the home of the poet, Amos Achimota. He was expecting them. Achimota led them outside. The three sat with their backs to the wall, facing the sea. The poet was an old man who began by reminding Professor Kwame Makola that his father and forefathers had been chiefs. Mason's eye was snagged several times by the up-turned tits of some young woman walking by. Usually carrying something on head-top. The poet talked of his meetings with Langston Hughes in the fifties. Was Mason impressed? Was Mason familiar with the works of Awooner, Soyinka, Senghor, Achebe, Ben-Gurion, Camera Laye, Mphahlele, Fanon? Mason lied—said yes. What did Mason think of Ghana? Did he know anything about its history? Well, yes: he *had* read Richard Wright's book: *Black Power* years before. Achimota spoke with gentle fervency. Two soldiers armed to the teeth strolled by giving them the once over. As Achimota spoke of the difficulty Ghanians had had since the fifties and before under colonialism, Mason remembered yester-day—his arrival at battered Kotoka Airport. Place filled with armed soldiers and police. Security check-points every five steps. Shirts and a suit stolen from his luggage before it even reached the baggage pick-up. Boys hassling him for money. Cab drivers—despite Professor Kwame Makola's presence—fighting over his luggage. Pathetic Makola, waving his sensitive hands in gestures of punctuation as he talked, trying to make the airport officials treat Mason as an "official visitor" and getting nowhere . . . and that so-called security-check just down the road from the airport where his luggage was searched again and where, finally, he and Makola were passed (and Makola saying, "Of course that was *not* an official security check. Outside Accra men often set up road-blocks just to, how do you say, rip off people... I hope your opinion of Ghana hasn't set yet....")... And now Achimota— with yellowed rotten teeth—was laughing as he reminded Makola (with his frozen grin) that he, Makola, had spent nearly two years in prison during the regime of Akuffo. "And just for having certain friends. Hey?" "That's right, Old Man." And was not the young Rawlings doing the best he could with an impossible situation? "Surely." Nobody questioned the integrity of the leader of the Provisional National Defense Council. Achimota looked directly at Mason. "Are you a political poet?" Of course. But the question left Mason feeling like somebody was about to throw a ball for him to go and fetch. The old poet was happy with the response then spoke again of Langston Hughes. Hughes, he said, understood how profoundly political the life of an individual in society was. Achimota hadn't met any Afro-American poets since Hughes but considered all of them his brothers. "Welcome home, Brother." "Thank you." But did Mason feel at home? How black was Blackface Hermes? The old man suddenly broke open a strange piece of red fruit Mason had never seen before and passed a piece of it to Makola and the other third to Mason. The three men chewed for a few minutes in silence. It was Achimota who spoke first. "I suppose you'll be having dinner with the American ambassador?" Mason shrugged. Said he knew nothing about such a proposal. "Well, it'd be unusual if you didn't." Achimota spat a couple of seeds into the dust. Two sullen policemen passed before them, followed by a pretty girl carrying a broken basket of rotten potatoes. Mason noticed a big man approaching. He was black. "This man you see," said Achimota, "is the Ambassador from Nigeria. Be careful what you say. He will not be your friend." After formalities the big man refocused on Mason. "Why are you in Ghana?" "To lecture on Monday at the University of Legon." "And your thesis?" Was this the third degree? The thesis was art. The Nigerian Ambassador did not squat down with them in the polite manner. He said a few hesitant words to Achimota about some meeting of the cultural body then excused himself. Three little girls dressed in white dresses with white ribbons on their hair went by. Mason remembered it was Sunday. Christians? Why had the ambassador been so hostile? Had he, like the airport officials, suspected Mason of being less than straightforward? Perhaps a pusher of seedless sinsemilla or a bringer of dangerous messages? (He did not know what was in that note for Q. Tee— but, well, that was for another country.) Professor Makola stood and their host got the message. He too stood. The three men shook. "Do not judge Ghana too quickly, young man. Your ancestors came from West Africa. . . . " As Mason and Makola approached the car a loud cracking sound and a scream, a cry, behind them broke across their necks. Whirling around, they saw a cop beating a young man. Even now Makola's smile did not vanish; it changed content though. It said: I trust. And in an urgent effort to distract, Makola asked, "How'd you like France? You know French people think you're stupid if you don't speak French." Mason chuckled. They got into the old battered car and Makola drove Mason back to the American Club. "Sorry you're staying here. You won't meet *the people* this way. But I guess you have no choice. IHICE, right?" "Right." Inside, the Housekeeper had a message for Professor Kwame Makola. The American Embassy's Cultural Director, Robert Astor, wanted him and Makola to come to dinner. Mason didn't know how to respond. Makola told him he'd like Astor: "He's a good man." A nerve-winged insect buzzed around Mason's head. The lobby was cool. "I'll fetch you at four. Curfew, you know. Everything starts early." A gust of heat came in as Makola left. Mason went to the bar. Americans were watching a variety show video-taped on the screen above the bar. The Ghanaian bartender had the in-scrutable face of a chaff sifter in a harvest sacrifice. Mason shifted to the screen. There, Painted Turtle hung from the mouth of an elephant. Then Edith appeared dancing with a snake curled around her hips. An earwig crawled in beer on the bar. After a couple of shots, Mason's legs turned to spiracles. As he walked to his room, his breathing was a parachute flapping in the wind. What'd that lice-faced sifter *put* in that drink? A maid was making the bed. He went in the toilet and threw up dragonflies and liquified antennas. In what seemed no time at all the maid finished, he slept and woke and Makola was there. They shot a game of intense pool in the rec room before rumbling away to the party. Death bones danced on the roadside. As they arrived in the driveway, a barrage of bullets swept the facade of the house, the cars, the stone steps. Mason and Makola hit the ground. Two other cars came into the driveway. A woman screamed. Mason looked out and up and saw eight or nine fatigue-clad soldiers crouched on the ledge of the front stone wall, aiming their machine-guns at the house next door. The heat of Makola's car poured its oil and gas smells down into Mason's face. The gravel beneath his belly had the pointed sharpness of a bed of nails. His knuckles bled. A jeep came into the driveway. The man next to the driver looked official as the keeper of Solomon's stables at Megiddo. He jutted a grim jaw. He was decorated. *"Halt your fire!"* he shouted to the soldiers on the wall. Risking the loss of his dignity, the official squatted a bit and beckoned to Mason and Makola. "Do come out! All is well!" He chuckled. "My men get carried away." They crawled out. As Mason and Makola beat dust from their clothes, a white man (Astor?) opened the big door and came onto the grand porch of the mansion, and down the marble stairway. The late afternoon smelled of gunsmoke and spurge blossoms. Mason had the vague feeling he'd reached some magical frontier. The official introduced himself as General somebody. His smile was full of humidity. The white man came and shook hands with the General. They obviously knew each other. He apologized to Astor for the stray bullets. "We have the house next door surrounded. An enemy of the people, this Major Okike! My advice to you, Mister Astor, is: You and your friends stay in your big fine house. It's safe!" Another car arrived. The Africans who'd gotten out of the other two were now walking up the driveway toward them. The General shook with everybody again then leaped back into his jeep. He went away in a cloud of dust, his helmet bouncing on his big head.... The dinner-party got on: Mason was soon cornered, with scotch in hand, by Kalmoni who invited him to dinner "tomorrow night." Mason mingled: Hourari, a silent young man who'd spent time in the states, gave him a secret handshake: it was more a slash than a thrust. Quickly, this place'd become a dungeon, hewn out of blood-slick walls. As the second round of drinks came, while the novelist, James Aburi, spoke to Mason of his two years as a political prisoner, a new round of gunfire rang out. A torpedo exploded. Janet Bu Karle, a dance teacher, joined Mason and Aburi. "Just remember we're getting there!" Mason laughed with them. Something beneath the nerve-bed and gymnastics of his sound echoed the little screech of the guinea fowl. It was not till one of the grand windows (through which the driveway could be seen) flew apart that Astor and his wife and twelve-year-old daughter quickly ushered Mason and the others down into the impenetrable coldness of their basement. It stank of fine wine and reptile skin. In the narrow passageway, the poet Jomo Danqueah joked: "All this for OAU!" On a dimly lighted wall, in passing, Mason saw this inscription: "This house constructed 1934 by MRF." What instrument of torture was this journey? Who was Astor—really? And these others? The pellet-like bones in his skin had him now in the grip of a deep chill. At the end of this submerged level, they descended to yet another. Okoto Nsawam, a journalist, was just behind Mason. He tapped Mason's shoulder. "Welcome home, brother!" His cackle was the crunch of a fish-eating gavial.

And so it went. Despite a weird dream about the kids he reached the next day without a bad head. Heading for Legon, Makola wanted to give the American a glimpse of Independence Square and the Arab market but Mason saw them through haze. Clusters of sidewalk vendors were everywhere. Their leather crafts, dresses, jewelry, masks, were spread out on sheltered tables along the main streets where the traffic was hectic, stalled, and where dust clouds lifted to the bat-filled grand old trees also lining the roads. Every street corner was a small community focus of solemn women and men and children who waited to sell their wares and produce: plantains and shrunken fruit and palm oil. Dogs lean and hungry wandered restlessly in the dust in and out of side-streets. Neighborhood women set up blocks to force drivers to pay to pass along their pitted, rock-laden dirt roads.... Part of the presentation was a flop because nobody'd heard of the Afro-American writers he referred to: Wideman, Shange, Reed, Charles Wright, not even Zora Neal Hurston. Cultural gap? Distance. It left him gloomy. Catching, huh, Makola was apologetic, reassuring. Then Mason read from his infamous work-in-progress:

" ... he touched Florence's shoulder. 'We have to go.' She was ready. 'You're on.' As they travelled they talked the past. 'Everybody in New York was serious in the sixties. The terror was not yours alone, then. The lost witch in the craft was rediscovered: politics, war, disillusionment were never the solutions. You could establish a forced logical connection between any two completely unrelated things: make a collage or cubist plot of yourself, your life.' Unable to find a suitable used struggle-buggy at Don's Easy-Terms Used Car Lot, they were on a Trailways. He spoke thickly, quickly. 'I tried that, too. Edith Levine lived with me then. ... ' Flo cut: 'Nobody cares about your dead past. Especially if you're not making the forced connections pretty and powerful. Listen, I knew an Indian girl who tried to resolve what she saw as a dilemma: by making a connection between herself and political ideas, specific ones—I forget which—.' Mason scowled. Flo: 'She stood, pink as puppy mouths, on a corner handing out leaflets for a cause she didn't herself fully understand; meant well as she stood on centuries of rage and corruption. Disillusioned, she went to work as a fast-food waitress at Quick Snack. She had the biggest, sweetest smile, back there behind the counter, with all those coffee cups, plastic plates, stainless steel knives, forks, spoons, sundae bowls, salt and pepper shakers, all, repeated dizzingly in the mirrors that surrounded her in her baby-green, snot-yellow uniform with its starched dainty collar decorated with tiny embossed elephants smacking on giant burgers. . . . ' Mason: 'Making forced connections in 1966 I first went to New York: felt intense among rug dye factories. You could be against racism without being against sexism and vice versa. Radical lesbians attempted to impregnate themselves with chemicals from their own bodies. There's no metaphor. Morality and moral fiction were in suspended animation. (Art hasn't saved anybody: appletrees, appletrees. Which appletrees?) Anyone could be shot or made. But you were there: you know—.' His memory was a thin layer of Matisse-green juxtaposed with a self-consciously brushed-in pink. But he could not now yank himself out of the climb: 'Look at me: I lost my *name* in that fucking place! My father was already dead and the iron years were behind me—those years: I punched a clock and welded metal together in a steel circus. . . . Before Attica—after the city of dirty el trains and Richard Wright's crash at Roosevelt Road when Cross got his chance to switch identities. I smoked cigarettes—a tough guy—and tried to look like Jack Johnson, act like Jack London, strike with the certainty of Jack da Ripper. Back then, Celt was with me often and guided me through the early stages—my apprenticeship. She hovered above me, bright as a Veronese Venus, editing, shaking her finger in my face when I lost intense concentration on the charged image, the driven word. Now, who knows where Celt might be: a halo over my enemy's head? I went on, Florence, raving about, say, the immortal leadership spirit of the underground railway, in poems, stories; in pictures—framing my chaos: brown men with glittering ornaments wearing gold and flat plates in their lower lips hundreds of years before slavery. On the Qt., I had a mission. I was going to *be* a writer: hadn't learned that illustration wasn't painting. You get it. Too much glutted-Glackens, not enough Pollack-pull or de Kooning-cool; too much ... I had something to *say* before I knew I had something to *make*. My forced connections hadn't registered. I cried out about poverty and death in Liberia. Imagine that! Felt my own face: it was a billboard facing a Liberian market place; beggars whimpering; hombres prowling; boney children crouched in damaged doorways and shitting in the sand by the death-river; everybody hungry, crazy; miserable. This, while tourists snapped pictures of them. I was pissed, Miss. I knew then I'd never known real poverty nor seen it. I was not Gauguin on a white horse under a red tree. ... ' Florence gazed beyond the window. She coughed. Kissed his cheek. There was challenge in her voice: 'Perhaps it's better to be quiet: as on a Sunday morning, quiet as it can be in a glass telephone-booth on a Sunday morning; quiet and unclear or clearly unfocused like an old senile woman I saw once searching the coin-return-slot in a telephone-booth; dressed in 1923-laced-up boots. I claim that view for all time. But you can share it with me, Key of C. She went into the booth almost too quickly: as though she was about something urgent; pretended to search for a *thing* in her purse and pockets. Her identity? Through her action she was creating it! It was winter: but the booth was a closure as "hot" as Henri's Red Studio—*as* familiar. And she was cool in a heavy black coat with her tiny pink face at its top above a big button. The phone to her ear, pretending to talk, then, on the sly, with the index finger of the free hand she searched, with real thrust, the coin-return-slot. I tell you, I was a witness to her draped-disappointment—and her warped dignity. But *silence* was her forte. I felt sorry. ... '"

Kalmoni lived in a house that was about two steps above a hut. That was all right. But he had electricity and gas. About half the guests who'd attended the dinner party at Robert Astor's were here. The most striking difference between this home and the Astor's was the degree of light. Kalmoni's dwellings were almost totally in shadows with dim pockets of either candle or soft lamp light with only two or three electric currents juiced. Everybody was more relaxed. Amos Achimota held forth from the rattan couch. He said, with British accent uppermost, "I apologize for not attending your lecture today, but my health . . . you know. I've heard, however, that it was not well received. I've also heard that the reason it was not had to do with your subject matter. . . . " Mason closed his eyes and faked falling asleep. The room was so dark nobody saw the gesture. Janet laughed and said, "Mister Achimota, with all due respects, Sir, I wish to interrupt: Our visiting writer is a *guest* in our country. Do you mind if we shift the mood of our little party and try to make him feel at home? After all, you know, he is—" five or six other voices rushed in, cutting off in mid-word: Nsawam felt Black people could be honest among themselves—Mason was not to be spared. Aburi said, "We're here to enjoy . . . " Kalmoni spoke: "Whatever you have to say, say it quickly: time is short. Remember the Revolution!" Now they laughed at themselves. And this was the moment that was needed. The mood of the party shifted and Mason became their friend. He may have survived The Middle Passage and returned whole but he was not so affected as to be without a sense of humor. And he could take *it*. Achimota was somber throughout the rest of the gathering. Near seven-thirty he said to Mason, "When you get back to America, I hope you'll keep in mind the seriousness of our plight. Langston Hughes knew. Richard Wright knew. Our African writers know. You must know. I'm happy to have met you. . . . " Also near the end of the party Danquah and Aburi and Kaneshire were locking horns in a raging argument over whether or not tribalism was valid in the face of a Marxist alternative for themselves as a struggling people. Aburi damned the notion of the Chieftain tradition ("No man should have to carry another man!" he said with exquisite theatrical poise). Janet described her work in the interior as "political"—she was teaching Ghanaian children to respect their own myths and ceremonies, their cultures and traditions, and, yes, their religions. The conversation left Mason crowded with misty secrets of his own unfinished transfiguration. These matters—their plight—were not his raw October. He shivered as Makola drove him back. His self-interest for the first time made snow fall in the ditch of his brain. He wanted to take somebody's hand but there was nobody. How could he come out of his fever and share his sickness? That search for The Impostor now lost had turned inward where the helpless wings of death beat in his night: making every effort, desire, mere specks in an endless constellation. For a moment he almost turned to Makola. But words were only dice in the shaking hand!

Now an air traveller from Accra to Monrovia must get there the best damned way he can—no, *no!* Start again. Sincerely: the plane must stop in Abidjan. Mason was mobbed by cab drivers and shoe shine boys at the airport. Serious-eyed skinny boys carrying boxes and rags clung to his legs. He could barely walk to the currency counter as he pushed his luggage cart. Ethiopian Airways flight number-what-ever had just landed and the whole place was buzzing with the itch for francs. While standing at the exchange window he shook a boy off his shoe. He was sweating so he thought he had malaria. Mosquitoes surely would win their war with chloroquine. His contained-mood was one of humiliation and rage: a freemason was not a victory but a question. . . . Ivory Coast was a shock: as he was driven into the city Mason felt as though he was in some modern European metropolis: massive traffic jams, skyscrapers, the whole bit. But he'd known . . . but, b-but why were the

French-speaking African countries so much "better off" than those ex-English and ex-Dutch and ex-German colonies?... The contrast to Accra was sharp: no need to put out the hearth fire before dusk here... Grande Hotel on rue De Gaulle faced the river, the bridge, on the big highways.... Settled, Mason went down to the bar to doctor—no, to perform surgery—on a scotch on the rocks. He got it okay despite accent. Then he held forth in great gloom.... Night life in Abidjan? A vague sense of urgency—remember?—drove Mason out into darkness toward mudfrog-cream, magic solutions, questions, linear answers; and he stumbled, first, into a bar where the scotch was really weird—tasted like celt-weed. A guru came over from shadows and sat next to him. "You have eye trouble. I suggest you try seven grams of curikon, a pinch of girongrie and ten grams of estravec." Mason said his vision was all right. The shady guru laughed derisively. Another figure, an obvious companion of the guru, came forward and perched himself on the stool next to Mason. "You want to add paprogue, too. Mix well. Then sit the whole *thing* outside on the terrace. In the morning stir in valainades—only an ounce. After an hour add two pounds of aromanout and six leaves of epicaselles. Let the whole mix sit in a cool place for six days then eat it at midi. You may feel it's a killer but it'll give you a kick—open your sense of reality, clear the—"... Mason was so shaken by the pregnancy of the moment he fled: dashed into the lighted-night: only to encounter people in the street responding to some sort of madness—crazed by music and the spirit of festival: was it disco or boogie woogie or, humph, polka! Certainly *not* African traditional drum rhythm! The city market area was lighted and busy. He found his way among unknown streets, unresponding people. In a night club he saw a black girl do a strip-tease. The show was billed as a See-Kript Act. Her stage name was Colt "Forty-five" Coo-Wow! At the end of her strip she shot two pistols into the audience. (Normally, a couple of dudes dropped.)

He was in the redhandedness of impeccable sleep when the pounding came at the hotel door. He struggled up, thinking he was in Attica and a prison break was in progress. About to piss on himself, he opened the door. Glare of light rubber-stamped his face. "You're under arrest," the officer said in French. The other two black policemen stepped forward and grabbed him: one by each arm. In his pajamas, they took him down in the tiny elevator, out through the bright lobby. The marble floor was cold. Only after he was in the hearse-like vehicle did Mason remember that he was in Abidjan. At headquarters tough black men in uniforms were speaking thick French and it was like listening to a record on the wrong speed. What'd they want with him? What'd he done? Suddenly he pissed in his pajama pants as they led him into a tiny room with a bright light suspended from the ceiling. Three big men in suits stood before him. "Remove your clothes," one of them said. Mason took off his pajamas. "Go down on ze floor." "Your rights they are not your rights. As a member of the PLA, enemy to Ivory Coast we hold you. You confess? You stranger. This is bad enough. In Ivory Coast this is impossible." No survival manual could save him now. He hadn't prepared well for the trip. Hadn't told anybody where he was going? He was alone? When moving into the wilderness one should take along more than a passionate search for self. Mason didn't even pack a compass. He had no map. Headgear? Never heard of it! Flares? Dehydrated food? Screwdriver? Except now he wouldn't have to wait for hypothermia or a loose rock to slide from beneath his foot. All the romance of Africa suddenly slipped away. Two of them took him down a steep, narrow, winding staircase. It was cold and dark at the bottom. A large key turned, in metal. Hinges squeaked like rats. He was roughly kicked and pushed into a cell. One of them spoke to the other in guttural French. The response was equally throaty. Mason'd fallen to the dirt floor. It was wet. He shivered. His masoned wall of faith? He was up against it now. The door slammed. His body-warmth lifted up out of his flesh like smoke from a smothered fire. His mouth was full of sawdust. Long streaks of pain like rubber tubing set afire shot through his body as he raised himself to his knees. He had to crap. No need to hold back. After a few agonizing motions, he was in a squatting position. It started slowly. Then burst out. The smell was a familiar vapor, not the least bit offensive. When he finished he crawled to a corner and curled up with his spine against the angle. Now what? Well, he could keep busy. Remember Satchel Page. Don't look back, something might be gaining on you. Keep rowing. Row row your boat gently. He slept for . . . who knows how long. When he woke his night-vision was better. A dim light beyond the cell? A large oblong object right here in the middle. He crawled over to it. Walking on his knees he felt its surface. No doubt about it: a coffin. He reached inside and slid his palm along the floor. Dry. He felt dizzy, terrified, hungry. Don't give in. Keep on keeping on. You survived the mirror. The prison. Being a clown. You name it. You'll get through this too. He climbed into the warmer space of the coffin and curled up again. He woke to the sound of hammering. Somebody was nailing a lid on? Losing control, Mason bellowed like a bull at the moment of castration. He beat at the lid with feet and fists. The holders of hammers responded to his outrage with laughter as they drove the final two nails in. Mason cried in long ropey sobs. As the men outside jabbered away in crude French, he whimpered and sniffed and ate his own snot. He farted and belched and continued to cry. . . . Some time later they went away. Then much later—days? weeks?—he heard the rusty door open again. Another presence came in. Weak and half out of his mind, he waited for a voice, a word, the sound of breathing. "When you're ready to tell us about the activities of the People's Liberation Army you'll be a free man. Do you *hear* me in there?" A new one! The cow jumped over the moon. High high the moon. Rise Sally rise. Mason didn't respond and before long the speaker of English went away. Another long stretch of time. Then two more of them came. He felt them lift up the coffin. He was being carried along the corridor, up the narrow staircase. Now they rested him on a flat surface. He heard and felt the hammers pulling the nails from the wood. The squeaking was like mice at play. When the lid was off he felt grimy hands lift him into blinding daylight. No moon, no sun: but a furnace of red light. Something like a grandfather clock was ticking. He smelled the old boots of a grave digger. They stood him up and he fell. Their harsh French couldn't touch the high spirit of guttbucket. He was sick of it. Their sneers too! He knew they were tying him to a tree but he didn't know he was in a courtyard of steaming tropical plants till time and a wind song helped him open his eyes. Silence and the sand of thick hands again greeted him. View: yellow teeth between grinning lips. Perhaps he was hallucinating but wasn't one of them standing there with a dead *antelope* around his neck? Blood dripping to the gravel! Mason had forgotten about his nakedness till one of the French-speaking Africans poked at his penis. It sent a sharp pain through his groin. The other one held up a huge Russian pistol. Mason's slit-view didn't cause panic. What the hell. You took the best so why not . . . He heard the distant sounds of celebration, gaiety, a banquet. Somebody was sipping excellent wine from a gold and crystal goblet. The sleep of pigeons hummed in his ears. Death? He thought he'd be objective about it. Why not. As the pistol carrier pressed the barrel against Mason's temple he whispered in Mason's ear, "Hello. Goodbye. How are you. Bang bang!" Then he pulled the trigger: it triggered the reshaping of Mason's inner wilderness: trees fell, Uncle Remus turned white, seas ran dry. Wouldn't you know it? No bullets in the gun. And these two clowns were laughing so hard their balls shrank up into their groins. . . . Well, so much for one day. They fed him and escorted him back to the cell. He heard them bring the coffin in later and place it exactly where it'd been. . . . It was perhaps a day or two later when the one who spoke good English came into the cell. He said, "You're the wrong man. An attendant will bring you clothes. Today you will be set free. However, if you find out anything about the PLA be sure to let us know immediately."

Liberia was hope. Here, as in Ghana, the airport was manned by a vaudeville of armed police and combat soldiers in fatigues. A menacing presence? Like American police ("Round up the usual suspects!") in the sixties. These guys though were brisk with the *new* spirit. Mason made his way at Robertsfield among hundreds of Muslims, Lebanese, Kpelle, Bassa, Gio, Bbandi, Lomo, Indians, Mano, British, Americans, even Japanese. Airports, he thought, are metaphors. A metaphor is, he thought further, never quite sure of itself. At the final paranoid-checkpoint (after every inch of his body—except for his asshole—had been searched) he found Professor Thomas Kakotu waiting at the gate. Kakotu held a sign. Horned-rimmed, Kakotu, flashed his gold tooth. The glitter of his smile was most welcome.... First impression at late afternoon—now—was haze and flatness. No sun yet you could feel it coming at you. In the car on the way in, Kakotu quickly proved to be a man of "like spirit." He was one who understood or accepted the notion that "the imaginative foundation of human existence had some basis in the secular 'dream' of our actual journey" yet... In Monrovia they stopped and parked in front of Diana's. Inside, two of Kakotu's colleagues (Jacquelyn Cloves and Samuel Roberts) were waiting for them. Diana's was a simple place in good taste. Round table. They sipped Liberian beer while investigating the menu. The waiter, a boy, wanted to know where Mason was from. Was it that obvious he wasn't from, say, around the corner?... On the recommendation of the waiter they all ordered potato greens— which was made with fish, chicken, bits of pork, potato leaves, peanut butter, palm oil and lots of spices and herbs. It reminded Mason of pungent Soul Food—turnips and hamhocks, black-eyed peas and cornbread. He washed the rich food down with tangy beer. Conversation? Timid and academic. As they were leaving the waiter grinned at Mason and said, "When you go back to New York America you tell strangers come enjoy Liberia everytime, okay." Yes. Back...?... His room in plush grandiose Ducor was cool. Then at the bar businessmen from Japan, England, South America, chattered away about rubber or iron ore deals. Mason smoked and sipped and wondered at the steamed flowers of his mood. He suddenly wished he had no face, no hands. No history. He took his quinine pill on the tide of a sip of scotch.... Those squatters in the Masonic Temple? Holy-moses, secret societies still. Hall of the oligarchy brought down by Doe: legacy plus a tight-grip of government by the old five-percent from 1821 Americo-Liberians, smashed, ended. Spirit of fourteen thousand originals placed back into the tribal context—no better than a Vai, a Kissi, a Lomo; compelled to take the same holi, barter with the charlies just like everybody else. What was "royalty" anyway? The in-breeding of royalty inevitably pro-duced in its line of offspring the off, the feeble, narrow, nervous, inferior. Real nobility could be found where it had earned its right.... It was relative, too; yes, in deedy. Well, drink up. He had the week-end free. But he *did* have to find Chief Q. Tee. But where...? He took the envelope from the inside pocket of his jacket. It looked innocent enough. Held it up to the light. Only one sentence typed on a folded sheet of paper. The words were not clear enough through the envelope to be read...

It was a Capricorn night: stubborn and grim. He knew he was out of his cotton-picking mind. And although he was in dirty, poor Monrovia—he remembered that for sure—the enemies had surely closed in. What could they want? He was drunk but not blind. And this taxi driver wasn't to be believed: smelling of bamboo and salted herring, he had a license placard with his grasshopper-face on it and his name was Wassily Bruno Ludwig Rottluff. Mason was suddenly afraid. Would they kill him, dump his body in some extragalactic space where nobody *but nobody* would ever find his remains? The guy was blue-rimmed and haughty even! In front of the dance hall, Mason got out. He reached into the uterus of the machine and pressed a filthy dollar into the crusty black hand. "Thanks." The joint was jumping. Called The Total Situation, it was on a side street off Broad, the main drag near the Chase Manhattan Bank. Natives were packed at the bar so deep it took Mason a full minute to recognize Reverend Jack Mackins tending them. Now *this* was some shit! Mason worked his way in and reached for Mackins' hand. The bartender gave him a dirty eye. Mason felt like a fringed-footed lizard. Red lights winked against blue darkness in the mirror behind the Man of God. Being here was like shopping in a supermarket. Mason looked up and down the length of the bar: a woman—the only white woman in the place—was eating peanuts from a bowl. A mug of beer in the other hand. Something about her rung a bell, nearly broke the ding and split the dong. He rubbed his pumpkin-colored eyes: this dame this lass was Little Sally Walker, the porno kitten. Nobody could tell him different. Damnit! The world wasn't *that* small. The man next to her was eating the placenta of some animal. Steaming hot, it superseded the double shot of whisky at his elbow. His black face was twisted and purple under the light. Mason turned back to the barkeep: "I know you, Reverend. You can't fool me. Remember Attica?" "Are you drunk? Can't serve you if you drunk. You from New York? Thought so." "Where can I find Chief Q. Tee, Reverend?" "Never heard of a chief by that name." Upstairs people were dancing and the weight of their festive display and desperate and absolute celebration of life had the lights in the ceiling rocking, releasing pearly iridescent specs of dust and crud. Mason ordered a scotch on the rocks. This place was more vulgar than he'd hoped for. Down the bar Little Sally Walker was licking her fingers. He remembered the tadpole-touch of her inner flesh. It gave him goose bumps and made eggs break against his spine. Later he'd go down and speak to her. She couldn't possibly be part of any plot against him. Could she? But the Reverend? Who could say. Little Sally Walker's glitter and glamor were throwing off a glazed inner rigidity she hadn't had back in Guy Flotilla's world of sentimental flesh and alienated genitals. Now now, be gentle. A commotion at the door pulled him around and his eyes snagged on the exodus: people were splitting like mad. It was moments before Mason could see the body of a bleeding man on the floor half way under a table by the front window with its winking bar sign. A hard muscle in Mason's head turned to spring flowers. His teeth felt like pine cones. He drank the scotch down in one gulp. In minutes uniformed police and soldiers filled the place. Like everybody else he had to show his i.d. People wearing German music hall costumes and American designer jeans and French fluff came down the stairs from sweating and jumping, herded along by the tips of billy-sticks. In the crowd was one white guy. He was German all right. And yes: believe it or not: he was none other than Taurus Heiner Graf with a black woman clinging to his arm. For a moment Graf was only inches from him. Mason reached out and touched his arm. "Graf!" Graf didn't respond. He kept right on as though he hadn't felt the tug. At the same moment little Sally Walker and her date were pushing their way past. He couldn't remember her real name when he opened his mouth. "Rise Sally rise." She gave him a smile and a wink. Well, well. On the way out Mason looked at the face of the man on the floor. He recognized it but he couldn't place it: it was too far out of context.

Saturday. Bopola-Ganori was a remote village reached by way of a good road built by foreign "investors" interested in you-know-what. Along the way were gigantic rubber tree plantations. A few scattered clouds hung above. It was not just another day drawn in charcoal. It had a conté sharpness, a certain verve.... They didn't arrogantly drive into the village, rather, they parked outside and walked in. Nothing much had started. The village chief, a slender old man wearing a white turban, greeted them with dignity and ceremoniousness. He didn't apply the customary, more casual, snap-of-the-finger-at-the-end-of-the-shake "handshake." Mason and the teachers walked about the area. A crowd was beginning to gather in the village square. Occasionally one of the professors explained something—how the huts were built, or—as they passed young girls cornrolling each other's hair—the process of braiding. They then ended up back at the square where the beer and food were spread out on tables under a shelter. Mason surveyed the feast, sniffed the pungent, spicy stuff, bean and sesame seed spread that smelled strongly of garlic; a wooden bowl filled with jumbo shrimp in red pepper paste; a big old pan of fried chicken in groundnut sauce that released little smoke clouds of chili and onions; some sort of baked thing with the aroma of ginger, nutmeg and cinnamon; then familiar potato greens. Kakotu said the chicken and rice casserole was a specialty of Ghana—called jallof rice. Ghana was his homeland. The professors paid their fee of twenty dollars to the old woman in the corner. The first thing Mason lifted to his plate was a baked dish of corn and okra then a wooden spoonful of sugared yams. His sweet tooth was calling. A bus load of people from Monrovia arrived at the moment they started eating. The dancers in costume out in the square were warming up, stretching their limbs. Mason and the professors took a table adjacent to the serving table and a boy placed a bottle of beer alongside each of their plates. Kakotu wanted to know if the writer's books were available in Africa. Mason didn't know. Something in the corn and okra was reaching under his tongue and burning all the way down through the root of his mouth and into the throat canyon. Besides, he felt sore and dizzy from a sleepless night. His host assured him that this food was a cut above Julia's Gurley Street place, the Lebanese joints, the Mandarin, and even better than what you'd get on Carey or Broad not to mention the so-called European places. Our wolf-in-sheep skin was enjoying himself out here among the "tribal" folk.... Before the dancing started, the visitors—Liberians mainly, an American couple, two British ladies—crowded the sheltered area. Mason wanted to know if Kakotu knew of a Chief Q. Tee in Monrovia. He did not. Some people from Sinkor and Paynesville arrived in a pickup truck. They came in just as a sprinkle started. The dancing was sort of casually beginning out there, though not with much kick.... A little man with an adult upper body perched on short legs—which were uneven—went to the center of the square, shooed the dancers aside, raised his hands against the drummers then addressed the visitors. Most of them were still eating as they stood or sat under the sheltered area. The deformed man explained the limitations of the festival: there were tribal secrets they couldn't share with strangers.... A grizzly fellow—obviously got-up to scare away evil spirits—wobbled into the square as the deformed guy stepped aside. Grizzle flopped about beating up dust despite rain. He ran toward the spectators in one direction then another. He was more comic then menacing. Not even the children flinched. Then two other bedeviled critters came from between huts and joined the old woolly bear. They beat around in the dust and tugged at each other with no apparent symmetry. A fourth one came forward from behind a cluster of old village women in plain cotton. Mason chewed on a shrimp dipped in ata sauce and watched the antics. (He was sure one of the English ladies was Cornelia in disguise!) About an hour later the thick dusty creatures were shooed away by the deformed man and the girls in grass skirts were ushered out. They moved their arms and twirled their hips and made all the turns and squats just right to the drum beats. The drummers, by the way, were clustered together at the other side of the square: also under a shelter of branches supported by four simple poles.... New dancers came and joined the present ones. Within minutes the girls were moving in a dusty storm as they pounded the ground with their bare feet. The drums talked. The sun came out sharply. Mason and his escorts continued to watch from beneath the thatched roof. The deformed man kept shouting to the dancers—urging them to move faster. Standing to the side, just inside the circle of viewers, he'd cut a little step himself to the drums. Cackling and gesturing toward his genitalia. He reminded Mason of Snake Hips....

"Tomorrow at noon come to Village Tabli-Gablah in Bomi Territory for official meeting. Essential you be there. You must appear in wooden mask. No one is to see your face. Q.T." This message awaited him upon his return to the Ducor. It was on letter-head stationary: Q.T. Secret Society. No address. No phone. Reader, for hours Mason was in a quandary! Yet he bought a mask. He didn't sleep well that night. The taxi trip to Tabli-Gablah would cost forty cruddy dollars. (Did the American government send all its dirty money to Liberia?) On his way, he thought how odd he'd felt to discover yesterday in the afternoon during the dinner party at Kakotu's that Kakotu had four wives. Mason'd known in the abstract that polygamy was still widespread here but to see it in action—all the wives busy in the kitchen—was different. The whole neighborhood came to Kakotu's home in northwest Monrovia to help him celebrate the visit of the American poet and novelist. It was also a party to honor the birth of Kakotu's first grandchild. Mason felt a little cheated. Scotch, rum, wine, beer, soda pop, a dining room table in a dark house filled with serving dishes of sizzling hot stews, fried meats, peppered baked dishes, salty, tangy, sweet meats and yams, overripe fruit. Guests chattered politely standing in line around the table, loading and reloading their plates. The cool darkness complimented the soft, low, sweet voices. As Mason listened to Jacquelyn Cloves tell of her adventures in New York, there suddenly came the clamor of something afoot out in the yard. Had Mandingo tribesmen come with unfriendly intentions? Had Camp Johnson Road been taken by the advanced guard of a new government? Naw. It was only The Devil: tall as a Georgia pine, with a red face! Mason, with the others, rushed out onto the screened porch to see what was up. The Devil was a sight standing there in the dust surrounded by a hundred or so awed and giggling children. Then His Satanic Majesty started a little sweet dance step. He had the charm of little Shirley Temple. A lifted foot, a lifted arm. His body was wrapped in yellow sacks all the way down his wooden—stilt-held—legs. The sucker was every bit of twelve feet! He had no voice but gestured toward his mouth with a webbed set of fingers—indicating thirst. Impatient with the slowness of spectators, The Devil snatched a bottle of beer from a man's fist. Toodleoo, beer. Whoa, now! Back up! But it was too late. He drained the bottle then snatched a glass of scotch from Robert's grip—spilled most of it in his clumsy effort to get the liquid in through his slit. Sort of wavering in a dust cloud of his own making, he accepted bits of meat, sips from bottles of soda pop, potato chips, crackers, pieces of chocolate. Even money. After taking Mister Nobody's scotch he demanded money—making his request clear by rubbing his thumb against his index and forefinger. The crowd roared. Mason gave The Devil a couple of dollars. He stuffed them into his shirt front then reached down and grabbed Mason by the shoulder. "Tonight..." he whispered through the mask. But there was something else. Mason missed it: a few words at the end: unclear, curved, clay-clogged, in a wheeze. A boy at the back of the crowd—perched high on a fence—was beating a drum to The Devil's dance. The Devil stepped now to the dreamy drunk sick rhythm of his Shirley Temple tap. Where was Big Bill? Calm as a clam, innocent as a curl, he danced his magic whim. He danced till he couldn't stand. By now the whole party'd moved outside. Then the poor-devil-of-a-guy dropped and leaned against the high terra cotta wall that separated the yard from the dusty road. As in novels of old, the afternoon wore on.... Tonight?

As he approached the Ducor to turn in for the night he felt like Moll Flanders ("Who was...Twelve Year a *Whore,* five times a *Wife*...Twelve Year a *Thief,* Eight Year a Transported *Felon*...at last grew *Rich,* liv'd *Honest*...") but he wasn't. Had he let his Hobby-Horse grow headstrong? Mason suddenly felt a breeze. The Prince without a principality was smooth as polished wood. His stride was indistinguishable from that of a man of noble birth. Then a hand reached out of the darkness and yanked at his sleeve. Mason swung around. It was The Devil, still on stilts. The diabolical fella stank of his own sweat. He hissed. He bent toward Mason's head. Whispered: "You be an irreligious—an infindel, like me: you no unspotted one. A circle will be drawn around you feet. Be careful where you stand. Don't cross the cross. The full moon watches you as you sleep. Stay away from swastikas: they be bad signs for a scoundrel the likes of you." As the demon whispered in Mason's ear Mason cringed, struggling to free himself from the fallen angel's powerful hold. "Hear me out! You'll go soon enough!" Two Chinese men got out of a taxi and went in the Ducor. Mason shuddered: he was a Francis Bacon figure in a bleak landscape: half-formed, trapped—deformed. The Devil's voice became sharp: "Don't let you dereliction go you to the wrong way: don't weave spells with them in Tabli-Gablah. It will be cause the end of you." Then before Mason could form the obvious question The Devil disappeared down the dark walkway alongside the Ducor. He thought of chasing but quickly realized how pointless it was since the archfiend's stilted footfalls couldn't even be heard on the stone.

The taxi driver refused to drive him into Tabli-Gablah. "They got a pact with The Devil. Me best not go there, Mister." He'd parked his Buick just outside the village at the mouth of the dirt road that led in. He held out his hand. Mason gave him four tens. Then got out. The air was heavy. It was eleven-thirty but felt like midnight. No sun. Giant trees caused a medley of shadows along the road. Goddamnit, had he so completely fallen out of Joyce Kilmer's? hurt himself? lost the formula? forgot his P's and Q's? his Z's? his C's? What the hell was a "smart" guy like Mason doing out here on a back road *alone* walking toward some unknown, uh, event? He started out. Heard the taxi leave. Then a vehicle on the highway a moment later. Looking over his shoulder, he saw a holi on its way to Monrovia—crammed with passengers. Absently, he felt the wooden mask in his shoulder bag. Should he put it on now or . . . ? He felt foolish. Sure. Why not now. He stopped and sat on a rock alongside the road. Opened his bag. He liked the mask a lot. It reminded him of the face of the woman who'd shown up at the Sommerfield party in Greece. Mason heard voices. But he saw nobody. Quickly he placed his mask over his face and adjusted the string around the base of his head. A weird tiredness gripped Blackface Hermes. He couldn't breathe properly with the mask on. Or . . . was something else . . . wrong? Then he saw three figures—men?—coming from the direction of the village—his way. The Prodigal son stood. His foolish wooden mask felt heavy like freshly grafted skin. His mouth tasted like Robert E. Lee's old boot. Mason waited—his eyes burning behind the slits. He watched the men approach. ("The *Man* Who Rode Away"?) No. You wouldn't get off *that* easily! Before the three were at arms' length he could see they too were wearing masks made of wood. He felt his mudfrog disappear. They stopped before him. The shortest one spoke: "Follow us." The tallest one quickly added: "We must hurry." Then they set off at a trot. Mason tried to keep up. . . . On first sight the village of Tabli-Gablah seemed normal: except there were no people. Mason followed the three toward the large hut at the base of the village square. They pushed him in. Inside, he couldn't see anything—at first. Then, by candlelight, he saw that the room was packed with people sitting on the ground in a circle: all wore wooden masks. An old man in a red robe came in. He told Mason to sit. Mason sat. The old man then sat on the ground next to him. The three escorts left. The circle was then complete. The old man spoke: "The envelope, please." Mason pulled it from his pocket and handed it over. The old man ripped it open and read aloud: "*Keep* this nigger!" He then looked with calmness at Mason. "Are you the person referred to here?" Mason didn't think to hesitate. He chirped. He felt the gravity of the situation—the serious presence of the circle of wearers of masks. Pastiché? Something linear about this circle . . . ? Mason scanned. He thought he recognized the flicker of an eye in a slit, the gesture of a body, the turn of a head, the shape of a set of breasts, the curve of a big toe. But he couldn't be sure. Not absolutely. Then the old man said, "One can carry the disease one covers oneself against on the fingers one uses to secure the cover. You, my son, have come to the end of your running." But by now his words were meant for himself alone. Far away in the distance they all could hear the sad bullhorn of a Muslim and shortly thereafter the crier with his mournful whining appeal from the upper window of a mosque. It was hot and muggy. The hut smelled of, of, cow rocks, turtle piss and smoke.